Acting COUNSEL

MORGANA BEVAN

ISBN: 978-1-916719-46-0

CHAPTER ONE

CATRINA

Bright and early Monday morning, I rolled into the office with a noticeable bounce in my step. I'd worked hard trying to prove my worth — weeks and months of late nights, early mornings, and endless briefs — and they'd finally taken notice.

Today, I started my first solo case: acquiring an LA film studio for one of the most popular actors in Hollywood. Not that I could put a name to the face if a celeb walked past me.

Even if I couldn't care less about the celebrity goings-on, one thing remained: I was one step closer to making partner.

At some point, I'd stop grinning like a loon each time the thought cycled through my mind.

It wouldn't be this week.

If my colleagues saw me, they'd blame my unusual pep on my boss's decision to trust me with the Starlight Studios acquisition, and I didn't care if they did.

Only I knew the truth.

Only I could feel the ache of disused muscles as I walked, reminding me with each step how I celebrated my step up.

I'd never been the one-night stand kind of girl, but I have to admit, it was exhilarating.

"Knowing my luck, I'd get swept out to sea and eaten by something."

"I could teach you, if you're up for the challenge."

"Are you going to stop a sea monster from eating me?"

"I'll keep you safe from any sea monsters." He grazed my cheek with his nose. *"Besides, I'm the only one allowed to taste you."*

Nathan.

I could feel the ghost of his hands mapping every curve of my body, leaving marks I wished would never fade.

Mike knocked on my door. Thankfully, I'd completed all of my preparations for this meeting and got myself as caught up as the sparse notes from my predecessor allowed.

"Catrina," Mike's voice boomed from the doorway, snapping me out of my thoughts. "I hope you're ready for a big day."

"Good morning, Mr Nelson. As ready as I'll ever be." I set my coffee cup down on the desk and stood, pasting a bright but confident smile to my lips. "I've been preparing all weekend."

"Good." He stepped inside, his tall frame taking up much of the space in my modest office. "I told you she was my best, Mr Logan, and I never lie."

A tall, blond man followed Mike into my office. My heart lodged in my throat.

Nathan. Those piercing blue eyes instantly found mine.

Two days. It had only been two days since I kicked him out of my apartment at dawn, banishing him from my home and my thoughts. Yet here he was, conjuring up memories I'd spent days savouring.

Nathan strode in casually confident as if he owned the place — and perhaps a part of me too, after a single unforgettable night. His blond hair was tousled, a reminder of tangled sheets and roaming hands. That knowing look in his eyes said he recalled my bed as clearly as I did.

"Cat," Nathan mouthed, his eyes widening briefly before a sly grin spread across his face.

Panic surged as the ramifications hit me. If he said the wrong thing, my career could be over before it truly began.

"Catrina Sinclair, meet Nathan Logan," Mike introduced us with a wave of his hand, completely missing the tension in the air. "Nathan is purchasing Starlight Studios. He's agreed to get you up to date on any additional details you might require."

"Nice to meet you, Mr Logan," I said, extending my hand for a firm handshake, but keeping my desk between us.

His gaze dropped to the hard surface, flaring with a look I recognised far too well. My breath caught as Nathan's heated attention raked over me, reminding me without words of how thoroughly he had explored my body. I fought the impulse to squirm under his scrutiny, composure wavering.

"Please, call me Nathan," he insisted with a warm smile, his eyes locked onto mine.

That accent. For a moment, I'd forgotten, but oof. I'd always had a weakness for a good English accent.

The memory of it whispering into my ear while he hovered above me sent a shiver down my spine. *"See, it's not so bad giving up control, is it, Icy?"*

"It's a pleasure to meet you too, Catrina," Nathan said, his lips quirking as he clocked the flush of crimson trying to break through my foundation.

I nodded, my voice trapped. I forced myself to release his hand, hyper-aware of Mike's eyes on us, and I refused to give him any reason to doubt my abilities.

Mike cleared his throat, clueless as to the cause of the tension thickening the air. "I need to make a call. I'll leave you two to get acquainted. Be back in a jiffy!"

The door clicked shut behind him, silence ringing in his

wake. I stared at Nathan, his knuckles white on the back of my guest chair, as a slow grin curved his lips.

"Surprised, Icy?" His gaze bore into me, hinting at pleasures we had shared mere days ago. "Did you miss me?"

I swallowed hard, searching for some cutting reply. But the sight of him left me tongue-tied.

Nathan rounded the desk. "No need for shy glances — we're well past that, aren't we?"

His cologne filled my senses as he leaned in too close, intent eyes catching me in their snare. He reached out, fingers grazing my flushed cheek. I stiffened as warmth sparked beneath his touch, threatening my composure.

"Mr Logan, this is highly inappropriate." I said sharply, putting space between us. "I'm your legal counsel, nothing more."

"You can drop the act. It's just us, Cat." His gaze softened, that charming smile fading as a glint of awe filled his blue eyes. "I never thought I'd see you again."

I faltered, caught by the earnest longing in his voice. His hand rose again, slow and questioning, giving me time to pull away this time. Instead, I found myself leaning into his touch, palm against my cheek as memories rose unbidden.

Nathan smiled, thumb brushing my lower lip. "There you are. I was hoping you'd come back to me."

I caught my breath, stunned by the tenderness in his gaze. His words slipped past my defences, hinting at something vulnerable inside of me.

"Don't look at me like that."

"Like what?" he whispered.

"Like I'm the only woman in the world."

Nathan smiled, free hand tangling in my hair as he tilted my chin up. "You are, for me."

His words struck a chord deep within me, prodding an ache I hadn't felt in years. The promise of being someone's centre. Actually caring about one another and not in the 'Oh good, you're still breathing' way my mother had me. It was a pipe dream I'd forced myself to stop living for.

And I won't start now.

I blinked, scrambling for a response that wouldn't reveal how much his unexpected appearance had shaken me. "I apologise if I gave you the wrong impression." My fingers caught his wandering hand, tugging it away from my face. "Friday night was a mistake and I have no interest in repeating it. Especially not now that I'm your attorney."

I stared up at him, all six-foot, five glorious inches of him, willing him to believe the lie. If only the complications of my job and the firm's rules against client relationships didn't stand in the way, I'd happily go back for a repeat of round two.

Nathan's eyes darkened, a spark of challenge in their depths. "Is that so? Because your body tells a far different story." His gaze tracked down the length of me, leaving tiny fires in its wake. "Admit it, Cat. You felt the same spark... and you want more."

My pulse leapt but I tilted my chin up, forcing an unaffected air. "My personal feelings are irrelevant. I'm here to represent your legal interests, nothing more."

Nathan's gaze dropped to my mouth, a slow smile curving his lips. "Your lips say one thing, but your eyes confess the truth. You want a repeat of Friday night... and so do I."

He reached out, knuckles grazing my cheek in a touch that momentarily wiped common sense from my mind. I swayed toward him before catching myself, panic setting in at how easily my body responded to his.

Nathan had slipped past all my defences with unfair ease, leaving me on edge and struggling against the pull of desire. I couldn't afford a single mistake if I wanted to achieve all I had worked so hard for, but part of me yearned to close the scant distance between us, regardless of the consequences. His tempting smile might just prove to be my undoing if I didn't find the willpower to resist.

I took a shaky step back, desperate to put distance between us before I did something I would regret. "I insist we remain professional. My career is at stake here, and I can't afford any... distractions."

Nathan's smile faded, expression sobering. "I didn't expect to see you here. But now that I have, I'm reluctant to let this go." His gaze bore into me, more serious than I had seen him. "Friday was more than just physical for me. I haven't felt a connection like that in a long time. Did you feel it too?"

I looked away from the intensity of his gaze, at a loss. I had told myself it was merely lust and impulse, refusing to consider anything deeper. But there were moments when we understood each other with no need for words.

"It doesn't matter." I straightened my shoulders, adopting a brisk tone. "We can't do it again, Mr Logan. My career depends on maintaining a proper distance from clients, and…"

"Nathan." His gentle rebuke gave me pause. I glanced at him to find a small smile curving his lips, but a hint of vulnerability in his eyes. "When we're alone, it's Nathan. And your career won't suffer, Cat. I want to do this right."

I stared at him, unsure how to respond. Doing this — whatever 'this' was — would go against everything logical.

"Have dinner with me tonight. No distractions, just two people exploring whatever this connection between us might become." He smiled, coaxing and genuine. "Give me — give us — a chance. I dare you."

A knock on the door interrupted us.

"I can't do that." I turned away from him, smoothing down my skirt. "From now on, I'm your attorney. Nothing more."

His smile faded before he nodded. "If that's what you want."

While Nathan rounded my desk and assumed a more natural position, I walked to the door, willing my hammering heart to settle down. *He's just a gorgeous but pushy man who gave you the best orgasms of your life—but he is now off limits. It's okay, he'll get bored soon enough.*

I opened it to find Mike waiting, breezing into the room with a thick folder under his arm. "Sorry about that." He sat in his usual seat without hesitation, missing the tension between Nathan and me. "Shall we?"

Nathan's expression smoothed into polite professionalism in an instant. "Of course."

"Absolutely," I agreed, settling into my seat and forcing my focus back to the task at hand. "Please have a seat, Mr Logan."

The sooner we got started, the sooner I could prove my worth to Mike and cement my position in the firm. I was prepared to do whatever it took to make this acquisition successful, even if it meant resisting the undeniable charm of Nathan Logan.

Nathan took a seat across from me, sprawling into the chair with a roguish grin. His expensive suit did little to hide the muscles beneath. I tried to focus firmly on my notes but felt his presence like a gravitational pull.

"Let me give you a bit of background on the acquisition," Mike began, leaning back in his chair and tapping a pen against the papers he held. "Starlight Studios is a major player in the industry, and they've been seeking a buyer for some time. Mr Logan," — he gestured towards Nathan — "is prepared to make that purchase."

I tried my best to concentrate on Mike's words, but I couldn't stop glancing at Nathan.

His gaze slid to mine, blue eyes smouldering with a heat that threatened to make me squirm. He masked it in an instant if Mike glanced his way. But in that fleeting moment there was a promise of passion waiting to ignite again, if given the chance. Nathan leaned forward as if riveted by Mike's words, but a sly quirk of his lips said his thoughts mirrored my own.

"This case is of the utmost importance to our firm," Mike continued, his voice firm and authoritative. "Our reputation is on the line, so we need to ensure that we handle everything impeccably."

"You can count on me." I forced myself to maintain eye contact with my boss.

"Good." He nodded approvingly. "Let's dive into the specifics of the deal."

I could feel the weight of Nathan's gaze on me, and I struggled to keep my composure under the pressure of his attention. Every time I looked at him, our shared secret seemed to shimmer in the air between us like an electric charge.

"Catrina," Mike's voice brought me back to reality. "Do you have questions about the agreement terms?"

"Uh, yes," I stammered, racking my brain for something relevant to ask. "Mr Logan—"

"Nathan."

"Right. Nathan." I forced a weak smile. "You've spent some time working on this deal. Besides the misfortune with your previous attorney, why do you believe the process has been so drastically delayed?"

"I believe the shareholders cannot separate fact from fiction."

"That's quite the accusation."

"Hmm. Is it an accusation if it's true?" He held up his hand before I could answer. "That was rhetorical. The gossip rags have made a sport of portraying me as a ladies' man, and the shareholders have used those rumours as an excuse to question whether I'm truly serious in my bid."

"I... see." I frowned, sorting through this new information. "And this perception has directly impacted negotiations?"

"To put it mildly." Nathan's smile turned wry. "My 'moral

failings' have been cited more than once as cause for concern in handing over the reins of their studio. As if my personal life has any bearing on my ability to run a company."

"That does seem rather absurd." I hesitated, unsure how much to reveal of my own opinions. "Tabloid gossip is hardly evidence of poor business sense or judgement."

"Exactly." Nathan threw up his hands. "Now, I'll be honest, once upon a time, some of them might have been true, but that hasn't been the case for some time."

His tone was sincere, and it left me feeling weak in the knees. We held each other's gaze. I'd never been one to shirk eye contact, but I might have had to start before I closed the lid on this purchase.

"Now the sad truth about Hollywood is that scandal sells, so where the lies about me weren't legitimately harmful to my reputation, I let them slide." He winced. "Unfortunately, the image of me the tabloids used to drive their site traffic does not lend itself to a level-headed businessman." He paused for a moment before continuing, his gaze still fixed on me.

"My priorities have changed, and I have instructed my agent to shut down any further rumours before they take root." He bit his lip and smiled at me, the sight of it making my core tense. "I believe that once the shareholders meet me, I'll be able to ease any of their fears."

His voice wrapped around me, low and intense as he focused all of his attention on me.

"I can understand why that would be aggravating." I met his gaze, pulse skipping at the glint of approval there. "Well, you can rest assured I have no interest in tabloid gossip or moral judgments. My only concern is representing your best interests in acquiring this studio, and ensuring all parties come to an equitable agreement as swiftly as possible."

Mike started to respond, but his words were lost on me. I stared at Nathan, feeling as if he had just let me in on something far greater than the acquisition of Starlight Studios.

"Have you ever been on a studio lot?" Nathan asked suddenly, his voice warm and inviting. The sudden change in topic caught me off guard.

"Uh, no, I haven't." My fingers nervously tapped on the table. "I've always been a behind-the-scenes kind of person."

"Ah, that's a shame. It's quite an experience," he said with a charming grin, then added softly, "Perhaps I could show you around one day? You know, purely for professional reasons."

My heart skipped a beat at the thought of spending time with Nathan outside the office. "That sounds interesting. Thank you for the offer, but I think we should focus on the acquisition right now."

Mike cleared his throat. "Exactly right, Catrina. You only have two days until the shareholder's meeting and it's taken nearly three months to get them to agree on a date."

When we finally finished, Mike shook Nathan's hand eagerly. "A pleasure doing business with you. We'll have the contracts ready for signing next week, hopefully."

Nathan smiled. "Likewise, thank you both for ensuring a smooth process." His eyes met mine briefly, regret flickering through them. "I appreciate your efforts on my behalf."

I nodded. "You're welcome, Mr Logan. I'll be in touch."

With a nod to us both, Nathan left. An odd mix of relief and disappointment filled me. I had done right... so why did it feel like I had let a once-in-a-lifetime chance go?

Mike chuckled, gathering his papers. "Quite the charmer, that one! But don't worry, you handled yourself well." He stood, smiling. "This was a big day, Catrina. The partners will be very impressed."

I returned his smile. "Thank you. That means a lot."

Mike headed for the door and my smile faded, doubts crowding in. This deal was everything I had worked for, yet Nathan threatened my ability to stay focused. Ten minutes in an office with him and I could barely ignore his draw. Our history — however brief — left him a distraction I couldn't ignore.

As difficult as it was, I had to be upfront with Mike — he deserved my unbiased best, and if that meant stepping aside, then objectivity demanded it. Even if the thought of losing all my progress stung.

"There's something I should tell you," I said to Mike before he could leave my office. "Regarding Nathan Logan — "

He turned, waving a hand and dismissing my concerns. "You worry too much. I know you've got this under control."

I frowned, thrown by his nonchalance. "No, that's not — there are complications —"

"Don't you start second-guessing yourself now!" Mike interrupted with a laugh. "You were born for deals like this." Mike smiled, placing a hand on my shoulder. "I never doubted for a second you were right for this." He chuckled.

"Mike, please listen— "

But he swept on, buoyed by enthusiasm. "You have my complete support, Catrina. Keep your eye on the prize. We'll make a partner out of you yet!"

Despite my misgivings, I couldn't help but smile at the praise.

"Before I forget…" Mike shuffled through his suit pockets, patting himself down with a look of pure concentration on his face. He reached into one and his expression smoothed out. "This is Mr Logan's agent, Maisy Michaels. Give her a call if you need anything." He handed me the card and spun away. "Keep up the good work, Catrina."

The door clicked shut behind Mike, and I sank into the luxurious leather chair at my new desk. I had to hand it to him, he knew how to motivate me when it mattered. His confidence in my ability steadied my nerves.

If Mike trusted I could handle the negotiations, who was I to argue?

Nathan's intoxicating cologne still permeated the air, tickling my senses and threatening my concentration. His confident voice lingered in my ears as I considered the high stakes of this case and my precarious position.

"Get a grip, Cat," I muttered to myself, raking my fingers through my hair, messing up my carefully crafted curls.

Focus on the promotion and the shiny new office.

Still my heart raced at the memory of Friday night, threatening to dismantle my carefully constructed facade of professionalism. I needed to get a handle on it. Letting the attraction run unchecked would not only jeopardise my ability to do my job but also my position at the firm.

Although with Mike's confidence in me, maybe it wouldn't affect my position as much as I'd first assumed.

You might as well give up now. You'll only fail in the end, and end up right back where you started: trapped here with me. My mother's voice echoed inside my mind, a replay of her goodbye before I left for law school in the States.

Growing up in a small town, the pressure to succeed and excel had been intense. Even with my mother's apathetic expectation that I would fail no matter how hard I tried, I had an entire town fixated on my smallest wins, pushing for more and more.

Moving thousands of miles away for law school had been the best thing for me.

I couldn't go back to that.

"Is it worth the risk?" I whispered, staring intently at the gold-lettered nameplate on my desk, Catrina Sinclair – Associate Attorney.

It had taken years of hard work, sleepless nights spent buried in law books, and countless hours to get me to this point. I was so close to making a name for myself. Was I willing to jeopardise everything for a tantalising yet dangerous attraction that might be one-sided?

Exactly.

No reason to believe Nathan actually wanted to see me again. Hotshot Hollywood actors probably had women offering themselves up to them on a platter.

Except he outright asked you out and just spent the better part of an hour eye fucking you with your boss in the room...

That meant nothing. It could have been nothing more than a game.

"Focus, Catrina," I chided myself, forcing my gaze away from the nameplate and onto the thick stack of Starlight Studios documents cluttering my desk. "You've got a job to do."

As the swirling storm of doubt and desire threatened to consume me, I replayed the meeting in my mind. Nathan had been nothing but professional in front of Mike, answering my questions with honesty and openness. The perfect actor with nothing on the line if his inappropriate interest ever came out.

Unlike him, I had everything on the line, and I had to find a way to ignore him. For the sake of my sanity and my career.

CHAPTER TWO

NATHAN

"Cut!" the director shouted as we rounded the corner of the street.

I slowed to a stop and my best friends followed suit, none of us so much as puffing at the exertion of our quick run.

The street surrounding us had become a collapsed wasteland, with steel beams jutting out of the ground where towers used to be and pieces of concrete strewn across the pavement.

As a film set, it was impressive. Especially when most studios these days preferred to demolish cities in the virtual world. There would be digital effects in the film, the director just didn't want to use them yet. After four editions of The Rogue Squad, he'd perfected his vision, and I was more than happy to go along with it.

"Jesus, it's hot." Finn McCarthy paced circles around us, angsty to get moving again. "I can't fecking wait to spend a real Christmas in Edinburgh with actual cold weather."

"You're full of shit." Jackson Levi laughed, his Scottish brogue making his outrage sound angry. "I bet the second you set foot on Scottish soil, you'll do nothing but complain about the cold and the rain."

"As long as he keeps his moaning away from my fiancée on our wedding day, he can feel however the fuck he wants," Shaun Martin muttered, his usually carefree but polished features hardened. The dirt smeared over us didn't help, but Shaun's clenched jaw told me there was something else going on.

Finn, Jackson, Shaun, and I had been friends all of our LA careers. We met as background actors on our first action film and stuck to each other like glue afterwards. I mean, what were the chances of four Brits making the LA move at the same time? It also helped that directors loved our *exotic* accents.

As our careers grew, they'd quickly dubbed us the Kings of Screen.

As a group, we ticked multiple boxes: Jackson's surfer look, Shaun's polished perfection, my generally cleancut-but-may-have-just-rolled-out-of-bed-after-a-steamy-night blond hair to Finn's out of control red corkscrew curls.

We could happily admit we represented the wet dream of Hollywood and we owned it. Mostly.

"Everything going alright with the wedding planning?" I asked.

Shaun nodded. "It's been a bit of a whirlwind." He pressed his lips together and glanced around, noting the crew setting up for the next shot. None of them were within earshot. "But the film's kept me so busy, Mona's had to handle most of it and I feel terrible about it. She keeps telling me it's okay, but what kind of man leaves his fiancée to deal with something so stressful alone?"

"You've got nothing to worry about." I clapped Shaun on the shoulder. "It'll be the wedding of the century."

"Yeah, she's no stranger to our world either, which probably helps you a lot," Finn said absently. He waved to a runner, gesturing for water. "Plus, she's just plain nice. She'd never begrudge you leaving her for work."

Something in his tone made us all turn to face him.

"Do I smell trouble in paradise?" Jackson asked, his tone blatantly teasing.

Finn spluttered. Just then, a runner stopped at our sides with a bag of bottled water. Finn's expression instantly morphed into a pleasant mask, but his eyes shot daggers at us.

"You're talking out of your arse," he said once the runner left. He crossed his arms and our brows climbed. He glanced down at himself and dropped them back to his side. "Abi and I are fine. Better than fine. We're talking about a vow renewal and she's meeting Da for the first time in Edinburgh. It's all happening."

A vow renewal? News to me, but I couldn't be happier for him. Finn's relationship with Abi had been a tumultuous one, but he'd finally seen the light and, well, here we were.

"That's incredible," Shaun said, echoing my thoughts before clapping Finn on the shoulder. "Who would have thought your agent actually had your back when he forced you onto Married Blind?"

We all, except Finn, sniggered.

"Yeah, yeah. The wanker expects me to name my first-born after him now." Finn rolled his eyes, but his lips curled slightly, betraying his annoyance.

"When are you two going to catch up?" Shaun asked, eying me and Jackson. "The bachelor image will get tired at some point."

"Not a chance." Jackson held up his hands, his face paling. "I'm more than happy to be the guy lapping up all the disappointed women you leave behind."

All eyes turned to me.

"Yeah, what he said," I muttered without a single shred of conviction.

"And they gave you an Oscar." Finn shook his head.

Jackson couldn't resist prodding me. "Come on, man, spill the beans. Who's the lucky lady this time?"

I hesitated. *Should I talk about her if she wants to keep our relationship professional?*

But that would be a major departure from my normal and they would notice. The questions would never end.

So sharing a few harmless details would help in the long run. Wouldn't it?

Who am I kidding? I just want to talk about her.

"Just someone I met at The Noir Bar on Friday night. We had a good time." The understatement of the century.

Her berry-stained lips and emerald eyes had haunted me since that night. The way she moved, swaying her hips in that figure-hugging skirt suit — I couldn't get her out of my head.

Finn raised an eyebrow. "Good, huh? If you're lying to us, it was more than a good time."

I rolled my eyes again, but couldn't deny the truth. "Yeah, well... I guess I'm not used to being turned down, and I figure there's no point talking about it."

Except I really wanted to talk about her.

The memory of her soft curves pressed against me, her breathy moans in my ear, tormented me. I could still taste her on my lips, feel the heat of her skin beneath my hands. The way she gasped my name, nails digging into my back as I drove her over the edge again and again...

God, I wanted her. The realisation slammed into me, my body tightening at just the thought of having her once more.

There was something about her smile, the way her eyes lit up with laughter and untold secrets, pulling me in. More than lust or curiosity, I felt a visceral connection to her I couldn't explain. As if she saw beyond the roles I played, glimpsing a part of me even I had stopped searching for.

It was madness, and yet I couldn't walk away from her now.

Someone needed to make sense of my head because I

couldn't. I didn't do relationships. Hell, I barely did one night, anymore. Yet, despite our fucked up situation, the thought of getting caught with Cat seriously revved my engine.

Sniggers floated around me as both Jackson and Finn lost it.

"You wanted a repeat with a lass and got rejected?" Finn asked, absolute delight shining in his green eyes. "Oh, this is too good."

I took their teasing on the chin. Heat crept up my neck, but I ignored it like the pro actor I was.

Of course, they'd find it amusing. I'd never been the sort to let a woman distract me, no matter the circumstance. Especially not when I was with my best friends. I'd always taken great pride in being fully present.

I forced a chuckle. "Ha ha, hilarious. Just drop it, okay?"

"Don't worry, we'll go easy on you." Finn clapped me on the back again, a little too hard for my liking. "Isn't that what you said to me before my Married Blind wedding?"

I raised a brow. "You still salty about that?"

"About my best friends not helping me escape?" His brows climbed. "Hell yeah, I am."

Jackson shook his head. "Don't let Abi hear you talking like that, man. She might kick you to the curb and swap your vow renewal for divorce papers instead."

"Christ," Finn muttered. He gripped his neck, staring at the pair of us like we were the ones talking about regretting meeting our wife. "I don't mean now!"

Nearly a year ago, Finn's agent forced him to join the cast of a reality TV show that married celebrities to civilians. He prided himself on keeping his distance from the media — a misplaced pride considering fucking the studio head's daughter in a bar bathroom landed him in image rehab — but the show had forced him to face up to his issues. It softened him in a way. Or more likely, Abi, his wife, had.

His transformation was a topic of much entertainment amongst our group.

"Stop distracting us." Jackson took a step toward me, excitement vibrating from him. For a man who swore off women, he was stupidly interested in my love life. "What's so special about this one?"

"There's something between us I can't explain." I sighed, shaking my head. "I know it sounds insane, but from the moment I saw her, I felt this connection like I've known her for lifetimes."

"Whoa, slow down there Romeo," Shaun laughed. "Love at first sight, huh? Never took you for the romantic type!"

"So it was more than a good time!" Finn chuckled. "Fucking knew it. You lying sack of shite."

I laughed, holding up a hand to stop their teasing. "As much as I wish I could see where this might lead, there's one rather significant complication." At their confused looks, I sighed. "She's not just some woman I met at a bar. As of yesterday... she's my replacement attorney."

Silence fell over the group, three pairs of widened eyes staring at me in disbelief.

"Your attorney?" Shaun asked. "As in, the one helping you buy Starlight Studios?"

I nodded, dragging a hand through my hair. "The very same."

Finn burst out laughing. "Oh, this just gets better and better! Trust you to fall for the one woman completely off limits, eh?"

"What are the odds?" Shaun asked, incredulous.

"Apparently, quite low." I shook my head. "But her charade only amused me. It made her more intriguing."

"Sounds like our boy's losing his touch," Finn teased, winking at me. "Can't even get a woman to admit she knows him after a night in the sack."

"Oi!" I protested, though I couldn't help but laugh along. "There's just something about her."

"Whatever you say." Jackson smirked. "Maybe it's time you embrace your new status as a mere mortal among women."

"Hardly." I crossed my arms, the challenge igniting a fire within me. "If anything, it's given me a reason to enjoy the chase again. I can't remember the last time I felt this excited about pursuing someone."

"Good on you, Nathan," Shaun said with a supportive smile. "Just don't forget us when you're off wooing your attorney."

"As if you'd let me." I nudged him with an elbow. "You lot are stuck with me for life."

"God help us all." Finn hung his head, feigning a sigh of resignation.

Finn and Shaun laughed, but Jackson brushed it aside with a swipe of his hand. "Yeah yeah. Details, please."

Chuckling, I gave in. "Canadian. Fierce, ambitious —" I hesitated for a moment, thinking back to our one-night stand, "— and undeniably captivating."

"When do we get to meet this captivating mystery woman of yours?" Shaun clapped me on the back.

"She's not mine though, is she?" I shook my head at him.

"Who's saying she can't be?" Jackson asked.

"Uh, the part where she's my attorney, and I'd like to own Starlight Studios sooner than the next decade."

"You're thinking too much, Nate." Shaun clapped me on the shoulder, squeezing as he grinned at me.

"Mona was once off-limits to me but we still got together."

True. Mona had been Shaun's assistant in Wales. They were meant to wait to get together until after the series wrapped, but couldn't resist each other.

"Not everyone is like you, Shaun. Some of us want to keep our professional lives separate from our personal ones."

Jackson chuckled. "Say it with a little more conviction and we might believe you."

I grinned. "Alright, so I'm tempted." The buzz of excitement said I was more than tempted.

"Plus, it's hardly revolutionary," Finn muttered with his back to us. He studied the approaching team of makeup artists, our first sign that the crew was nearly ready for us. "Loads of celebs have dated their attorneys."

"Good for them. I'm not looking to date anyone."

Lie. If I could convince Cat, I'd bloody jump at the chance.

"Keep telling yourself that," Jackson said, his voice low, trying not to be overheard. "I'll put money on you falling into bed with her again by the end of the week."

I shook my head, amused but keeping my mouth shut so he wouldn't realise I agreed with him.

"Alright, enough teasing," Shaun interjected, clapping his hands together. "We've got a scene to shoot, boys. Let's get back to work!"

CHAPTER THREE

CATRINA

I stared down at my salad, picking at the greens with my fork as if they held the answers to all of my problems. Across from me, Sam chatted animatedly about her weekend plans, but I could barely focus on her words.

All I could think about was Nathan Logan and the case that now entwined us. His latest round of texts might have had something to do with it.

I didn't need to look at the messages to guess their contents. More offers of parties, dinners and coffee dates, all hidden beneath the guise of getting caught up on the case.

Naive I was not. But stupid? If I didn't stop seriously considering his offers, definitely.

A sudden sound snapped me back to reality. Fingers clicked in front of my face and my body jerked in surprise.

"Are you even listening to me?" Sam asked, her tone sharp but her eyes swimming with concern.

"Sorry." I sighed, stirring my dressing into the lettuce leaves aimlessly. "I've got case notes running circles inside my head." I forced a smile and put my fork down, leaning forward in a silent promise to pay attention. "What were you saying?"

"What do you take me for?" She shook her head, then a devious grin curled her lips. "Who is he, and why have you been holding out on me?" she asked, her voice ringing out loud and clear in the tiny but busy bistro.

"Could you keep your voice down?" I hissed, ducking my head.

She ducked hers too, her brows climbed in surprise. "Is it a secret?"

I bit my lip. The truth or a lie? My heart raced as I struggled for an answer I didn't fully understand myself.

"Oh my god, is he married?"

"No!"

I closed my eyes for a moment, taking a deep breath. Sam meant well, but her questions only muddled things.

"Fine. I'll tell you."

"So there is a guy?" At my nod, she bounced in her seat. "I knew it! Where did you meet him? What's his name? Is he hot?"

The chatter of the bistro faded into the background as Sam bombarded me with questions. I stared at the cup of coffee growing cold between my hands, my stomach churning.

"Slow down, Sam. Let me just think for a second, please." I took a sip of coffee and mentally prepared myself to spill the beans. "I met him at The Noir Bar on Friday when you ditched me. His name is Nathan. He's too hot for sanity and he's a client." I stared at her, my eyes conveying the meaning my mouth wouldn't let me.

"Shit."

"That was my thought when he walked into my office with Mike on Monday."

"Wait!" Her hands flew up, begging me to stop. "You didn't know?"

I took a deep breath, steeling myself for the confession.

Leaning as far forward as I could without lying in my lunch, I caught her up.

"So, after you ditched me Friday night, I decided to stay and drink a glass of bubbly to celebrate anyway. On my way to the bar, I tripped and this shockingly good-looking guy saved me from face-planting."

Sam's eyes got bigger as she listened. "No way. It was Nathan Logan?" At my nod, a smile came over her face that was impossible to ignore. "Aw. Your knight in designer armour!"

"We started chatting, and the next thing I knew, we were doing tequila shots. He was charming and funny, and so close I could feel the heat of him through my clothes." I sighed, remembering how they had flashed when I teased and goaded him. "Every time our eyes met, it felt like an electric shock passed between us. I didn't stand a chance."

Sam sighed. "With moves like that, who would?"

I laughed. "The bar was closing and I didn't want the night to end. So I asked him back to my place."

Sam's eyes went wide. "You minx! I never thought you had it in you."

I shook my head, biting my lip. "Neither did I. But those eyes, that smile, the way he made me feel... I couldn't resist."

Sam leaned in, her voice dropping. "So how was it? As mind-blowing as I'm imagining?"

I nodded, warmth rising in my cheeks. "Even better. That man's hands should be registered as lethal weapons."

"Lucky girl!" Sam whistled, drawing far too much attention.

"Sam," I growled, keeping my voice low.

"Oops. Sorry." She glanced around. Then her focus returned to me and she lowered her voice again. "No wonder you were off in dreamland. I'd be replaying that night too if I were you."

"Believe me, I was." I sighed.

"And now he's your client."

"A client who won't stop flirting with me." I glanced to the side, assessing the crowd around us for eavesdroppers or familiar faces. There were none thankfully and everyone appeared engrossed in their own lives. Still, I kept my voice low as I said, "As stupid as it is, I'm enjoying it."

I shook my head. "If the partners find out I had a one-night stand with Nathan Logan before he became a client…"

"They won't find out," Sam said firmly. "Your personal life is none of their business. You're a damn good lawyer, and this won't change that."

I raked my hands through my hair, torn between longing to see Nathan again and fear of the mess I'd landed myself in. "What was I thinking?"

Sam shrugged. "You were thinking that for once in your life you deserved to walk on the wild side with a gorgeous man. And now fate, or whatever, has dropped him in your lap again. Maybe it's meant to be!"

I laughed at her optimism. "Or a disaster."

"You never know unless you see where it leads," Sam said. "I know you, Ms Responsible. But not every risk ends in flames." She grinned. "Sometimes they end in passionate flames. And I know which one I'd bet on here!"

Perhaps she was right. Perhaps I should throw caution to the wind and just see where this unexpected twist might lead. After all, life was short. And Nathan Logan was temptation itself, already proving near impossible to resist.

I sighed, shaking my head. "The responsible thing would be to recuse myself from this case altogether. Start fresh with a new client and avoid potential scandal."

"Since when has anyone at that old boys' club we call a law firm cared about responsibility?" Sam scoffed. "Please, attorneys at our firm have done worse and still kept their jobs."

"What do you mean?" I asked, brows furrowing.

Sam shrugged. "Let's just say your little indiscretion is small potatoes compared to the assistant in litigation and the new client in family law."

"Are you serious?" My eyes widened.

No wonder Mike hadn't been concerned when I'd tried, and failed, to talk myself out of the job.

Sam nodded. "At least you didn't know him as a client at the time. Those two idiots should have known better, but as usual, different rules apply. Don't punish yourself for seeking a little pleasure, Cat."

I sat back in my chair. Maybe Sam was right. Recusing myself seemed like an overreaction. Mike had brushed me off. And though I knew I should avoid entangling my personal and professional lives, the thought of handing Nathan's case over and never seeing him again caused an unexpected pang of regret.

"You've given me a lot to think about."

"Besides, if they ever question you, you just throw the truth at them. Friday night, you didn't know who he was." She winced. "Although, how you'd sell that in this town full of celebrity chasers, I don't know, but I digress." She shook herself and smiled. "You didn't know then. Now you do, and you're maintaining a professional distance — not that I think you should — they can't ask more of you, Cat."

I stared into Sam's eyes, searching for any doubt in her words. But all I saw was unwavering confidence in me and my abilities as an attorney. Still, the lingering fear of jeopardising Nathan's case and my career gnawed at the edges of my mind.

"I appreciate your faith in me." I sighed, toying with the salad on my plate. "But I can't shake this feeling that I'm walking a tightrope here. If anyone finds out about that night... it could destroy everything I've worked so hard for."

"Babes, you can't let fear hold you back," Sam said, her voice softening. "You've always pushed through every obstacle that's come your way. This is no different. Trust yourself."

Her words resonated with me, echoing the same determination that had fuelled me throughout my career. I thought about Nathan — his undeniable charm, his heartbreaking vulnerability hidden beneath the surface, and the spark that had ignited between us.

Then, I thought about the promotion I'd spent years fighting for. If I backed away now, I'd be letting go of my dreams.

"Okay," I whispered, my decision solidifying like steel in my chest. "I'll stay on the case."

"Really?" Sam asked, surprise flickering across her face.

"Yes." I nodded resolutely. "I won't let my personal life dictate my professional decisions. I've ignored charming men all my life. I can resist Nathan Logan."

Sam smirked. "You think you can resist a Hollywood heartthrob with a British accent?"

Mischief glinted in her eyes, giving me pause. *I could, couldn't I?*

"Yes," I said with slightly less conviction.

She grinned. "Well, this is going to be fun."

*T*he lingering scent of roses filled the air as we stepped off the elevator. Sam and I shared a confused look before turning in opposite directions to return to our offices.

As I approached my desk, I saw a stunning bouquet of red and white roses sitting in a crystal vase. Their velvety petals were carefully arranged, and their beauty was undeniable.

A warmth spread through me as I spotted a handwritten note tucked among the blossoms.

'Thanks for all your help, Cat. You're a lifesaver! And a heart-stopper, too ;)'

I bit my lip to suppress a giddy smile, his playful words making me feel like a smitten teenager.

Do not get gushy over this. It'll only lead to trouble.

But my frown quickly melted into another grin as I took in the roses' sweet fragrance, memories of our night together rushing back in full force.

His hands skimming my skin, his lips turning my knees weak as they claimed mine, the feel of his hard body moving above me. Those eyes that seemed to stare directly into my reckless soul as we tangled together beneath the sheets.

The tequila had knocked down my walls, allowing me to throw caution to the wind and give in to a temptation I usually resisted.

Nathan had been charming, playful, pushing my buttons until I could stand it no longer.

"Wow, those are gorgeous," a passing intern said from my open door. "Who sent them?"

"Uh, just a friend," I mumbled, my cheeks heating as images of Nathan's wicked smile and wandering hands flashed through my mind.

I busied myself with paperwork, struggling in vain to shake off thoughts of throwing caution to the wind and reliving that passion all over again.

"Must be a really good friend," she said before leaving me alone in my office.

I let out a soft, conflicted laugh. Friend? Was that what Nathan was now? Or was he still simply a client who needed a reminder of the new line in the sand between us?

He was proving impossible to resist. The roses seemed to mock me, a reminder of our smoking hot night together and the mess I now found myself in.

I paced the office, torn between the need to call Nathan right that second and the voice of reason warning me to run far away from this smouldering spark before it ignited into an inferno.

"Get it together, Catrina," I muttered, forcing myself to focus on work and not those ocean eyes that saw straight into my reckless soul.

Yet no matter how hard I threw myself into reports, I couldn't let it go. Taking a deep breath, I composed an email to him.

Subject: Thank You

Dear Mr Logan,

I wanted to take a moment to express my appreciation for the lovely roses you sent to my office. They are beautiful and brighten up the office perfectly. However, I suggest a more professional tone should you need to send handwritten communications to my office again.

Warm regards,

Catrina Sinclair

I hesitated for a moment, my finger hovering over the mouse before finally pressing send. With that small task complete, I turned my attention back to the case files scattered across my desk.

My phone buzzed with a notification, breaking my focus.

NATHAN

Roses are red, violets are blue, I'm glad I could make your day brighter, just like you do. ;) —N

A grin stole across my face and warmth flooded my cheeks.

NATHAN

Sorry, was that too cheesy? I couldn't resist.

Before thinking better of it, I typed a quick reply.

CAT

Corny but cute. You're lucky you're charming.

NATHAN

Glad you liked the flowers. Just wanted to
brighten up your day, just like you did mine.

Joy warred with reason, even as I glanced at the roses and questioned what people would think. Nathan had a knack for catching me off guard, his teasing texts rekindling barely extinguished sparks.

I shook my head yet smiled all the same, frustration and yearning vying for the upper hand. The temptation to throw caution aside and give in to him wrestled with my need to play by the rules.

However, the reminder of the potential implications to the case flooded back, causing a wave of guilt to wash over me.

"Focus." I shook my head to clear it.

I put my phone aside, determined not to let Nathan's flirty texting derail me from my work.

But even as I tried to focus on the legal documents in front of me, my fear and joy tangled together, freezing me to the spot – fear of what this growing attachment could mean for both my career and my heart.

"Damn him for making me feel like this."

As I attempted to refocus on my preparations for the Shareholder's meeting, I couldn't escape the nagging feeling that I was standing at a crossroads, forced to make a decision that would shape not only the outcome of the Starlight Studios case but also the course of my future.

CHAPTER FOUR

CATRINA

"I'm five minutes away from the Shareholder's meeting," I said, as I pulled up to the entrance to parking beneath Starlight Studio's law firm. "Is there anything else I need to know, Maisy?"

"Hmm, we just received news that The Rogue Squad is getting a fifth movie," Maisy, Nathan's agent, said, her Southern voice warm and full of life. "It's going to be shot in Budapest so Nathan won't be in LA for the summer."

A potential argument for neglect.

"He'll have staff so I can argue that easily." I started to descend the ramp. "Anything else? I'm going underground so we might cut out."

"Not at the moment. I'll call if I think of anything."

"Thanks, Maisy."

We hung up and optimism surged through me. I had spent the entire week meticulously preparing for today's meeting with the Starlight Studios shareholders, poring over contracts, financial reports, company profiles into the early hours of each morning and questioning Maisy until we were both exhausted. I was determined to prove my worth on this high-profile case.

Sleep had been an afterthought compared to preparing for every possible scenario.

I parked and gathered my briefcase, my mind racing over the details of the deal. Somehow I needed to figure out why the shareholders had gone out of their way to throw every roadblock imaginable in the way of the sale. There had to be more to it than just Nathan's reputation.

Piece of cake.

With a deep breath, I stepped out of my car and straightened my blazer. *You've got this. All those late nights and double-checking will pay off.*

As I made my way across the dimly lit garage toward the bank of elevators, a figure in the distance caught my eye, waiting by the silver doors. My heart fluttered as I recognised Nathan's muscular body's far too familiar lines… even in a suit.

That should be illegal.

All other thoughts fell away. A sly smile teased the edge of his lips as he spotted me. A hint of stubble along his jaw only enhanced his irresistible charm.

Nathan Logan was a force of nature, sweeping into my life without warning and threatening to derail everything in his path. And though I knew it was foolish, there was a part of me tempted to let him.

But I had never let my love life get in the way of my career and I wouldn't start now… no matter how much he could make me ache with a single glance.

As I approached, I took a steadying breath, pushing aside all thoughts of what might be for what must be. Nathan flashed that devilish smile, and I felt its pull deep inside me.

"Morning, Catrina." His accent curled deliciously around

my name, threatening to unravel the tenuous hold I had on my composure. "Don't you look lovely today?"

I flushed at the compliment, struggling to maintain a professional air. "Good morning, Mr Logan."

"Nathan." His eyes drifted appreciatively over my figure as I approached. "That's a stunning suit."

I pressed my lips together, willing myself to find a little patience.

"Remember, we're here to focus on the shareholders' meeting. No flirting."

"How could I forget?" He fell into step beside me, leaning in with a conspiratorial whisper. "Though if the shareholders get too boring, we could always sneak off for a coffee. There's a great coffee shop right around the corner."

I bit back a smile. "Behave yourself. This deal depends on today going well."

He sighed in mock disappointment. "And here I thought you enjoyed our little back and forths, Icy. You're all business today."

"Exactly. No distractions. Follow my lead in there and stick to the key points we discussed. Convince them this deal is in their best interest, and we'll get Starlight Studios by month's end."

Surprise widened his eyes. "You really think it'll be that fast?"

"There's no reason it shouldn't be. I can't imagine what else they could throw out to stop it."

"That changes things," Nathan muttered to himself, rubbing the scruff along his jaw.

The elevator arrived with a soft ding and Nathan turned away from me, but not before I caught a thoughtful yet calculating gleam in his eyes.

What is he up to now?

As the doors slid open, I gave Nathan a pointed look before stepping inside.

His hand grazed my back as he reached out to press our floor. A tingle raced up my spine at his touch, warmth pooling in my cheeks.

His eyes gleamed with mischief. "You know, if you keep blushing like that around me, people will start to wonder if my Ice Queen is going soft."

I scowled, ignoring the acceleration of my pulse as he tacked on *my*.

"Don't call me that ridiculous nickname in front of people. And there's nothing for anyone to wonder about."

The doors slid shut and Nathan's gaze drifted over me, a smile teasing his lips. "Now that's too bad. I find myself rather fond of making you blush."

I shook my head, fighting the urge to laugh. We could never cross the line between business and pleasure.

And yet, a part of me thrilled at this game we played — and longed to surrender.

"Of course, Icy. You're in charge here." His eyes glinted with mischief. "Though I have to say, I like it more when you let me take control."

I sighed. "Do you ever stop?"

He chuckled, the rich sound warming me despite my best efforts. "Not when there are such... compelling reasons to misbehave."

The doors slid shut, and I gave him a stern look of warning.

"Behave."

Nathan held up his hands again in surrender, though his smile remained incorrigible. "As you wish, counsellor. I'm at your command."

He really was impossible.

❄

NATHAN

The conference room was stifling, filled with too much cologne and thinly veiled suspicion. I tugged at my collar, resisting the urge to loosen my tie as six sets of judgmental eyes watched us from around the long oak table.

Cat began her presentation with calm confidence, highlighting the key terms of our offer and the benefits to Starlight. But as she spoke, the shareholders' gazes drifted to me again and again, sizing me up like vultures eying a carcass.

Or more, searching for signs of the tabloid-loving playboy beneath the perfect veneer of my suit.

All lies of course, but gossip rags never had cared all that much for fact-checking.

I should have kept my mouth shut. Let Cat work her magic as I charmed them with little more than a smile, as we had discussed. But twenty minutes in, I couldn't stand their poorly concealed judgement another second.

"While gossip rags may question my character," I said, interrupting Cat mid-sentence, "my business dealings have always been ethical and above board. I want to assure you all that Starlight Studios will be acquired and managed legally and responsibly."

The Director of the Board, Miranda Chambers, raised a sculpted brow. "We are well aware of how you conduct your... *affairs*, Mr Logan. Excuse us if we seem hesitant to hand over control of this company to a known philanderer."

"Those rumours have been greatly exaggerated." I steepled my hands on the table in front of me, forcing myself to remain calm. "I built my career through dedication and hard work. My personal life is of no concern here."

Miranda smirked. "Forgive us if we seem hesitant to hand control to one better known for late-night carousing than professionalism."

Her accusation stung. My jaw clenched, a retort on the tip of my tongue. Cat silenced me with a look.

Cat smiled apologetically at the shareholders. "Excuse us for a moment." She met my gaze, her voice firm but low. "Not another word. You've caused enough damage."

I started to protest but swallowed the words at her quelling look.

When Cat turned back to the table, her tone was warm and gracious. "Tabloids provoke more than inform. An actor's reputation alone should not determine their dedication or work ethic."

Miranda frowned.

Cat's gaze flicked to me, a teasing glint in her eyes as if sharing some private joke. "Just look at Mr Logan's long list of accolades. He started on the lowest rung in his acting career, relocated to a foreign country to better himself and pursue a career in an industry he loved. I think that is far more telling of his character than fantastical scandals created on the basis of random witnesses and blurry pictures."

A grey-haired shareholder frowned. "The stories we've read suggest otherwise."

"And those stories are meant to generate website traffic, not report truthfully," Cat said. "I understand your concerns but urge you not to judge based on speculation alone. While finalising Mr Logan's business dealings for this acquisition, I have found him professional, serious about his craft, and committed to operational responsibility — the qualities most important in a role such as this."

Miranda pursed her lips. "You ask us to ignore years of questionable headlines for your brief assessment?"

"Not ignore, simply look beyond." Cat's smile was earnest. "Consider the acclaim and respect of Nathan's peers, those who judge him based on skill alone. Their high praise speaks to the calibre of actor — and man — he truly is."

A heavy silence fell. I scarcely dared breathe, afraid to hope Cat's clever reasoning had swayed them.

Miranda gave a brisk nod. "Your perspective is appreciated, Ms Sinclair. We will discuss the proposal's terms now."

By the end, the shareholders seemed placated if still unconvinced. I shot Cat a remorseful glance. She responded with a subtle nod, forgiveness simmering in her green eyes. Relief washed through me followed quickly by gratitude.. She had rescued this meeting from disaster, proving herself my champion even when I deserved it least.

I mouthed a silent "thank you."

No praise or achievement could inspire me like her belief in me. She was worth any price to my reputation or career.

My Cat. My saviour. My secret addiction I couldn't give up, even if I wanted to.

CATRINA

As we left the conference room, Nathan caught my arm. "I'm sorry. You were right; I should have kept my mouth shut."

I sighed. "You need to control that temper of yours. This won't be the last time you're judged for your reputation, fair or not."

Nathan brushed my cheek, gratitude evident. "Thank you. For seeing the truth…" His fingers traced my jaw, coaxing me to meet his gaze. "And for defending me when I don't deserve it."

I leaned into his touch before catching myself. We couldn't cross lines, no matter the connection between us. And definitely not when people could see us. I took a step back, ignoring the loss of warmth where his hand had been.

Thankfully, the hallway was empty, but I couldn't expect to always be that lucky.

We made our way to the elevator, a heavy silence between us. Nathan's gaze drifted to me, a small smile teasing his lips.

The doors slid open and we stepped inside.

"You were bloody brilliant in there," Nathan said, shifting closer as the door closed. His eyes gleamed with admiration. "I'd call that grounds for celebration."

I couldn't help smiling, despite my best efforts. His enthusiasm was contagious.

"I appreciate the vote of confidence, but we still have a lot of work to do."

"Come on, Icy," he said with a dramatic sigh. "You can't tell me you're not at least a little thrilled by today's progress."

I glanced at him, taking in his polished hair and bright eyes. He was captivating and he knew it.

"Of course. But let's celebrate when the contract's signed."

He nodded in understanding. "Fair enough. But you know what would be a great way to celebrate once we're done?" His grin turned mischievous. "A date with me."

For a moment, I considered giving in. How would anyone find out? I could drink my fill of him and get this fascination out of my system.

But I would know.

"I don't think that would be a good idea."

"Why not?"

I sighed, exasperated by his refusal to understand. "I could lose my job."

Although, would I actually? Sam seemed convinced attorneys at our firm regularly broke that rule and none of them had been fired.

Plus, if I give in, maybe he'll get bored and move on.

"Then we'll be discreet."

"Nathan," I sighed, the sound far too wistful.

The floors flashed by, the elevator racing to free us. Only the longer I spent with him the less I wanted to be free.

Stupid. So bloody stupid.

"Why me?"

"Why not you?" He ran a hand through his hair, holding my gaze. "You're different. Refreshing. Honest and unimpressed by my status. That doesn't happen a lot."

My pulse raced; I was lost for words. He saw something in me I didn't.

"Do you want me to keep going? It's like you don't see what you bring to the table," he said softly. "A breath of fresh air."

I wished I could give him the answer he wanted. But if I agreed, he'd never stop.

Instead, we stood in silence as I searched for the words to end this.

"I appreciate you explaining, but it doesn't change anything. We need to remain professional."

"About that…" He reached out and hit the emergency stop button, the elevator lurching to a halt.

I grabbed the railing to steady myself, staring at him in disbelief. "What the hell are you doing?"

"You were staring at it with panic."

"I was not."

"You couldn't stop looking at the thing." Nathan shrugged, stepping closer, gaze searching mine. "I figured that meant you didn't want this conversation to end and if the doors open, there might be people around to see it continue." His fingers traced my jaw, coaxing me to meet his eyes once more. "Now you don't have to worry because no one can see us."

I swallowed hard, torn between rebuffing him and giving in to desire. His touch left me powerless to resist, my objections fading into memory. "My office… would have sufficed."

His smile turned wolfish. "It'll start moving again soon enough." He brushed his lips against my cheek, stubble grazing my skin. "I couldn't resist stealing a moment alone… with you."

"This is highly unprofessional." My protest sounded feeble even to my ears.

Nathan's eyes gleamed. "Then hit the button to restart the lift." His fingers traced down my neck, setting my skin aflame.

My pulse raced at his touch. "We really shouldn't. Not when the studio deal's at stake."

Nathan stepped closer, a coy smile teasing his lips. "It'll be done in a couple of weeks. You said so yourself. Then you'll be free as a bird?" His thumb grazed my mouth; he leaned in close. "You'll have no excuses left to keep us apart."

"This is crazy." I turned away, grasping at self-control. "We're supposed to be sorting the contract details, not…"

"Not what?" Nathan nuzzled my neck, hands sliding down my back. "Giving in to pent-up longing?" He chuckled, his breath warm against my skin. "Seems I just couldn't help myself."

I gasped, my resolve threatening to crumble under his touch. "We have obligations to fulfil first."

"The contract will be signed before you know it." Nathan grasped my chin, forcing me to meet his gaze. "But right now, rules were made to be broken, right?" His eyes gleamed with mischief.

The sincerity in his voice caught me off guard. He pressed tender kisses along my jaw and down my neck, his five o'clock shadow grazing my sensitive skin. I leaned helplessly into him.

We shouldn't be doing this.

"Tell me you feel it too." Nathan's whisper grazed my lips. "Tell me, and let's start living for the moment."

I trembled, clinging to self-control by a thread. "If the Board knew we were—"

Nathan's mouth captured mine, hungry yet gentle; I gasped, control snapping. His touch ignited a slow burn I'd fought so hard to ignore.

My fingers grasped his shoulders for support. Nathan

growled in approval, pulling me closer still, his fingers tangling in my hair.

When he finally broke the kiss, I could only stare up at him, breathless.

Nathan smiled knowingly, tracing my damp, swollen lips with one thumb. "So what do you say, will you have dinner with me?"

"I can't," I gasped, scrambling for coherency.

"Not right now." Nathan chuckled. "When the deal is done."

I swallowed heavily, pulse still racing. "What?"

"When we close the deal on the Studio, will you have dinner with me?" His eyes gleamed with determination.

My breath caught at the sincerity in his voice. "Are you... asking me out?"

"Trying to, if you'll let me." Nathan brushed my hair back, tone turning coaxing. "What do you say, Cat? Think you could bear an evening of wining and dining if I promise to be on my best behaviour until then?"

I shouldn't be tempted and yet…

"It wouldn't be professional."

"Sod professionalism." Nathan grasped my hands, leaning in close. "I'm asking if you'll give this a chance once we've inked that damn contract." His forehead rested against mine, his sigh warm against my skin. "I won't be your client anymore. There'll be no more need for professionalism between us."

Going on a date with Nathan Logan — it was crazy to even think about. He was a notorious playboy, used to charming women way hotter than me. No way would someone like him stay interested in a lawyer from Ontario. The second this job together ended, so would this little crush of his.

And yet... the way he looked at me made me feel like the only girl on earth. When he touched me, I couldn't breathe.

He brought out this hunger in me I'd been ignoring for so long. What would be the harm in grabbing dinner, just once?

I exhaled slowly. "If you're still interested once this deal is closed... then yes, I'll have dinner with you."

Nathan's eyes lit up at my answer. "You won't regret it."

I held up a hand to stall his enthusiasm. "But let's be clear — this is just dinner. I'm not promising anything more."

His smile turned cocksure. "We'll see about that." Nathan leaned in close, nuzzling my neck. "You won't be able to resist me."

A shiver ran through me at his touch. "Don't be so sure of yourself. I don't fall that easily."

Nathan chuckled, undeterred. "Is that a challenge, Icy?"

"A warning." I folded my arms across my chest. "I'm agreeing to dinner, that's all. So you better bring your A-game if you want anything more."

He grinned. "Game on, then." Nathan pulled me close again as the doors opened, brushing his lips against my ear. "You're in trouble now, darling."

I swallowed hard, hoping my bravado wouldn't come back to haunt me.

CHAPTER FIVE

CATRINA

The sun shone brightly through the window of my office, casting a warm glow across my desk as I carefully reviewed the legal documents for the Starlight Studios acquisition. After Friday's meeting, I had a firmer grip on the situation and any lingering doubts about my abilities had completely faded.

The buzz of my phone cut through the silence, pulling me from my concentration. Almost without thought, I unlocked the device, swiping to the new message.

> **NATHAN**
>
> Did you know that your smile has the power to light up an entire room? ;) x

A blush crept along my cheeks — damn him and his charm. My stomach twisted with a combination of desire and frustration.

Trust Nathan Logan to continue his incessant flirting even after I agreed to his demands.

I silenced the notifications and refocused on my work. This project was too important to be sidetracked by idle charm and tempting blue eyes.

Even if said eyes had coaxed more kisses from me and persuaded me into a date I would likely regret.

"You're different. Refreshing. Honest and unimpressed by my status. That doesn't happen a lot."

His eyes lit up with a thrill of victory would forever stick with me.

With a sigh, I shook off the memory and redoubled my focus. My career was at stake, and I refused to be swayed, no matter the effect those blue eyes might have.

The next day, armed with a little distance and a carefully crafted list of issues, I drafted an email to Nathan. And deleted it. And retyped it. Over and over again. Never before had I given so much consideration to an email.

He was not going to like it, but what could I do?

Chewing my lip, I hit send, just barely stopping myself from closing my eyes.

Dear Mr Logan,

I hope this email finds you well. As per our discussion, I've reviewed the terms for the acquisition. In the attachment, you'll find a summary of the key points, but in addition to these, I have received a formal request from the shareholders of Starlight Studios regarding your signature on a non-disparagement and non-competition clause. Upon careful review, I will be pushing back on the non-competition clause as it appears to be impractical and unrealistic.

However, I would like to confirm your willingness to sign the non-disparagement clause, which is a common and reasonable provision in such transactions. Please let me know your thoughts on this matter at your earliest convenience.

Thank you for your attention to this matter.

Sincerely,
Catrina Sinclair
Associate Attorney
Hudson, Wallace & Associates

With the email sent, I leaned back in my chair, holding my breath. I shouldn't be feeling so uneasy about a perfectly normal request.

Nathan's constant flirting made it increasingly difficult to separate my personal feelings from my professional responsibilities. I couldn't indulge in those emotions — not now, and perhaps not ever. For the moment, all I could do was hope that Nathan would take my advice, and we could proceed with the acquisition as smoothly as possible and detangle ourselves from this emotional no-man's land.

Five minutes later, my phone pinged.

NATHAN

I'd rather you talk dirty to me but I guess formal will have to do it for me for now. *winky face* What am I signing?

I sighed. Of course, he would.

Torn between annoyance and the fluttering excitement his words stirred within me, I pursed my lips and considered the best way to keep him on track.

Taking a deep breath, I typed my response.

I hit send, hoping he would take the hint.

While I waited for his reply, I couldn't help but imagine the warmth of his hand in mine and the mischievous glint in his eyes.

Would it be so bad to break the rules just once?

My laptop pinged, saving me from the dangerous thought.

A new email loaded from Nathan. The subject line read, "Re: Non-Disparagement Clause," and a small sense of relief washed over me.

Dear Ms. Sinclair,

I hereby confirm my agreement to sign the non-disparagement clause as requested. If there are any further documents that require my attention, please do not hesitate to let me know.

Yours sincerely,
Nathan Logan

I exhaled slowly, grateful for his change in tone. It appeared that he had finally recognised the importance of keeping things strictly professional between us — though why did a tiny part of me feel disappointed?

Then a knock sounded on my office door, making me scowl.

"Come in," I called out, minimising the email window on my screen.

The door swung open. Nathan strolled in, the picture of casual nonchalance in jeans and t-shirt that hugged his unfairly toned physique. He closed the door behind him, smiling as if dropping by to see his girlfriend. Except I wasn't his girl.

Yet.

My heart kicked into overdrive at the sight of him.

"What are you doing here?" I asked, rising from my chair.

He approached my desk with a grin meant to dazzle and disarm, wielding his unfair share of charm as a weapon against my composure.

"Thought we should talk about the deal face to face. Make sure we're on the same page."

I folded my arms and arched a brow. "We were doing fine over email."

"Were we?" He chuckled. "Admit it, you'd rather hash this out with me in person."

He had me there. I fought a smile and shook my head as I sank back into my seat. "That suggests we don't agree. We just had a... difference of opinion."

"Is that what they call it in Canada?" Nathan moved closer, eyes dancing as he rounded my desk. Nerves fluttered in my stomach as the scent of his spicy cologne hit me.

He settled himself on the edge of my desk, towering over me but his muscular thigh within tantalising reach.

Thank God my office door was shut and lacked windows into the open floor.

I tilted my head back to meet his mischievous gaze. "Your email said you'll sign the clause. Anything else we need to discuss now?"

"A few things." His smile faded. "Listen, the bigwigs know my reputation. They're waiting to make trouble."

I frowned, confused. "What's that got to do with me?"

"I trust you, Cat." He met my gaze. "And I want them to see that. So if it helps, I'm okay with you accessing my phone tracker. But only you."

I blinked. "You want me to track your phone?"

He grinned wryly. "Who else would I trust with that?"

His words struck deep. I hadn't realised he trusted me that much already.

"You don't have to do that. We'll figure something else out."

"I want to." Nathan leaned in close enough for me to take a full on whiff of that spicy scent — the man was a walking temptation. He took my hand, eyes earnest. "We're partners now, like it or not. Might as well prove that to the doubters."

Heat rushed to my cheeks. I swallowed hard and nodded. "I appreciate your trust."

"I know you will, darling." He lifted my hand to his lips, smirking. "And when you need a break from that lawyer act…" His smile turned devilish. "Feel free to track me down. I could use some fun after all this dull work."

Before I could reply, he tugged me up and out of my chair until I fell into his arms. His mouth captured mine in a kiss that seared me to my core. I gasped against his lips, free hand grasping his shirt to pull him closer as my body ignited.

Nathan deepened the kiss slowly, teasing my mouth open with his tongue. All my reasons why it was foolish of me to give into him at work scattered to the wind. How did he unravel me so completely? His hands roamed down my back, urging me closer until I was pressed flush against him. The kiss went on until we were both breathless. I stared up at him, reeling, as reality crashed back in.

I was at work.

"Catrina, are you blushing?" Sam teased a couple of days later with a mischievous grin on her face.

She stood in the doorway, leaning her hip against the frame. *How long had she been there?*

I quickly locked my phone, hiding the latest string of flirty texts from Nathan.

"Absolutely not." My cheeks betrayed me as they flushed an even deeper shade of red. "It's just... warm in here."

A week had passed since Nathan had kissed me in this very office. Keeping myself focused proved difficult, especially when my desk served as a reminder of how easily I could give in to him. For the first time ever, I found myself counting down the hours until work ended for the weekend.

"Uh-huh, sure it is." Sam's grin only grew. "I've noticed you blushing and biting your lip a lot in the last few days. Did you make a decision on that thing we talked about?"

"No." I shook my head, pasting what I hoped was an innocent smile to my lips. "Absolutely not."

She studied me, her eyes narrowing. "I'm not sure I believe you."

Just then, my phone buzzed with another text from Nathan. He'd sent me two pictures of himself in different suits – one a deep navy blue, and the other a classic black.

The first clashed with his eyes, but the second made them pop. The sight of him, broad shoulders straining against the shirts and blond hair swept back, polished yet carefully mussed, it stole my voice and, momentarily, my common sense.

Why am I resisting a snack like him again?

NATHAN

Which one do you like best?

CATRINA

Why?

NATHAN

It's for the premiere next week. I can't pick and I trust your judgement.

"Wow," I muttered under my breath, staring my fill of him

in both perfectly tailored suits. He looked every bit the Holly-wood heartthrob that he was, but there was something more to Nathan — an intensity behind those blue eyes that hinted at a vulnerability he didn't often reveal.

"Wow indeed," Samantha echoed, leaning over my shoulder to catch a glimpse of the photo. "That man certainly knows how to wear a suit."

Don't I know it.

She rounded my desk, smirking. "So, which one are you going to pick for your 'client'?" She added air quotes around the word, making her scepticism clear.

"Neither," I replied curtly, typing out a response to Nathan.

CATRINA

I'm your attorney, not your stylist. Good luck tonight.

"**C**at, I appreciate all your hard work on this," Nathan said, his British accent making even mundane updates sound far more enticing than they should. "It sounds like everything is moving along nicely."

I held the phone to my ear and for just a second, I allowed myself to shut my eyes and let his warm English accent wash over me. He could read me the phone book and his voice would make me shiver.

We were hashing out what would hopefully be the final details of the acquisition, just the two of us on the line. Miranda had tried to throw up more roadblocks through the week, requesting more unnecessary audits, some of them ones that had already been completed. I successfully knocked them all down. We were so close to closing the deal, I could almost taste it.

"Of course." I forced my voice to stay steady and professional. "That's what I'm here for. I'll make sure we close this deal as smoothly as possible." I glanced at my watch. "Well, I think we've covered most of the legal technicalities. I've got a bottle of merlot calling my name so if there's nothing else, I'll touch base with you next week."

"Before you hang up, there's something else I wanted to talk to you about."

My brows rose. "Oh?"

"I have an upcoming film premiere and I would love it if you could join me."

My mind instantly flashed to the pictures he'd sent me. I'd be lying if I claimed to have not studied them until I had every line of his body memorised. *Wonder which one he chose.*

I hesitated, my fingers tightening around the phone. "Thank you for asking me, but you know I have to say no, right?"

"But do you really?" His honeyed voice filled my ears.

"Yes. I'm representing you legally in an important business transaction. Appearing together socially could undermine perceptions of my objectivity and professionalism."

"Is that really such an issue these days?" Nathan argued. "Attorneys date clients all the time in this town. Need I remind you about Brandon Cooper's lawyer, or Charlie Thor's? No one batted an eye."

I sighed, more frustrated that his examples hit close to home, weighing in his favour, than by his persistence.

"My firm isn't as... flexible in their views." As far as the employee handbook stated. In practice, I couldn't be so sure. Just yesterday, I'd heard whispers of one of the partners cheating on his wife with a high status client. "And this deal matters too much for me to take chances."

A beat of charged silence passed between us and when he spoke again, resignation tinged his words. "You're right, of course. Wishful thinking. I need to borrow some of your patience."

"After the deal, we'll see where things stand," I promised softly. "For now…"

"For now, it's business only. I hear you, counsellor." Nathan's voice regained its charm. "You sure drive a hard bargain." A lingering pause. "Goodnight, Cat."

"Have a good weekend," I said softly before hanging up the phone.

As much as I longed to share in the glitz and glamour of his world, I knew that our partnership demanded boundaries.

While the silence enveloped my office again, I leaned back in my chair, staring at the phone in my hand. The weight of our conversation hung in the air, leaving me with a sense of longing that I struggled to squash.

Why did it have to be like this? Why couldn't we just be two people, free to explore the connection that seemed to spark between us?

My gaze drifted to the window and the warm glow of the sun setting reflecting off the skyscrapers surrounding me. For a moment, I allowed myself to imagine a different life — one where Nathan and I could walk the red carpet together, hand in hand, unburdened by the complexities of our professional relationship.

But as quickly as the fantasy appeared, I forced it from my mind, reminding myself of the responsibilities I had to my clients and my career. It wasn't fair to entertain such thoughts when there was work to be done, deals to close, and dreams to fulfil.

CHAPTER SIX

NATHAN

"So, is it true you once trashed a hotel room in a drunken rage after a breakup?" Cat peered up from her laptop screen, brow furrowed in concern.

I sat in the leather chair opposite her desk, hoping that her inquisition would wind down at least before lunch. When she'd asked me to clear my morning to go over the case, I'd honestly been hoping it was code for something much more fun.

"No, Icy, that's as false as the rest." I shook my head, amused despite the endless stream of questions. "That footage was manipulated. I don't binge drink or riot."

She arched a brow. "And why should I believe you?"

"You have my word." I held her gaze, hoping my sincerity showed through. "I value privacy too much now to do something so stupid."

Her brows rose. "And five years ago?"

I laughed.

"You caught me — I was young and stupid then." I raised my hands in surrender. "But we all grow up sometime, right?"

"Really?" She studied me, a challenge in her eyes. "Leopards don't change their spots so easily, Nathan."

"When there are a million cameras pointed at them, they do."

She pursed her lips, considering. "And the latest gossip rags? All lies too?"

I nodded, hoping she'd believe the truth over tabloid trash. "You know better than to trust those vultures, Cat. They need to sell papers."

"I didn't realise you were so camera-shy." Scepticism laced her tone.

Those curves and that sass were going to be the death of me.

I held back a sigh. "Look, things change. Priorities change. I got smarter — grew up and wised up. Not everything needs to be a public spectacle."

Her full lips pursed as she studied me, her green gaze boring into me.

"Okay, let's try again, since you need more convincing." I shook my head, smirking at her stubborn determination. "I have never and will never trash a hotel room."

I leaned back in my seat across from her desk with forced casualness, pulse kicking into overtime under her scrutiny. I fought not to fidget, hoping she glimpsed what she did to me without my saying a word. This push and pull between us was maddening, but I wouldn't give it up for the world.

"You buying any of this?" I arched a brow, anticipation building as pink tinged her cheeks. I lived for those rare moments when I caught her off balance.

Her lips twitched. "I'm reserving judgement. Your promises don't match your reputation."

I chuckled, pride filling me that I could make someone like Cat blush. "Then give me a chance to change your mind, counsellor." I winked, thrill rushing through me as she fought a smile.

"What about emotionally abusing an ex then?" she asked.

I shook my head. "There was no relationship. She wanted fame at my expense."

A familiar little line had formed between her manicured brows and her lips pressed tight as she considered me. She brushed some loose strands of long golden brown hair back, her fingers tapping on the desk, fidgeting as she puzzled me out.

"So you don't date at all?" she still looked doubtful, making me laugh once again.

"Not properly, no. My agent started those model tales to make me seem unattainable."

Cat studied me before nodding and continuing. "Alright, how about being reckless or an arrogant diva then?"

"Lies spread to threaten my reputation." I grinned at her.

"What really happened with that model in St. Tropez?"

I stifled a groan, raking my fingers through my hair. "Not that I don't enjoy spending my mornings with you, but why are we rehashing my past when the deal is all but signed?"

She shot me a look that broke no argument. "They caught us off guard before. I won't have them blindside us next time."

She wouldn't have the shareholders blindside *her* she meant. Those stuck-up bastards needed to focus on the job of approving this deal instead of digging into my personal life. As if my reputation had any bearing on business. Never mind that I was one of the hardest-working actors of my generation or that this studio would be lucky to have me.

"I have to be sure of who I'm representing."

"Fine. Ask me anything." I held her gaze, hoping she could see my sincerity. "I'm an open book for you. Question me as long as needed."

Her breath caught, her eyes bright with what I hoped was longing. "This may take a while then."

My smile widened. "There's nowhere I'd rather be right now than with you."

A ghost of a smile graced her lips.

I picked up my chair.

Cat blinked at me in surprise. "What are you doing?"

I flashed her an unrepentant grin as I set the chair down by her side. "It's easier to refresh my memory seeing what you're looking at."

She tensed up as I settled in, our shoulders and thighs brushing. She shot me a look that said she saw straight through my flimsy excuse but a blush stained her cheeks all the same.

"Must you?"

"Yes." I winked, delighted when she cleared her throat and turned back to the screen.

Cat dove into the next question, her voice slightly higher pitched than before. I bit back a laugh, leaning in to glimpse the article on her monitor. The subtle floral scent of her shampoo filled my senses, along with the warmth radiating from her skin.

"Alright, the model in St. Tropez."

"We shared a drink, posed for some photos. That's it." When her brow rose in disbelief, I held up my hands. "On my honour, Icy. I was there for work, she wanted the press. We parted as strangers."

Our legs touched under the desk and I let my knee rest there, pressing closer. Cat inhaled sharply, clutching the table edge.

"A stranger you kissed?" She tried to shuffle her chair away, I hooked my ankle around hers under the chair and held her there. She huffed in frustration, biting her lip.

"Purely for show." I shrugged, not even bothering to hide my amusement.

"The photos make it look pretty real."

"Studied them closely, did you?" I smirked. "If I couldn't sell a fake kiss, I'd be a shitty actor."

I brushed my fingers along the bare skin of her arm. Her breath caught, eyes darting to mine. Reaching up, my fingers lingered against the curve of her neck. She leaned into the touch, pulse leaping under my fingertips.

"If I'm to believe your comment about changing," she said, her voice breathy, "I presume earlier rumours of your… exploits are true?"

"Look, I'm not going to deny that in my early twenties I got swept up in the flash and wasn't too picky about who I hooked up with." She shivered as I grazed the sensitive skin behind her ear, eyes flashing dangerously. I grinned, ready to push my luck. "I was an idiot, and it took time to grow up."

When she looked away, flustered, I laughed under my breath. She shot me a glare that promised trouble.

"That's putting it mildly."

"You're right. But the guy I was then isn't the one sitting here now." I caught her chin, making her meet my gaze, willing her to see the truth. "I grew up and my priorities changed."

Cat studied me for a long moment before nodding, seemingly satisfied. A few tendrils of honey-coloured hair escaped her messy bun, catching the light. I reached out and gently tucked one loose strand behind her ear. My fingers lingered, tracing the curve of her cheek. Her breath caught, eyes locking with mine.

We stared at one another, the world narrowing to just this — her green eyes searching mine, my heart pounding wildly against my ribs.

My gaze dropped to her mouth as she wet her lips, thoughts scattering. I was vaguely aware of leaning closer, powerless to stop myself. So close I could see the faint freckles dusting her nose and the gold flecks in her eyes.

Her eyes drifted shut. Her hands clutched the arms of the

chair and she swayed forward. I froze in place, mentally begging her to close those last few inches between us.

She cleared her throat and pulled away. "So what about the drunken brawls?"

Disappointment slammed into me but I forced it away. There would be plenty of time to tempt her to my way of thinking.

"When I was younger, yes. Anything more recent..." I leaned back, closing my fist tight against my thigh like I could hold on to the warmth of her skin. "Nothing but lies. I told you at the bar our first night that I prefer quiet nights in to courting tabloid attention these days. I'm also much more level-headed than I was in my early twenties. "

"And the ever changing stream of models and socialites?"

"In the last few years?" I shrugged. "Publicity stunts orchestrated by my agent."

Cat's gaze dropped to where my knee brushed hers against. "So you don't chase fame and beauty over substance?" she eventually asked, her voice strangled.

Oh, to see inside her mind. *What's got you worked up, Icy?*

I shook my head. "Not anymore."

This inquisition was proving more enjoyable by the second. My methods might be unorthodox but they got the job done. She could protest all she liked but the tension sparking between us with every accidental touch told another story. I was breaking through those professional boundaries, slow but sure. Any objections she raised were feeble at best.

"Must you persist in crowding me?" She shot me an exasperated look, though there was laughter dancing in her green eyes.

"If it bothers you, I can always move." I held her gaze. "Just say the words."

Cat's lips parted in surprise before pressing into a thin line, saying nothing. I chuckled, keeping still. As if she wanted me to leave. The blush staining her cheeks and her quickened breath gave her away.

This little game of ours was proving too much fun to end now. I leaned in, pulse racing at her sharp intake of breath.

"Well?"

"Must you?" Her voice was barely more than a whisper, her eyes dropping to my mouth.

I smiled slowly. "Must I what?"

After a few minutes, Cat cleared her throat. "You never did say if there's anyone special now."

I raised a brow, surprised by the question after asking her out just last week. "Did you forget about our plans already?"

She bit her lip, but didn't answer.

I reached out, touching her hand. "There's only you, Cat, since that night. I thought I made that clear when I asked you to dinner." I smiled. "Or do I need to stop another elevator to convince you?"

Her gaze dropped to our joined hands, then glazed over. I gave her fingers a gentle squeeze.

"Where did your mind wander off to?"

Cat flushed, clearing her throat and pulling her hand away. "Nowhere, I should keep going through these links."

She turned back to her screen, clicking the next headline the firm's assistants had compiled. Her computer chimed as the page opened — and she gasped, eyes going wide.

I glanced over, suppressing a groan at the sight of those damn photos from years back splayed across her monitor. Trust the tabloids to keep dredging up relics from my reckless youth.

Two photos filled her screen, one a perfect shot of my backside while I was sprawled out across a bed and in the other I'd just stepped out of the shower. I had a towel pressed to my hair, water still running down my very naked body. They left absolutely nothing to the imagination, but the second was the press's favourite. My junk was on full display.

Cat gaped at the images in shock before glancing away, her whole face scarlet.

She peeked at me from the corner of her eye. "I didn't expect to see quite so much of you."

"No need to blush, Icy. You've seen it all in person already — and given me a far better review." I flashed her my panty-dropping smile, pleased when she laughed.

"Care to explain?" She gestured at the screen, keeping her eyes carefully averted from the screen.

"It was a few years back, after an afterparty for a music awards show. I went home with a girl and a mediocre night and left her place the next day none the wiser." I dragged a hand through my hair. "A few hours later, I had Maisy on the phone breaking the news."

Cat winced. "She sold nude photos of you to the tabloids?"

I shrugged. "Apparently so. Took me by surprise at the time but with the benefit of hindsight, I should've known better."

"Did you press charges?" Cat asked.

"Thought about it, but Maisy convinced me not to." I sighed. "Said the girl was young and made a mistake, and a lawsuit would ruin her life."

Cat's eyes narrowed. "How charitable of you."

I held up my hands. "Don't give me that look, I know how naïve it was now. But I was a bloody idiot in my twenties and thought avoiding more bad publicity was the smart move."

Cat scoffed. "More like you didn't want to seem ungrateful, given how much you benefited."

"You're not wrong. Turned out posing in my birthday suit landed me the role of a lifetime. All press is good press, right?"

Cat rolled her eyes. "Only you could turn a compromising photo scandal into a career opportunity."

"What can I say, my fans seemed to approve of the view."

I winked. "Sales of those tabloids skyrocketed, the studio execs took notice, and the rest is history."

"Yes, your 'view' certainly benefited you, didn't it?" she muttered.

I laughed. "Are you sure you weren't a fan yourself, Icy?" I dropped my voice, leaning closer. "After all, you studied those photos awfully closely. Find anything… interesting?"

Cat spluttered. "Don't be absurd." She shoved at my chest but I caught her hand, linking our fingers.

"No need to be shy, love." I brought our joined hands to my lips, brushing a kiss over her knuckles while holding her gaze. "Plenty of women would kill to trade places with you right now."

She shook me off, swatting at my chest, the colour still high in her cheeks. "Must you always tease?"

"If it makes you smile? Absolutely." I winked.

She shook her head at my antics but her smile remained. I grew serious, catching her hand once more.

"I joke about how they helped me, but I need you to know, I made sure to never put myself in that situation again."

"How could you possibly guarantee that?"

"I stopped picking up strangers in random places after those photos." I searched her eyes, willing her to grasp my meaning. *Until her.* "I hope this doesn't change things between us."

She studied me in silence before she smiled softly, threading her fingers through mine.

"The past is the past. You're not defined by your mistakes, even such… memorable ones." Her eyes danced with humour.

I pulled her into my arms, nuzzling her neck. She wrapped her arms around me, holding tight for a moment before she stiffened.

She pushed against my chest. "Stop. We can't do this again."

I searched her eyes but she glanced away, cheeks flushing. She cleared her throat and focused on her screen again, quickly shutting down the nudes.

"Were you arrested on a DUI charge?"

Cat peeked at me and quickly looked away, but not before I caught the hint of a smile curving her lips. The crease between her brows had smoothed out. I settled in, confident I could outlast her questions. She was worth the interrogation.

CATRINA

"Of course, he'd say that." Maisy chuckled. "Men, no sense of the damage one wrong move could do."

I waited no more than two minutes after Nathan left my office before calling his agent, Maisy. He could swear every rumour was false until he turned blue, but without corroboration, I would always struggle to believe him.

"But he really didn't know about the photos?" I asked, needing to be certain.

"Absolutely not." Maisy tutted. "Honestly, Cat, you should have seen him back then. He was in my office, running circles between full blown panic and vindictive rage. He might pretend it all worked out for the best, but he didn't always feel that way."

I smiled despite myself. "I wonder why he didn't tell me that."

Of course, I already knew why. There was no bigger turn off than a man descending into panic in crisis.

"You know he wants you, right?" Maisy asked, her tone light and friendly. "I've tried to talk sense into him once or twice, but it goes in one ear and out the other with that man."

"I'm aware. I've also tried the talking route." I chuckled.

"I don't know how you handle him, but it's impressive all the same."

"I'll admit I might have lowered myself to bribery once or twice."

I snorted. "How did that go?"

"Not well," Maisy grumbled. "If he keeps pushing his luck, I'll take a leaf out of Finn McCarthy's agent's book and sign him up for a reality TV show. He'll never question me again."

I couldn't help but smile at her disgruntled tone. We chatted for another half an hour. I've never laughed so hard in such a short period of time.

CHAPTER SEVEN

CATRINA

A week passed and I had successfully managed to resist Nathan's attempts to tempt me. Somehow I'd also avoided spilling all of the details to Sam. Not for lack of trying on her part, mind you. Every lunch and coffee date for a week, I sat there, baring my teeth in some semblance of a smile while Sam tried to force me to drill into my feelings.

Honestly, not something I needed help with. I'd dissected every moment I spent with Nathan, every lapse in judgement, every kiss, every long glance. I went over it all, searching for weaknesses.

Mine mostly.

Why couldn't I resist him?

The easy option would be to blame the accent, but something told me it wasn't that. Something I didn't want to acknowledge. Especially not on a Friday afternoon with a mountain of paperwork waiting for my attention.

My phone lit up just as I opened the first brief. I sighed at the name flashing across my screen.

Ignore it.

I picked it up and unlocked it, holding my breath for some stupid reason.

NATHAN

Sure you don't want to come to the premiere?
There's still time.

With just two weeks until the office closed for Christmas, I needed the deal done and signed asap. My sanity demanded. If we got it closed out, I could spend Christmas with Nathan. I wouldn't have to avoid him when he offered to take me out or invited me to red-carpet events I desperately wanted to experience.

The thought of walking the red carpet by his side, feeling his arm wrapped around me, filled me with an unexpected thirst. A longing that Miranda fucking Chambers was preventing me from quenching.

I closed my eyes and allowed myself a fleeting moment to imagine being there with him before shaking my head and begrudgingly returning to reality.

CATRINA

Thanks. I have a mountain of work to finish.

NATHAN

Okay, but I promise it won't be fun without
you. ;)

I tried to focus on the stack of legal documents in front of me, but my thoughts kept drifting back to Nathan.

※

I was curled up on the couch Sunday night, scrolling through social media mindlessly. A picture stopped me in my tracks. I scrolled past it, gasped, and then frantically scrolled back hoping I hadn't seen what I thought I'd seen.

Of course, when I wanted my brain to trick me, it didn't. Just reality slapping me for being stupid.

Nathan's charming smile filled my screen. He stood on the red carpet at his film premiere, wearing the classic black suit.

That wasn't the arresting detail.

No, the sight of him in a close embrace with a gorgeous blonde supermodel, his hand resting naturally on her hip, both of them laughing as if they had no cares in the world.

As more pictures flooded the media, showcasing the glamorous couple posing together on the red carpet, the small stab of jealousy grew.

With each new image, my heart twisted painfully in my chest, an unwelcome reminder of just how much I had grown to care for Nathan.

"Ugh, why am I doing this to myself?" I muttered, closing the app and refocusing on the book I'd abandoned hours before. But no matter how hard I tried, I couldn't shake the envy taking root inside me.

"Damn it, Catrina," I scolded myself. "You're the one who insisted on keeping things professional until the deal is done. You can't have it both ways."

I lasted five minutes, reading the same paragraph over and over again. One click and the browser reopened, throwing an image of Nathan and the supermodel back in my face.

Without pausing to consider the consequences, I pulled up our message thread and texted Nathan.

CATRINA

Looks like you had fun last night.

I hit send, immediately regretting the impulsive text. Nathan's response was almost instant.

NATHAN

I did, thanks. Tabloids loved it.

I gritted my teeth, my fingers flying across the screen before my brain could catch up.

CATRINA

Glad you had no problem finding a suitable date.

Nathan

Ah, Icy. It was just business. Wished you were with me the whole time.

Why did that make me feel better? Of course I was jealous, but I didn't want him to know that.

The phone rang in my hand, startling me. For a second, I stared at it, my heart in my throat. I sighed and accepted the call.

"Catrina, Catrina, Catrina." Nathan's delectable accent caressed my ear, making me shiver as it curled around my name. "Tell me, baby, are you jealous?"

With a sigh, I answered. "You wish."

He chuckled. "You're a terrible liar, love. Those pictures got under your skin."

I gritted my teeth, refusing to give him the satisfaction of a response.

He exhaled slowly. "It was just a publicity arrangement to boost our profiles. Nothing serious."

I frowned, tension easing slightly. "You seemed quite cosy for an 'arrangement'."

"Don't be like that." His tone gentled. "There's only one person I wanted with me. It killed me, pretending when you're the one I can't stop thinking about."

My pulse raced as I grasped for a reply. Even as logic

warned he had to remain off-limits, my resolve weakened. "We agreed to be professional."

He scoffed. "There's nothing professional about how I feel about you." Nathan's voice dropped to a husky whisper, sending a shiver down my spine.

I pressed a hand to my forehead, willing my heartbeat to slow. "Stop it. We can't go there yet." The words tripped off my tongue, lacking any strength.

"Are you sure?" His teasing echoed in my ear, tempting me

"Yes." But as I said it, longing hit me.

You're his attorney, not his girlfriend. No matter how tempting he is.

Why was I jealous? We couldn't happen. Yes, he claimed to be seriously interested in waiting until after the deal closed, but would he actually?

I wasn't naive enough to believe it.

Nathan was a means to advance my career. I couldn't see him as anything else.

Liar.

Frustration boiled over. Why did it have to be complicated? Why was he so perfect, and why was I his damn attorney?

With a groan, I paced the room, trying to work off my frustration. It wasn't just Nathan — the case, the deal, work stress, our attraction. I needed a break to figure out what I wanted. But time was running out, and the Starlight deal loomed.

"Talk to me, Cat."

I stopped pacing, the sound of his voice soothing me despite common sense saying I should hang up. *How did he do this to me?* I was unravelling, and the blasted man knew it.

"Sorry, I'm crabby." I dragged a hand through my hair, tugging hard as I cursed myself.

Why the hell are you apologising?

"I'm just tired and I've got a busy day tomorrow."

For a second, silence filled the line and I glanced at my

phone to check he hadn't hung up. Then his voice floated through, caressing me all over again. *He's irresistible, even through the phone.*

"Do you need a distraction?"

I flopped back onto the couch, my mind working itself into knots trying to figure out if being on the phone with Nathan Logan for personal reasons was really a safe choice.

"What kind of distraction?" I eventually asked.

"How about twenty questions?"

I rolled my eyes at the suggestion but smiled. His playful side chipped away at my defences, helping me relax. "Seriously? What are we, twelve?"

"Come on, Icy. Live a little. You go first. Ask me anything."

With a sigh, I gave in. Chatting with Nathan wouldn't hurt, and would distract me from everything else. "Okay, fine. Favourite film of all time?"

We went back and forth, questions growing personal. Nathan wanted to know everything from my favourite colour to the most embarrassing moment. His curiosity was infectious, and soon we were laughing over details of each other's lives. The stresses of work and my jealousy were forgotten.

At some point, I shut off the lights and crawled into bed, cradling the phone to my ear. I refused to think about Nathan joining me. Or at least I tried.

"If you could instantly become an expert in one subject, what would it be?"

"Cooking. I can barely boil water. You?"

"Astronomy. I've always been fascinated by the stars." I laughed. "Not surprised. You do have a dreamy, faraway look at times. Like you're gazing at distant galaxies."

"Very poetic, Icy. Have you been reading my screenplays?" His laughter echoed down the line. "So, want to hear about my ridiculous holiday plans?"

"Of course, what are you up to?"

"Heading to Edinburgh for my mate's New Year's Eve wedding. The city will be crazy busy and honestly, it's a bit stupid us going at that time of year, but we've been friends since university. I couldn't miss it."

"Wow, that sounds amazing. Edinburgh is supposed to be incredible."

"It is, especially lit up for holidays full of revellers. We always sing Auld Lang Syne at midnight under fireworks. I love how Scots celebrate. Mum will still expect me for Christmas dinner."

I smiled wistfully, imagining cheerful holiday scenes. His plans sounded chaotic and heart-warming. "Your mum is lucky to have you home for Christmas."

"I'm lucky to have her. Family is important." The statement sent sadness through me. His family closeness made me feel envious.

"Do you have any big plans for Christmas? Americans really celebrate, don't they? Are Canadians the same?"

My smile faded. Christmas was a sore subject for me. Most years, I avoided it.

"I don't actually have any plans. I'm not big on holiday traditions."

"Really? Why not?"

I hesitated. Did I want to open up? His concern made me want to, but it left me vulnerable. I imagined his cosy family Christmas and felt a pang.

"My family isn't really close, so holidays were never a big deal for us."

"I'm sorry to hear that. Family troubles are never easy."

His sympathy caught me off guard, and I blinked back unexpected tears. Nathan seemed to understand without details, his compassion easing the old ache in my chest. I took a shaky breath, steadying my nerves.

"It's alright. My parents divorced when I was young, and

holidays were tense after. I guess I got used to not really cele-brating.”

“That must have been hard. No wonder you avoid cele-brating. If I weren’t in Edinburgh, I’d help make new memories.”

“It was, but it’s past.” I bit my lip, pushing back the burn of lingering tears. “So Edinburgh for New Year’s, huh? Should be fun.”

We talked for over an hour, about everything and nothing. Until the sun had truly set.

“I wish I could hold you now,” Nathan said, his tone wistful. “As much as I love hearing your voice, it’s not enough. I want to see you.”

“You know why that can’t happen.” I rushed on before he could attempt to talk me around. “And before you try to use last week to weaken my resolve, I’m going to sleep. So good-night, Golden Boy.”

Nathan’s chuckle was soft, intimate. “If you say so, baby. I’ll be dreaming of you.”

I hugged the phone to my chest.

CHAPTER EIGHT

CATRINA

Nathan and I walked out of the elevators after meeting with Miranda yet again. Frustration thrummed through me. I could see our completion date slipping further and further into December. If we weren't careful it would be January before we escaped from under that woman's thumb.

Would Nathan still want me if it dragged out or would he lose interest like I thought he would?

"Do you have a dress?" Nathan asked, his lilting voice echoing in the empty parking garage.

I kept heading for my car but shot him a confused look.

"A dress for what?"

"I have another red carpet thing in June, a charity gala." He flashed me that smile. The one that made my knees go weak and made me question my ethics. "You'll need a dress."

He pulled out his cell and started typing out a text as he walked, effortlessly keeping pace with me.

"I'm not going to your gala."

"Yes, you are," he said, without looking up or slowing. "I'm setting you an appointment with my stylist for the end of January. She'll make sure you've got everything you need."

"Nathan." My exasperation got the better of me and his name came out like a growl. But it achieved its goal, I had all of his attention. Too bad having all of it made me ache in frustrating ways.

We stopped in front of my car and he stared down at me, his brow furrowed.

"Cat," he said, mimicking me, only his tone was very much amused.

"I'm not going."

"Why not?" His brow quirked.

"Because we can't."

"The deal will be done well before June." He pocket his cell but his gaze never wavered from mine. "You said you were hoping before Christmas."

"Were you even listening to Miranda?" I gestured towards the elevator bank. "That woman is determined to drag this into next year."

"I heard her." He shrugged. "That doesn't change the fact you agreed to a date when it is done. Are you changing your mind?"

"No, but —"

"Then I'll text you the appointment info." He turned away from me, heading for his own car.

"Nathan," I called after him.

I ignored the edge of panic in my voice and unlocked his car.

"I'll see you soon, Icy." He shot me a devilish grin over the top of the car before climbing in.

"Fucking men." I threw my arms up but climbed into my car before my exasperation could get the better of me and I did something I'd regret.

A dress. For a charity gala. Where people would see us. Together. Six months from now.

Why did that make me feel all fizzy with excitement?

You're a lost cause.

"Correct me if I'm wrong but you did say Bon Jovi was your favourite band growing up, right?" I stared at the handset in my hand like it might bite if I made even the slightest move. "Cat? Are you there?"

Hesitantly I placed it back to my ear. "Yes, I did say that."

"Good. I got us tickets for the next tour."

My eyes widened. "The next tour isn't until September, Nathan."

"I'm aware, Icy. I had to pull some strings but I also got us backstage passes."

If my eyes weren't already bugging out, they might have started. Backstage passes?

What the hell is he playing at?

"That's incredibly thoughtful of you, Mr Logan," I placed extra emphasis on his name, "but I can't accept."

"You don't have to right now." Nathan chuckled. "These are for *after.*" His voice dropped on the last word, dragging it out and grating it over my nerves with unspoken promise.

"Nathan, I... we haven't even had a first date yet." I cleared my throat and forced my shoulders back, chiding myself for sounding so breathy and interested.

You are interested.

He doesn't have to know that!

"You can't buy concert tickets nearly a year in advance!"

It's unprofessional and people could see it as... oh who was I kidding, I couldn't stop toeing that unprofessional line every time I found myself in a room with the man.

"Why not? I told you, Cat, I'm serious about this. About you and me, after this bloody deal is done. I want to do this right." His declaration left me breathless.

My protests died on my lips. How could I argue when part of me was thrilled at his words? Nathan wanted me, was willing to wait and plan an entire future together. It was terrifying, moving too fast — yet it felt right.

Still, I had to be practical. "You're getting ahead of yourself. We have no idea how long this deal will actually take, or what might happen after. I can't make promises."

"I know what's going to happen after." His voice dropped to a sultry whisper. "The evening after we sign, I'm taking you to dinner and then, day depending, I'm going to whisk you away to a villa in Napa where no one will disturb us while we make up for lost time."

My body clenched at his promise and I squirmed in my seat.

I thought my mouth had gone dry before, it was nothing compared to the Sahara it turned into with images of us in seclusion. *What is he planning?*

"Well, now I know how to get your complete attention." Nathan chuckled. "I'm aware of the risks, Icy. But some things are worth fighting for. You're worth it."

The line went dead before I could retort.

Impossible, stubborn man.

"*I*ncredible progress with the Starlight deal." Mike's voice made me jump. "Thank you, sir."

Mike smiled, shifting restlessly in place. "The partners are thrilled with how fast you've turned things around. Keep it up."

With that, he was gone. But his unexpected compliment

left me grinning like an idiot, tension melting from my shoulders.

To know the partners — and Mike — approved of how I was handling it filled me with relief. My job was safe; I was proving I deserved to be here.

NATHAN

I ended the call with the director, finally wrapping up for the day. Cat sat on the small sofa in my trailer, typing away on her laptop.

Watching her work, seeing her so at ease in my space, filled me with a contentment I rarely got to feel. Her golden brown hair was draped over one shoulder, her expression open and unguarded. She seemed perfectly at home here, and having her with me made even this cramped trailer feel warm and welcoming. I never wanted the moment to end.

"Thanks for coming by. I'm sorry I couldn't get away to meet you at your office." I tried to keep my tone casual, not reveal how much I'd been counting the minutes until filming finished and I could see her again.

Cat glanced up, green eyes warm and relaxed. A smile played about her soft lips. "It's no problem. I had work to catch up on anyway, and your trailer has fewer distractions than my office."

She turned back to her work and I hesitated for all of a minute.

"Do you have any big plans for February next year? Any holidays or trips you usually take around then?" I tried to ask casually, not wanting to give away my surprise just yet.

Her brows rose at my question. "Not at the moment. Why do you ask?"

"Just curious how much leave you get from the firm each year. And how much notice they require if you take time off."

Cat's eyes narrowed in suspicion. "Nathan Logan, what have you done?"

I sighed, shrugging my shoulders in defeat. The blasted woman knew me too well already.

"Finn's having his vow renewal ceremony in New York in February and then we're going to Bora Bora for a private celebration. I booked us a week in a bungalow for after the ceremony."

"You did what?" Cat stared at me in disbelief. Then she pinched the bridge of her nose, her eyes falling shut as she muttered to herself.

"You alright there, Icy?"

I shouldn't have prodded her.

"No, I'm not alright." She exploded out of her seat, pacing towards me. Those gorgeous green eyes flashing just the way I liked them. "We have no idea if this deal will even be done by then, or where we'll be. You can't just book surprise holidays!"

"I couldn't help myself." I sat down beside her, taking her hands in mine. "I have to go anyway," — Finn would murder me if I didn't — "and I figured there was no harm. After so long waiting, the thought of an entire blissful week alone together was too tempting. I had to plan something, even if it's still months away."

"What happened to Napa?"

I kept my face perfectly natural, containing the gleeful smile desperate to break out. She'd listened to my ramblings about our first date? That had to mean something.

She shook her head, though I could see her exasperation fading. "You're utterly mad. Buying concert tickets is one thing, international holidays are another!"

"What can I say?" I stood up and met her midway

through her third lap of the room, catching her hand in mind. "My heart knows what it wants." I brought her hand to my lips, brushing a soft kiss over her knuckles.

Cat sighed, and I could see her resolve crumbling.

She wasn't mine yet, but the day would come and when it did, I had no intentions of letting go.

CATRINA

I glanced up to find an intern at the open door, clutching an enormous white box in her arms. "Delivery for you, Ms Sinclair."

I blinked at the size of the thing. "Are you sure that's for me?"

She checked the label. "Addressed to Catrina Sinclair, yes."

"Okay, you can just set it down over there." I gestured to the table by the window.

"I hope I get gifts like this once I've passed the bar!" She set it down and flashed me an envious smile before leaving.

I eyed the box with suspicion. The name *Juliette's*, was printed across the top in silver lettering.

What on earth was Nathan up to now?

I lifted the lid to find a gown nestled under layers of tissue. And not just any gown —a stunning emerald evening dress that likely cost more than my rent. No receipt, no note. Just a small envelope tucked into the folds of the fabric.

I opened it to find a single sheet of heavy parchment inside. In Nathan's unmistakable scrawl were two lines:

You'll be needing something for my next premiere.

Anything less than perfection won't do.
- N

My jaw dropped. The premiere for his new film was two months away. *Is he still going to be interested then?*

I shook my head. The man never ceased to surprise me.

CHAPTER NINE

CATRINA

"Catrina, darling, it's Miranda." Her voice oozed false sweetness, like a snake draped in velvet.

I'd managed to go nearly a week without speaking to the two-faced Director of the Board at Starlight Studios. I should have known it would be too much to ask that we get through another weekend without scrutiny.

"Hello, Miranda." I tried to keep my tone professional. "What can I do for you?"

"Have you seen the latest gossip about your client?" she asked, her voice dripping with fake concern. She breezed on before I could so much as hum. "He's been spotted at a strip club."

My eyes widened and I sat forward fast. "I'm sure that's not true."

He'd promised me his playboy days were over. Why would he go to a strip club?

"It's all over social media, Catrina. There are pictures of him entering." She clucked her tongue. "I'm sure I don't need to remind you of the impact something like this could have on the Starlight Studios deal."

My heart sank. This wasn't good. Nathan's reputation was already precarious, and any scandal could jeopardise our delicate negotiations.

"Okay, thank you for bringing it to my attention." I clamped the desk phone between my shoulder and ear and picked up my cell to thumb through the apps, chewing my lip at the urge to click into Find My Friend. "I'm sure it's not what it looks like, but I promise you I'll get to the bottom of it tonight."

"I trust you'll handle it discreetly. I'd hate to see all your hard work go to waste." With that thinly disguised snide comment, she hung up, leaving me to stew in my frustration.

Despite the urgency buzzing through me, I couldn't bring myself to open the app. Nathan had given me access to his phone tracker for emergencies, but was this really an emergency? The thought of invading his privacy made me uncomfortable. If I could avoid it, I would.

My fingers trembled as I dialled Nathan's number, hoping he'd pick up and set the record straight. The phone rang once. Twice. Three times. And then it went to voicemail.

"Damn it, Nathan," I muttered under my breath, my mind racing with possibilities.

Was he really at a strip club? Or was this just another fabrication by someone eager to bring him down? A gossip rag jumping to conclusions?

I needed answers, and I needed them now. As his attorney, it was my job to protect him — not just from legal troubles, but from himself as well. And if there was even a hint of truth to these rumours, I had to confront him before it spiralled out of control.

Repeating the routine for a good twenty minutes, I redialled his number and listened to his voicemail almost to the beep in the hopes that this time he'd answer the phone. He didn't.

With each unanswered call, my resolve grew stronger and my hesitations faded. I couldn't let this jeopardise everything we'd worked so hard for, and I couldn't let Nathan throw away the deal over some thoughtless indiscretion.

I paced my office, my heart racing as I searched for another option. His agent. His friends. Someone had to know where he was.

"Get a grip, Catrina," I whispered to myself, trying to quell the anxious energy that coursed through me. "This is why he gave you access in the first place."

Taking a deep breath, I opened the app on my phone and pulled up Nathan's location.

NATHAN

The microwave meal sat untouched, steaming on the counter. As appealing as cardboard. A year ago, I'd have been at some posh restaurant, the lads in tow. The things I do to keep up appearances.

With a sigh, I lifted my fork, resigned to a dismal Friday night in.

The wall phone rang. Brow furrowed, I glanced at the clock. Who could it be at this hour? I abandoned the grim excuse for dinner and crossed the open-plan space with long strides.

"Mr Logan, there's a Catrina Sinclair here to see you. Shall I send her up?" the guard asked.

Cat? Without calling?

But then I hadn't looked at my phone in hours. I glanced around the open-plan space. *Where is my bloody phone?*

"Are you sure?"

"I checked her ID, sir."

She'd driven from downtown Los Angeles in rush hour traffic on a Friday night. To see me?

"Let her through," I said, barely keeping my tone even.

I hung up the phone and paced from one end of the foyer to the other. My mind ran through a million possibilities. I opened the door, pulse racing.

Cat emerged from the car, lips pinched, eyes blazing. "Have you gone mad?" Face taut with worry, she demanded, "A strip club? After everything we've been through, after all the work we've put into protecting your reputation, why would you risk the deal now?"

"Cat, wait —"

"Social media is buzzing." She breezed past me and into the house. "And Miranda just called me, frantic about the potential damage to our deal. You know how important this project is to both of us." She paced my entryway. I shut the door and crossed my arms, waiting patiently for a lapse in her shouting. "How could you jeopardise everything like that?"

So much for patience.

"Catrina!" I shouted, the sound echoing in the marble foyer. Her lips slammed shut as she stared at me and her wide, questioning eyes met mine. "I don't know what you're talking about. I haven't left my house today."

Her expression hardened and she growled my name. "Don't lie." She paced away again. "There are photos everywhere."

"Bloody hell. Stop." I caught her by the shoulders, forcing her to stop and look at me. "I didn't go to a strip club, alright? I wouldn't. Not after…" I let my eyes convey my meaning and she blushed. "It's just another bloody rumour. You have access to my phone, Cat. Didn't you look at it?"

She scowled at me. "Of course, I did. But they have *photos*, Nathan. Photos of you walking into a strip club when you're meant to be doing everything in your power to protect your reputation and Starlight Studios."

"Well it wasn't me." I crossed my arms and fixed her with an unwavering gaze. Either she'd believe me or she wouldn't. *God, I hope she does.* "I haven't left the house tonight."

"How do you explain the photos?"

I sighed. "There's a guy in LA who looks vaguely like me. In the dark," I shrugged. "You know how these things go — one person sees me, or someone who looks like me, somewhere and suddenly, it turns into a scandalous story. It's ridiculous."

The anger in her eyes faded, replaced by a flicker of something else — relief, perhaps, or maybe even guilt for jumping to conclusions.

"Alright," she finally said, her voice quieter now. "I believe you. But we need to be careful. We can't afford any more scandals, especially not now."

"I don't want to jeopardise your progress any more than you do." My gaze locked on hers, willing her to understand the depth of my sincerity.

If anything, I wanted it to move faster. The sooner I signed on the dotted line, the sooner she stopped being my attorney and I finally got my date. And possibly a weekend away with her.

Cat's shoulders sagged with relief, and I released her from my grip, but she didn't move immediately. Instead, she searched my eyes as if looking for something.

For a brief moment, the world around us disappeared, and we were the only two people in the room. My pulse quickened and my mouth went dry. What thought flickered behind those fiery intelligent eyes? Was she remembering the feel of my lips on her too?

But just as quickly as it came, the moment passed, and Cat stepped back, breaking our connection.

She cleared her throat. "I'll handle Miranda. But the gossip—"

"Will fade." I shrugged. "If we avoid drama this weekend. Maisy will shut it down though, just to be safe."

Nodding, gaze distant, she finally met my eyes. "I should go. Calls to make... paperwork to handle before Monday."

"Just give me a second…" I held out my hand, silently imploring her to stay. I took a step toward her when she didn't make an immediate run for the door, my classic flirty smile curling my lips. "Now that I have you…"

"You don't have me," Cat argued, stepping back toward the foyer wall.

"You drove to Malibu on a Friday night to set me straight." I grinned but my brows climbed. "You checked my location. You knew I wasn't in a strip club, Icy. You could have easily gone home, content with that knowledge." I leaned forward, pressing my arm against the wall above her head, caging her in. "Tell me again how I don't have you?"

Her breath hitched as I leaned in, the heat from my body radiating toward her. Her gaze jumped to my lips before quickly darting away, a blush staining her cheeks. But her resolve didn't falter.

"I'm not yours to have," she whispered, her tone and expression uncertain.

"Yet," I whispered. "And even while we wait for the deal to close, I thought we were friends at least." I pulled back slightly, giving her space. "We text constantly. Do you share details about your personal life with all your clients?"

Cat's mouth opened and closed as she scrambled for an answer, her cheeks still flushed. She was used to being in control of every situation, but right now I had the power and she wanted it back.

"We don't talk about anything outside our attorney-client capacity," she finally said, her voice wavering slightly.

"Exactly." I smiled knowingly and shook my head, leaning

in again. "You'd never mention your love of Hallmark Mysteries or your hatred for Christmas."

"I don't hate Christmas," she grumbled.

I grinned, victory in sight. I stepped closer; my index finger traced a line along her jawline as I spoke in a low murmur. "Do you wish your other clients would fuck you over your desk?"

I'd seen the way she blushed when looking at her desk far too many times not to put the pieces together. One day, I'd make her wish a reality.

Her eyes met mine, heat flaring in the green depths. I could see the struggle clear as day. The desire for something more was there, but so was the fear of what it could mean for us.

"Why can't I shake you?" Cat muttered beneath her breath.

"Maybe it's fate." I bit my lip, considering her, enjoying her close proximity. "Or maybe we're secretly gluttons for punishment."

"Maybe." She shook her head with amusement. "Or maybe you need to get laid more."

I smirked. "Or maybe..." My fingers trailed down her neck, grazing over her pulse point but featherlike. "We need a repeat."

She swallowed hard but her gaze never left mine. "Or you could find someone else."

"Eh, I'm good." I canted my head to the side, considering her determined yet needy expression. Such a contradiction was my Cat. "I have my hands full with you."

"You're ridiculous." Cat chuckled, the sound delighting my senses.

I smiled as I reached out and brushed her cheek with the back of my fingers. She closed her eyes at my touch, leaning into me. The air between us shifted, becoming charged with electricity.

I leaned forward, hovering my lips near hers and whispered, "I still only want you."

Then I pressed my mouth against hers.

At first, the kiss was gentle, a tender exploration that quickly escalated into a fierce inferno. I couldn't resist.

It was intoxicating, the heat and intensity of our connection igniting a fire within me. I wanted more, to pull her closer and explore every inch of her body until we were nothing but a tangled mess of limbs. Enact every one of her fantasies, starting with bending her over my desk.

The room seemed to grow hotter and heavier with each passing second, the heat between us becoming almost unbearable. But Cat broke the kiss and ducked under my arm, backing away from me.

"Nathan—"

Her phone rang, interrupting whatever excuse she planned to throw at me.

She pulled the device from her pocket with a furrowed brow. One glance at the screen and she sighed.

"It's Miranda." She grimaced as she turned off her ringer. "I'll call her back in the car."

"The deal is nearly done and you won't be my attorney forever."

"I can't think like that right now." She shook her head. "It's too risky."

"You've perfected the Ice Maiden persona, baby." I smiled softly as I pushed a piece of hair behind her ear, unable to keep my hands to myself. "How would anyone know if we pretended the deal was done?"

Before she could respond, her phone rang again.

She stepped away, answering Miranda's call as she walked towards the door. I watched her disappear, my jaw tightening.

Catrina Sinclair wanted me as much as I did her. She just needed to stop hiding behind excuses.

CHAPTER TEN

CATRINA

A week after I lost control with Nathan again, I sat in my office, the AC droning. The building was empty. Everyone else had already left for their holiday break.

Save for me. The usual pressures still weighed heavily on me, and I had no interest in going home to an empty apartment.

The week had been hell. Miranda and Starlight's shareholders kept throwing more obstacles in my path.

And I was. Not. Having it!

They had no idea who they'd pit themselves against. My determination knew no bounds. I would prove myself and I would break for Christmas with all the pieces in place for a quick exchange of contracts in the new year.

The faint glow of my desk lamp cast shadows on the legal documents laid out before me. My fingers danced across the keyboard, trying to keep up with my racing thoughts.

But my mind kept wandering to Nathan. How could I have been so stupid?

I let my guard down, gave into temptation and almost destroyed everything I'd worked for.

Of course, I was angry at myself, not Nathan. Because that would be irrational of me to place all the blame on him when I'd kissed him back like a woman starved.

And oh, what a kiss it was...

He was just being himself — charming, persuasive, impossible to resist.

This was on me.

I knew better, yet still played with fire.

The memory of his lips on mine, hands roaming, threatened my concentration. Each lapse in control revealed what I really wanted, deep down. The truth I tried so hard to bury each day I spent working with him.

I couldn't afford to slip up again. Had worked too hard to achieve this dream. One moment of weakness could bring it all crashing down.

But Nathan had awakened something in me I couldn't ignore. This intense need that refused to fade.

Still, giving in wasn't an option. Not yet at least.

So what if I'd lost control a couple of times? I had come too far to throw it all away on an impulse. I just needed to bury my misplaced feelings for him until the deal was done, double down on being a professional.

If I repeated that mantra enough times, I might start to believe it.

Might forget the fire in his eyes as he hovered over me, whispering that I was the only one he wanted.

Might forget how badly I wished that were true.

But I couldn't afford to forget. My determination was the only thing standing between me and disaster. I just needed to keep my distance from now until the deal signing, no matter what tricks Nathan pulled to weaken my resolve.

I wouldn't make the same mistake twice. I was stronger and smarter, not some foolish woman who lost her head over a charming smile and skilled kiss. And talented hands and drool worthy abs and a delectable cock and…

Fuck.

I rubbed a hand across my tired eyes. Who was I kidding? I could deny him all I wanted and alone in my darkening office, I could pretend to believe it.

But the truth of the matter? I needed this deal done as much as Nathan.

More even.

I held no illusions that as soon as the thrill of the forbidden faded, he'd be on to the next challenge. Even with all his distant bookings. But I couldn't find it in me to care. I wanted the opportunity to experience another mind-numbingly good night with him. Even knowing that if the deal dragged out too long, his impatience might get the better of him and he'd lose interest.

Just when I thought I might never see the bottom of the mountain of paperwork on my desk, an unexpected knock echoed through the room. Startled, I glanced up to find Nathan standing in the doorway, holding a brown bag of food. A mixture of confusion, surprise and shame washed over me.

A blush burned up the back of my neck as I met his happy gaze.

Somehow, I'd naively convinced myself that I'd get three weeks without seeing Nathan. I told myself he'd get on the plane to Edinburgh and when he came back, we'd sign the deal, bang, and then all of our feelings would resolve themselves.

"Evening, Cat." He didn't wait for an invite, just breezed across my office with his signature charming grin playing on his lips, leaving my office door open. "You still haven't texted me back, and I assumed you'd be working late again. Thought you could use some sustenance."

My heart fluttered at his thoughtful gesture. Careful!

"That's nice of you, but I'm swamped with work right now."

"You can't work on an empty stomach." He waved the bag temptingly and the delicious fragrance of Indian food quickly filled my office.

His concern for my well-being warmed me from the inside, but I knew accepting his offer would only tempt us further.

Tempt away. Who's going to tell? my libido cackled.

It had a point. Everyone else had gone home hours ago. I was the last one left on our floor.

"Alright," I relented with a sigh. "But only for a moment. I really need to finish this."

"Deal," he said, his eyes twinkling in satisfaction. "Actually," he paused, the bag of delicious food tantalisingly close. "Do you consider sharing a meal over paperwork unprofessional?" Nathan asked, mocking me. "Should I eat outside?"

I hesitated, feeling the familiar flutter in my stomach that always seemed to accompany his presence. It was dangerous territory, sitting in a dark room with him alone after hours.

I glanced at the open door, chewing my lip. If anyone were to stumble across us, I'd have a hard time explaining.

Then my stomach growled, reminding me that I hadn't eaten since breakfast and stealing any pretence of a choice from me. *There's no one here anyway.*

"Food is harmless," I murmured, trying to convince myself as much as him.

"Exactly." He moved to help me clear a spot on my cluttered desk, pushing aside stacks of documents and contracts to make room for our impromptu dinner.

As we settled in to eat, I got lost in the easy conversation that flowed between us. We chatted about our respective weeks — the script readings he'd attended for future projects, the cases I'd worked on — and it felt like we were just two friends catching up.

Eventually, the conversation turned to Christmas plans. Nathan would leave for his friend's wedding tomorrow, and I couldn't help but feel a twinge of jealousy. The idea of escaping LA, even for just a few days, sounded heavenly.

"Are you excited for the wedding?"

"Excited, if slightly panicked at how fast it's arrived. Shaun and Mona wanted an intimate Hogmanay wedding, so of course that meant planning it around multiple family Christmases and Hogmanay parties across the city."

"An intimate wedding for an A-list actor?" My brows rose. "Is there such a thing?"

"Well…" He scratched his jaw. "It was intimate for all of a month. Not so much anymore."

I laughed. "A New Year's Eve wedding in Edinburgh does sound wonderful but mad."

"Mad is the perfect word." Nathan grinned. "We've a stag do and the rehearsal in the two days before, tux fittings and suitcases to pack, not to mention my best man's speech still to finish. I'm not sure a Hogmanay wedding was the most practical choice, but Shaun's determined to make it unforgettable."

"I'm sure it will be. Celebrating new beginnings in such an iconic place, surrounded by friends, and ringing in the New Year as a newly married couple." A wistful sigh caught in my throat.

Nathan's eyes softened as he looked at me. "I wish you could be there with us."

"I have a date with my couch, don't worry about me." My words sounded more regretful than intended.

He frowned. "You're still not going home?"

"Nope."

A furrow formed between his brows. "So when you said you weren't doing anything for Christmas, you meant…"

"I'd be spending it alone." When his gaze softened with

something akin to pity, I pointed my fork at him and scowled. "Don't look at me like that. I told you I don't have the best relationship with my family."

"I didn't think that meant you'd be alone." He dropped his fork and picked up a napkin, furiously wiping his hands.

"I don't have a great relationship with my mother. We haven't spoken in years." I pressed my lips together, trying to bite back the words before I spilt all of my secrets. I failed. "I don't really miss the small town I grew up in either. Better to live my life without the pressure of a hundred nosey neighbours and spend my holidays without someone passing out drunk while the turkey burns."

Nathan reached out and squeezed my hand, sending a comforting warmth through me. "I'm sorry."

I shrugged, trying to play it off. "It's fine. I'm used to it by now."

But the truth was, I wasn't fine. The constant tension between me and my mother had always been a sore spot, and the thought of spending Christmas alone in my apartment was depressing.

"That's it." He picked up his phone and started swiping.

"What are you doing?" I asked, my eyes narrowing while concern bubbled in my chest.

"Getting you added to the passenger manifest for Edinburgh."

My eyes widened in shock. "What? No, Nathan, I can't go to Edinburgh with you."

He paused, brows furrowing in confusion. "Why not? You just said you'd be alone for the holidays. Come celebrate with us, keep me company during the chaos. It'll be fun."

I stared at him in disbelief. "You want me to go to Edinburgh with you and your A-list friends who I've never met?"

"Yeah, why not?" Nathan said, his eyes sparkling with excitement. "We could use an extra person to keep us all in line. And they aren't all A-list. Mona and Abi are perfectly normal unlike the four of us."

For a moment, I was tempted to say yes.

But then I thought about the potential consequences. Spending Christmas with Nathan and his friends would only make it harder to keep my feelings in check. And what if something went wrong? What if someone snapped a picture of us and started a brand new rumour that derailed all the work I'd put into getting the acquisition done?

I took a deep breath, choosing my words carefully. "That's a very generous offer, but I can't go."

Nathan set down his phone, leaning forward with determination. "Cat, I don't want you sitting here by yourself over Christmas. Just come — we'll dress up, dance at the ceilidh, laugh when Jackson inevitably gets knocked over in 'Strip the Willow,' drink whiskey, set off fireworks at midnight. You work too hard and deserve a holiday. Please?"

For a second, all I could do was blink at him. *Dance at the what?*

My heart clenched at the enticing image he painted and the pleading in his eyes. How I wished things were different, wished I could throw caution to the wind and escape with him. But that simply wasn't possible.

"It sounds wonderful." I gave him a sad smile. "But what happens when someone notices us together and the tabloids start another rumour? I literally just need ink on the page in the New Year and I'll have pushed the acquisition over the line."

He opened his mouth to protest, but I held up a hand. "I appreciate your concern, but I'll be fine. A few days of peace and solitude while catching up on reading and TV shows sounds perfect. I don't need an extravagant vacation to be happy."

Nathan searched my face, frustration creasing his brow before resolve slipped into his expression. "Alright, I understand. But I don't like the thought of you here by yourself. At least promise me you'll call if you need anything?"

"No need to worry about me. Go, enjoy the wedding and New Year's celebrations with your friends." I gave him a teasing wink and smile to lighten the mood, hoping to convey I would be okay on my own. "I'll keep myself entertained by re-watching Hallmark Murder Mystery movies."

He chuckled, tension easing from his shoulders. "If you insist. Though that does sound like cruel and unusual punishment. I suppose I'll allow it on one condition — you save 'It's A Wonderful Life' for us to watch together when I'm back."

"It's a deal," I said.

I had made the right choice in saying no. But a deep pit of regret still formed in my stomach.

We ate in companionable silence for a few minutes. Then Nathan wiped his hands and leaned back in his chair, regarding me with an expression I couldn't quite read.

"So are we going to talk about what happened the other night?"

I froze, my fork halfway to my mouth. "What night?" I asked cautiously, knowing full well what he meant. "You know exactly which night." His eyes glinted with humour and something more heated. "The one that started with a kiss against my foyer wall and ended far too soon for my liking."

My pulse accelerated.

I scowled at him as he leaned in closer to me. "That was a mistake."

Not because I didn't want him closer still.

No, I enjoyed the way his voice dropped to a sultry whisper that sent shivers down my spine.

What I didn't appreciate was the continual reminders of my weakness.

"Tell me you haven't thought about it since," he said, his eyes locking onto mine with a challenge I couldn't ignore.

The memory of our stolen moment played at the edges of

my thoughts, tempting me to give into the desire that threat-ened to consume us both. But I shouldn't risk it — not when there was so much at stake and we were so close to being free.

"Nathan," I said, fighting to keep my voice steady, "we can't… I can't let this happen again."

"Ah, but Cat," he countered, a wicked grin spreading across his features, "I never said we should right now. I merely wanted to know if it had crossed your mind as often as it has mine."

Before I could respond, Nathan reached into the bag of food he'd brought and produced a small container of choco-late-covered strawberries. The rich, dark chocolate glistened under the dim office lights, and I found myself drawn to the treat.

"Would you like one?" he asked, his tone playful yet seduc-tive. "Or would that be crossing a line?"

My heart raced as I considered his offer. It was just a strawberry, after all — a simple indulgence that couldn't possibly harm my career or jeopardise the acquisition. And yet, if I gave him an inch, he'd take another yard. "Alright," I agreed despite knowing better. "But just one."

With a triumphant smile, Nathan selected a plump, choco-late-covered strawberry from the container and held it out to me. My eyes never left his as I opened my mouth, allowing him to feed me the surprisingly decadent treat. The moment his fingers skimmed my lips, a wave of pure desire washed over me, leaving me breathless.

"Incredible, isn't it?" Nathan murmured, his voice low and inviting as he leaned in closer, his warm breath tickling my ear.

"Absolutely."

As our eyes met once again, I knew that we were both teetering on the edge of temptation, fully aware of the poten-tial consequences that lay just beyond our reach. But for now, all that mattered was the sweet taste of forbidden fruit and the intoxicating allure of a love that could never truly be ours.

The intensity of Nathan's gaze pinned me in place, his azure eyes a storm of emotion that I couldn't escape. My heart raced, pounding like a drumbeat.

"Catrina," he whispered, as if my name was a prayer he'd been holding back for too long. The sound of it sent shivers down my spine, weakening my resolve.

We leaned in simultaneously, our lips meeting in a soft, tender kiss unlike any other we had shared. It felt like time slowed, allowing us to truly savour this stolen moment.

Nathan's hands gently cradled my face, his fingertips tracing the curve of my jaw as our mouths moved together in perfect harmony.

"God, you're gorgeous," he breathed into the kiss. I could feel the walls I had built around my heart beginning to crumble, replaced by the warmth of Nathan's interest and the aching need to be closer to him.

But just as quickly as the floodgates opened, reality came crashing down. The repercussions of giving in to this forbidden romance loomed over me, casting a dark shadow on the reprieve we had momentarily found in each other's arms.

My career, my family's expectations that I'd fail, and the public scrutiny that would follow — they all threatened to drown us both.

We were so close to closing the deal. Rushing things now would be foolish. We just had to wait another couple of weeks.

I pushed Nathan away, my chest heaving as I struggled to regain control, conflicting feelings warred within me.

"We can't do this yet, Nathan." I stood, unable to meet his gaze. My voice was fragile, betraying the doubt that was eating away at my resolve.

"Cat, please," Nathan said softly, reaching out to touch my arm. But I couldn't let him — every ounce of strength I had left went into maintaining the distance between us.

Heavy suffocating silence stretched around us as Nathan searched my face. I could no longer deny the truth– my feelings for Nathan went beyond an easily quenchable fling.

"We both know this isn't a mistake," he said, his voice a gentle plea.

My heart raced in my chest as I tried to gather my thoughts, to find the right words without revealing too much of the vulnerability I so desperately fought to conceal. But there was no denying that the magnetic pull between us had become impossible to resist — and I could see it in Nathan's eyes, too. He felt it just as strongly as I did.

"I can't do this right now," I whispered, my voice shaking. "My career, my visa… I can't risk losing everything."

He reached out to brush a stray strand of hair from my face. His touch sent shivers down my spine, and I struggled not to lean into his warmth.

"There's something here, Cat, and we can't just ignore it. We owe it to ourselves to at least explore what this might mean and if the day ever comes when your visa's in jeopardy, I'm sure I could find a way to help."

I appreciated the sentiment, but I'd never be able to delude myself into thinking I'd let him help me. I had never been the sort to take a handout. I took great pride in working for every single opportunity given to me.

"Or," I countered, forcing myself to push my chair back and my shaky legs to support me as I stood, "it could destroy everything I've worked so hard to achieve. I won't let that happen." The words tasted bitter on my tongue because deep down, I didn't want to let Nathan go either.

"Is that really what you want?" Nathan asked, his voice tinged with sadness. "To walk away from something that could be amazing?"

"Sometimes we have to make tough calls for the sake of our priorities." I blinked back tears. "Right now, I need to focus on myself and the path I've chosen. In a couple of weeks, we can revisit it."

"Catrina —" Nathan tried again, but I couldn't handle hearing his voice, couldn't stand another second in that office with everything unsaid hanging over us.

"Enjoy Edinburgh."

I turned and walked out of my office, leaving Nathan behind.

CHAPTER ELEVEN

CATRINA

*C*hristmas rolled around fast. I wish I could say I'd put all thoughts of Nathan in a box, but then I'd be lying. Fortunately, a couple of days after the big day, I found myself wrestling with my conscience for a totally different reason. A break, if you will, from obsessing over what my off-limits client was getting up to during his holidays.

On the one hand, I'd already eaten more nanaimo bars than I care to admit.

On the other hand, it was Christmas, and I should indulge.

Cloistered in my tiny one-bed flat, who would know?

No one. Screw the waistline.

As I reached for another bar, the phone rang, interrupting me before I could even touch the delicious dessert.

Maisy's name flashed up on the screen.

"Hey Cat. Do you have a minute to chat?"

"Sure, has something happened?"

"I wouldn't normally call one of Nathan's girlfriends, but

since he's in the middle of wedding preparations with Shaun and I can't reach him, I'm making an exception."

"Girlfriend?" I scoffed. "I'm his attorney, Maisy. "

"Of course, honey." Her tone suggested she either didn't believe me or didn't care. "I have some rather… urgent and potentially upsetting news for you."

"Upsetting how?"

"Well, that depends on you," she said, clearly stalling and frying my patience.

All I wanted for the week was to hide out in my flat and pretend there weren't people on the other side of North America bitching about me.

That involved being left in peace. Not being teased with bad news.

"I don't need to be coddled. Spit it out."

"Okay. A tabloid has a photo of you and Nathan kissing. They're running the story in a couple of hours."

I blinked at my off-white kitchen cupboards. Her matter-of-fact but rushed tone shocked me for a second even though I'd asked for it. When the words registered, it didn't matter anymore.

Tabloids had pictures?

Of me?

My stomach dropped, and my pulse quickened.

This wasn't good.

Not just for the deal, but it threatened to shatter the carefully constructed image I had built as a determined, unyielding attorney. My grip tightened on the phone.

"Can you stop them?"

"Unfortunately, no. They only informed me as a courtesy." Maisy sighed. "I know this isn't ideal, but there's nothing we can do other than damage control once it releases."

Panic seized my lungs, threatening to suffocate me. But I couldn't let it win. I couldn't let this situation tear down everything I'd worked so hard for. I took a deep breath and shoved the anxiety aside, focusing instead on the task at hand.

Reluctantly, I asked, "How bad is it?"

I mean really, unless someone had snuck into my flat the first night it couldn't be that bad. I'd been careful to keep my distance.

"You're both clothed if that's what you mean."

I blew out a breath, embracing the tiny rush of relief. It wasn't enough.

"The best I can offer is a press release." Maisy paused, the silence almost deafening. "But honestly, I'd advise against commenting."

"You want me to just pretend some tabloid isn't about to release a story that'll destroy my career?"

"That's not what I'm saying at all." She sighed. "If you and Nathan do want us to address it, I'm going to need a story to spin and if you're not together…"

Then downgrading the truth wouldn't work and lying might not be possible. Unless…

"Can you see my face?"

"Yes."

My stomach hit the floor. Fuck.

"Can you see Nathan's face?"

"No."

A rush of relief.

"Could we claim it's someone else?" Another lengthy pause sent my heart rate back up. "Maisy?"

"Your face is clear, but they don't have your name yet. It's in your office, Catrina. Someone will recognise it."

Shit.

"If I could reach Nathan, maybe I could find an innocent angle." She hummed. "Leave it with me. I'll see what I can come up with to reduce the fallout, but watch your back in the meantime. The paparazzi attention can be… unnerving." Her voice shuddered on the last word.

"Thank you for telling me."

"Good luck. We'll figure something out," she said, her determination loud.

❄

"I thought you were going to keep a tight leash on your client, Catrina?" Miranda said, her voice grating against my already frazzled nerves, her tone falsely sweet, setting my teeth on edge.

"Why would I need to do that?"

She tutted. "Haven't you seen the tabloids in the last hour? There are photos of your client in a compromising position. Kissing some mystery woman in his office!"

I pulled up the news article, the photo loading on my screen. There was Nathan, in my office, his hands tangled in my hair, his lips on mine, but his face completely obscured. My face on the other hand was recognisable — to me, at least. The angle made it a little difficult.

In any case, there appeared to be one small mercy in all of this. Miranda had no idea I had kissed Nathan. I swallowed hard, steadying my voice.

"Nathan's private affairs have no bearing on his role at Starlight and, in any case, you can't even see his face in that photo."

"We have shareholders and sponsors to answer to. Your client needs to understand his actions have consequences."

"Ordinarily, I would agree, but I would hardly call a kiss between two people in private compromising," I said, tone dry and toeing the road to scornful. "If this photo turns out to be Nathan, he is entitled to a personal life."

Really, did she have nothing better to do with her holidays?

She scoffed. "If that's your version of damage control, then God help you both. We're just trying to protect Nathan's reputation and investment here!"

I pinched the bridge of my nose in frustration. "On the contrary, Miranda, finalising this deal should be the top priority, as it is mine. I suggest we remain focused on that."

Until she realises it's you in the photo. Then what?

I couldn't think about that yet. If I gave that part too much attention, I'd be next to useless fending off someone as vindictive as Miranda Chambers.

"And how exactly are we to focus when your client can't keep his hands to himself?" Miranda snapped. "The sponsors are already asking questions, worried how much control he really has over that 'personal life' of his."

I took a measured breath, refusing to rise to her provocation. "Nathan has proven himself an adept and responsible businessman. One ambiguous photo will not change that, unless you and your shareholders continue to make a habit of blowing things out of proportion. May I suggest giving the tabloid frenzy a day or two to die down before drawing conclusions?"

Miranda huffed. "A day or two could do irreparable damage. But very well, it seems I have no choice but to trust your judgement in reining him in. For now."

As soon as the call ended, I forced myself into fixer mode. I could come up with a thousand excuses but without corroboration, none of them would stick. I needed to find Nathan and face it head-on.

I'd gotten lucky *this time.* But someone would connect the dots. Then what?

Bye bye Mike's approval?

How could I let this happen? I lowered my hands, staring at the photo on screen of us practically mauling each other. Nathan's back was to the door. The door I stupidly forgot to close because I thought I was the last person in the building that night. *Stupid.*

I scrambled for my phone, flicking through the lock screen and to recent calls while my stomach churned with dread.

"Hey there. You've reached my voicemail. I'm busy at the moment, so leave me a message and I will get back to you."

I stared at the phone. It didn't even ring.

I hung up and without hesitating this time, I opened Nathan's phone tracker. Once I confirmed he was in fact in Edinburgh, I booked a flight. Better to be in the air with a plane of people with zero internet access than wait around for his return. I'd be a sitting duck for the paparazzi.

Together, we had to figure out how to navigate the chaos that was about to unfold in both our lives.

NATHAN

The things I do for my friends. No one else could have convinced me to wear a baby blue tuxedo.

"Smile," Isla whispered, barely moving her lips as she side-eyed me. "Better." She pinched my arm and I just about held back a glare.

"What was that for?" I hissed.

"For potentially ruining my sister's wedding photos." She smiled sweetly at an older woman off to our right with tears streaming down her face. "I don't care how you screw up your love life. Keep it away from my baby sister's special day."

The side door opened, and in stepped Cat, almost like she'd been summoned. *What have I done now?*

"Stop," Isla growled. She pinched me again and nodded towards the fast-approaching altar and my perplexed best friend. "You're an actor. Act."

Cowed, I blocked out the burn of Cat's gaze against my neck and focused on Shaun. The lucky wanker looked normal in his black suit and tails compared to the rest of us. The only patch of blue on him came from his bow tie.

Isla left me with a warning look before stepping up onto

the dais to Shaun's left. The moment I stepped into line beside him, he swayed towards me, a flicker of concern in his gaze.

"I'm fine."

His brows rose. "That's why your lawyer's crashed my wedding? Because you're fine?" He nodded to where Catrina leaned against a wall, her arms crossed as she watched me.

Finn and Abi reached the end of the aisle, clinging to each other until the very last minute.

A couple of months ago, I would have sneered at the sight. I would have had immense fun ribbing Finn for his sappy moments.

Now, things had changed. My gaze tracked to Cat again.

At least, for me they had. The damn woman had far too strict a sense of propriety for my liking.

All the more rewarding when I finally fuck it out of her.

"I don't want drama at my wedding, Logan," Shaun said, a warning note in his voice. "This is a drama-free space. Do not stress Mona out today."

"What are we talking about?" Finn asked, joining us with curiosity painted plain across his face.

"Nothing," I grumbled.

I eyed Finn. Somehow he pulled off the baby blue suit. How? I bit my tongue on the whine of frustration dying to get loose. Hollywood royalty does not whine.

"Nathan's brought his drama to my wedding."

"Oh, did he, now?" Finn grinned, his brows climbing as utter delight skittered across his face. "Are we taking bets on how long it takes for them to fall into bed?"

"Don't waste your breath." I turned to face the crowded hall.

Ornate, antique chandeliers hovered above their heads. The Assembly Rooms barely needed decorating with their decorative walls and original features. The place looked like a fairytale come to life.

Shaun had to pull some serious strings to get the venue for

New Year's Eve but he'd managed it. Despite the chaos of the annual Hogmanay street party outside, they made the entire space over into their very own Winter Wonderland, with ice sculptures, faux furs, and every white, blue, and icy-looking flower on the planet.

They'd even dressed us to look like Jack Frost. Every single one of our protests fell on deaf ears.

Once Jackson and Mona's friend Tilly had made it to their positions, the orchestra switched pace and the room collectively held their breaths. All eyes turned to the door, ready to watch the bride make her way down the aisle.

Mine didn't make it. I got caught up in the shimmer of moisture in Cat's.

For a second, I thought my mind deceived me, but no, the Ice Queen had melted. For a moment, at least.

A fanciful dream crashed into me, stealing my breath. One where I got to watch Cat walk towards me in a flowing white dress and a soft expression of utter joy on her face.

Fuck.

I never thought I'd be the commitment guy, but for her, maybe I could be brave enough to feel what Finn and Shaun did towards Abi and Mona. Pure, endless love.

The thought of it both terrified and excited me.

There was just one problem. We were still client and attorney, and Cat — my beautiful, fierce and rule-follower Cat — was still determined to resist me until the deal closed.

CHAPTER TWELVE

CATRINA

When the ceremony ended, and the applause rang out, Nathan stepped down from the platform, his questioning gaze fixed on me. Laughter followed from his friends and they called after him too quietly for me to hear. The grins on their faces screamed teasing.

After more than a week, I couldn't stop my eyes from devouring every detail of him like a woman starved.

His suit hugged his broad shoulders and accentuated his toned physique. I'd seen him in a suit before of course, but never in person. There was something overpowering about it. Never mind the interesting baby blue choice. He looked so good, my anger towards him momentarily faded.

"I'm surprised to see you, Icy," he said as he stopped in front of me. "What brings you here?"

Those kissable lips captured my attention for a brief second. *Stop it.* That's what got us into this mess in the first place.

"We need to talk," I muttered before spinning on my heel and marching out of the hall.

Nathan followed me away from the chatter of wedding guests gathering at the bar. As we walked his steps echoed behind me in an uneven rhythm. I did my best to ignore him, but the sound of his polished shoes on the marble and the burn of his eyes on my back was like a beacon calling to me.

We passed an empty reception room and I ducked inside, trusting he'd follow.

The room was devoid of all furniture. Just an open dance hall with polished hardwood floors and a ceiling so high it made me dizzy to look at. I only cared that it was empty, giving us the privacy that we so desperately needed for this conversation.

The door clicked shut, and I turned to face Nathan.

Words collided on my tongue. Far too many things desperate to escape my mind.

"Where have you been?" I hissed, my eyes darting around as if someone could have snuck past me and remained hidden in the empty room.

"I told you I'd be here, in Scotland, for Christmas."

"Yes, I know, but why didn't you answer your phone?" Before he could reply, I rushed on, my panic quickly spiralling and destroying any attempt I made to project a professional calm. "Maisy was trying to reach you and what if I needed to talk to you urgently about the acquisition? What if there had been an emergency? Why wouldn't you answer the phone?"

Nathan's expression hardened. "One, I'm eight hours ahead of LA right now." He counted it off on his fingers. "Two, Maisy called me while I was asleep. Three, I called her back as soon as I woke up. Four—?"

"So you know about the photo?"

He nodded. "Maisy told me."

"Don't you care?" I spat out, my anger returning. "This is my career on the line! My job, my visa, everything!"

"Of course, I care," Nathan said calmly, stepping closer to me. "But this sort of thing is common in my industry. I promise you it'll blow over fast, but I already have Maisy working on the best response. She's figuring out whether releasing a statement to deny it will do more damage and then we were going to call you."

It wasn't lost on me that his words virtually mirrored my assurances to Miranda. Funny how I couldn't find comfort in it coming from someone else.

I frowned. "Why would it cause more problems?"

"I've made a point of shooting down every false rumour in the last few years." He dragged a hand through his almost pristine blond hair, wincing. "If I stay silent, it confirms it. If I shoot it down, I'm lying." He shrugged. "Either way, we can't win."

"So we're fucked either way?" I whispered, horrified.

"No. Maisy's a genius at these things. She'll figure something out." His blue eyes softened on me. "It'll be fine. In a week, some other scandal will replace us on the headline crawl."

"Your industry might be used to scandals, but I'm not!" I snapped, anger and fear lacing my voice. "It's not normal for me! Do you have any idea what this could mean for me?" I barely let him get a word in. "Starlight Studios could pull out of the deal, my boss could fire me, I could be deported back to Canada. This could ruin my entire life!"

"None of that will happen," Nathan said, placing a hand on my shoulder. "We'll get through it. We'll handle it together."

For a moment, I allowed myself to get lost in his eyes, our faces mere inches apart. His words brought me some comfort. His confidence was intoxicating.

But the reality of our situation still loomed over my head and I couldn't let his charm distract me from the potential disaster that lay ahead.

I shook his hand off my shoulder, taking a step back. "How could you let this happen?" I bit out and guilt instantly stabbed me in the gut. That was unfair.

"How could I let it happen?" Nathan repeated, his voice hollow with disbelief. "You kissed me."

"That is not how I remember it."

"Handy that." He glared at me. "It doesn't change the facts, Cat. Your name's not out yet but it will be."

"We don't know that." Desperation and optimism clashed in my voice. "Maybe no one will notice me. How long has it been now?"

"I don't know, fifteen, twenty hours maybe."

"And they still don't have my name." I nodded firmly, trying to convince myself. "Maybe they won't figure it out."

"You're not that naive." He sighed and reached for me again. With a firm grip on my shoulders, he shook me. "Someone in your office took the picture. Your face is partially visible, and yes, maybe only those close to you will be able to ID you, but that person knows it was you, and your colleagues know what your office looks like."

My knees went weak and I slumped against the wall.

"Maisy said she was going to spin the story." My head tilted as I considered the slowly developing glimmer in his eyes. "Is that why you're so calm? She's come up with something?"

"I'd be calm anyway, but yes." He nodded. "For now, she's staying silent while we wait to see if anything else comes out."

"Anything else like what?" I asked, my voice weak.

"Eyewitness interviews, family members grabbing their five minutes of fame."

The riot of nerves in my stomach settled for the first time in hours. My muscles finally relaxed but Nathan continued to stare at me like I was a snake about to bite.

"What's that look for?"

"Just making sure you're all angered out before I keep going."

My eyes narrowed. "What's that supposed to mean?"

He sighed. "You don't have a good relationship with your family."

I shook my head hard. "No."

"Is it bad enough that they'd throw you under the bus for a quick buck?"

"No."

"Is that 'no, they wouldn't' or 'no, I'm not considering it'?"

"They wouldn't and I'm not considering it." I squared up to him. How I expected to intimidate a six-foot-five giant, I had no clue but that didn't mean I wouldn't try. I pushed my shoulders back and stared up at him, my jaw clenched and my eyes narrowed. "Leave my family out of it."

Nathan shook his head. "Fine. I won't mention it again."

"Cat, I'd like you to meet some of my closest friends," Nathan said, a triumphant smile claiming his lips after he'd convinced me that hiding out in a hotel room waiting for things to get worse was pointless.

While we'd been gone, the room had been totally reconfigured. Now instead of an altar and rows of chairs, there was a long table at the front of the room and a sea of circular ones.

Nathan moved through the dwindling crowd with ease, smiling and shaking hands with people as he passed. I followed behind, keeping a careful distance and walking with far less confidence. The last thing I needed was some fame-hungry wedding guest snapping more pictures of us.

"Everyone, this is Catrina Sinclair," Nathan said when I finally caught up to him. Reaching back, he gripped my wrist and tugged me in front of him.

With six pairs of eyes fixed on me, my mouth went dry.

For once, I had no issue letting Nathan do all the talking. He introduced everyone, friends, spouses and siblings.

"Hey!" Finn McCarthy, the Irish actor with a megawatt smile, stretched out his hand for a firm shake. His wife, Abi, waved cheerfully beside him.

"Catrina, it's lovely to finally meet you," Shaun Martin said, his Welsh accent adding a melodic lilt to his words. He was tall and broad-shouldered, with piercing green eyes that seemed to bore into your soul. Beside him stood Mona Baines, the Scottish bride, her warm smile inviting me in.

"Last but not least," Nathan continued, gesturing to the final member of the group, "Jackson Levi, our dashing bachelor."

"Well aren't you a vision," Jackson replied with a roguish grin, taking my hand and pressing a kiss to my knuckles. "If you ever decide to bin the Englishman, I'm all yours."

Everyone laughed but Nathan. I peeked at him, surprised to find him scowling at his friend. Nathan pushed Jackson away from me, only making his grin widen.

"You like that test far too much." Mona chuckled.

"I'll say, didn't he try it on me and Abi?" Finn asked, his eyes sparkling with amusement.

Jackson made a show of studying the couple, his brows climbing at their proximity. "I'd say it worked, wouldn't you?"

More laughter followed, briefly freeing me from the pressure of our situation.

"How do you all know each other?" I asked, trying to hold on to the light mood.

"Ah, well, it all started on the set of our first LA job." Jackson glanced at his friends, smirking at them. "First legit Hollywood jobs on a shitty action film. Luckily, we bonded over the long hours on set and formed a lifelong friendship that audiences just can't get enough of."

"You don't need to make it sound so weird." Nathan

covered his face. "Maybe I shouldn't have introduced you to these lunatics."

They ignored him, their amused and friendly gazes firmly fixed on me. A waiter appeared with a tray loaded with champagne flutes. We all accepted a glass with muttered thanks.

"Abi and I met on Married Blind," Finn chimed in, slipping an arm around his wife. "We were matched on the show. The first time we saw each other was at the altar. Turned out to be the best thing that ever happened to me."

"Really? That's amazing!" I said, genuinely impressed by their unlikely love story.

Nathan chuckled. "Don't let him fool you. He wasn't that happy about it to start."

"And Mona and I..." Shaun glanced down at his new wife, eyes lovingly caressing her. "We met on the set of Mystery Lines. She was my assistant at the time."

Mona grinned. "We were meant to wait until my contract ended before getting involved."

Shaun grinned. "We couldn't resist each other long enough to finish the show."

I looked around at these couples who had defied the odds and found love in the most unexpected places. It gave me pause. If the deal survived the picture scandal and I didn't lose my job, could we actually make it work after the acquisition closed?

Without a clear answer, I didn't want to dwell on it.

"Cheers to that!" I lifted my champagne flute in a toast.

The group clinked glasses, but not even the happy energy surrounding me could totally eradicate the ball of worry inside of me.

"Can I ask you something, Abi, Mona?" At their nod, I spat it out, not chancing a glance at Nathan. "How would you react if the tabloids were threatening to ruin your career?"

"Cat," Nathan hissed, his mouth close to my ear.

When had he gotten so close? I shuffled forward and tried to ignore him.

"I've had my fair share of rumours printed about me." Mona sighed, her shoulders drooping. "You learn not to take it too seriously after a while. People forget and move on."

"Really?"

"Absolutely," Mona assured me. "You develop a thick skin, especially when you're in a relationship with someone in the public eye. The important thing is to remember who you are and what really matters."

I nodded, appreciating her candour but still feeling unsettled.

"Personally, I think it's a big deal," Abi admitted. "Our lives are so exposed as it is — we deserve to have some control over our own narratives. If there were false rumours that could potentially damage my career, I'd want to do something about it."

But could I truly claim the tabloids were printing false stories? We weren't in a relationship, but we had kissed.

"And what would you do?" I asked Abi, ignoring Nathan for now.

She shrugged and exchanged a look with her husband. "We just try to stay true to who we are and hope that the truth will eventually come out. People hear both sides of the story before they form an opinion — and as long as ours is genuine enough, it can be quite powerful."

Shaun nodded in agreement. "I think you need to focus on what is real and important — family and friends who will always have your back no matter what comes up in the press." He smiled lovingly at Mona before continuing on. "Be resilient but don't let them define you or your happiness. The most important thing is staying true to yourself."

Before I could ask more questions, Nathan stepped in front of me.

"Let's dance," he said before grabbing my arm and pulling me away from the group.

He led me to the dance floor. I tried to protest, but he shot me a pissed-off look that froze the words.

"I don't know what you were trying to achieve there, but letting this overshadow the entire evening will only make it worse."

We stopped on the dance floor, each of us glaring at the other.

"I don't want to dance," I muttered, my tone embarrassingly petulant.

He pinched the bridge of his nose. "Fine. Then what do you want to do that doesn't involve questioning my friends?"

My throat tightened. "I want to figure out how we can stop this from getting worse," I said, my voice wobbling slightly. "But I don't know how."

Nathan sighed heavily before saying, "Come back to my room with me so we can talk about it in private? That way you won't have to worry about being overheard by anyone here."

CHAPTER THIRTEEN

NATHAN

"Remember, you don't have to stay," I said as the door to my hotel room swung open. "I can book you on the first flight to LA in the morning and call you a taxi any time."

She brushed past me into the room, freezing as her gaze landed on the single bed. Her face paled, and for a moment I thought she might change her mind. But when she turned to me, her expression was resolute.

"Thanks for the offer, but I'm staying. This is my job, and I won't let anything come between me and my success."

I sighed, noticing how she avoided directly mentioning the bed or our lingering tension. Her determination to ignore the obvious amused me, even as I admired her perseverance.

"Here we are."

I set down her bag and watched her stare at the bed, unmoving, her face pale and almost ghostly against the muted colours of the room.

Biting back a smile, I asked, "Are you alright?"

"Yes. I guess I just didn't expect..." She gestured at the bed, eyes wide. "There to be just one bed."

"Look, if it makes you feel better, I'll sleep on the sofa." I gestured to the plush seating area across from the bed. It wasn't really long enough to take my six-foot-five frame, but I'd do it if it made her comfortable.

Cat worried her lip, considering. I could see the indecision in her eyes and knew she was battling the desire to run versus proving she could handle this. My fingers twitched, longing to run through her silken hair and draw her into my arms. Instead, I kept still, giving her space to think.

Finally, she asked, "Why would someone like you, with your kind of money, book such a small room? Why not a suite?"

I laughed, the sound echoing in the quiet room. "Believe it or not, there's a lot of Hollywood's finest in town for the wedding. I don't need loads of space." Though at the moment I would give anything for a larger suite, if it meant easing the awkwardness between us.

She eyed me sceptically but seemed to relax, her shoulders losing their tension.

I smiled, hoping to reassure her. "Sharing a room will be fine, Cat. And remember, it's your choice to stay. If you ever feel uncomfortable, you can leave at any time."

"Fine." She shifted, hugging her arms around herself. "We need to establish some ground rules."

I nodded, keeping my expression neutral. "You set the rules, and I'll follow them."

She met my gaze steadily. "First, no touching. We're sharing a room, but that's it. Nothing's changed."

"Understood."

"Second, our relationship remains strictly professional."

"Agreed." The word tasted bitter on my tongue.

She took a breath, as though bracing herself. "Lastly, we

don't discuss this with anyone. No one needs to know about our arrangement or any... tension between us."

"Your secrets are safe with me," I assured her, my hand instinctively reaching for hers before I remembered her first rule. I quickly clenched it into a fist at my side.

She studied the floor, shoulders tense. "I think that's all I have to say for now."

I opened my mouth to argue, to tell her how badly I wanted to touch her, but nothing I said would change her mind. My pride also wouldn't let me. So instead, I settled for a nod and a weak smile.

"Sounds good to me."

We stood in silence, the rules forming an invisible barrier between us.

I sighed, rubbing the ache building behind my eyes. "You must be tired after your flight. Would you like to rest or come back to the wedding? Dinner's in half an hour."

Cat studied me, her lips pursed for some reason. *What did I do now?*

"Any updates from Maisy?"

"No, nothing yet. Do you want me to call her?" I kept my tone light, though her coldness stung.

She stared at me, eyes hard. At last, she nodded. "Yes, I think that would be best."

I swallowed a sigh, fingers tightening around my phone. Her meaning was clear — call Maisy now, so I can be sure you're not lying.

Maintaining a casual smile through gritted teeth, I tapped Maisy's number. "Maisy, hi! It's Nathan…"

CATRINA

Guilt churned in my stomach. This disaster was my fault. Why did I assume my office was safe?

My fingers trembled as I scoured social media.

I listened intently to both sides of their conversation, since Nathan put it on speaker, desperate for information. Nathan paced back and forth, his voice a calming balm that spoke to something deep inside of me.

That calm stood no chance against the anxiety of reading speculation online. With each article, another brick was laid in the wall separating me from my dreams. The threat of losing all I'd worked for weighed on me, though I knew I couldn't control others.

"So what do you advise we do?" Nathan asked.

"If you don't want to admit you're in a relationship or let it fade on its own?"

"We don't," Nathan said, resolute.

"Then denial is your best strategy." Tapping sounded over the line. "Currently, no one has names or an angle showing your faces. I assume they think it's you only because the person who took the photo said so."

Did the fact my name hadn't been given to the tabloids on a silver platter mean the photographer didn't know me?

Surely someone who knew me, and my working relationship with Nathan, would have supplied my name.

My fingers clamped around my phone as anxiety warred with a flicker of hope.

"Denial is your best strategy. " Maisy paused; the silence making my focus zero in on the phone in Nathan's hand. "Now don't shoot the messenger but I made a couple of assumptions after speaking with Cat and have already started the process of denying the story."

"What does that mean, Maisy?" Nathan asked.

"I hinted to a friend you weren't even in LA that week."

"And the other thing?"

Maisy sighed. "I left an anonymous comment on one of the news sites denying it was you two in the photo."

My breath caught as I processed her words. "That's it?"

"For now. If you want to deny it, then do nothing and let my anonymous comments do their work," Maisy said, her voice gentle yet firm. "It will throw some doubt into the situation and if we are lucky, this could all blow over by the end of the weekend."

"And if it doesn't?" Nathan asked.

Maisy sighed. "You've set a precedent in the last year, Nathan. If it doesn't die down on its own, we'll have to issue a press release putting it to bed. But—"

"We'd be lying," Nathan said, interrupting her, tone resigned. "And if someone ever figured out that we lied, it would become a bigger story."

"I'm afraid so."

Nathan rubbed a hand across his tired face.

"What do you think?" he asked, turning to me.

What *did* I think? I didn't have a better solution that was certain.

Quietly denying any relationship and relying on Maisy's cunning felt like our only choice. If we were lucky, sidestepping the spotlight's glare could allow this mania to fade into yesterday's news. Admitting the photo's authenticity seemed destined to cause more damage.

Except there was one problem with the plan...

"Miranda won't be content with silence and letting it blow over." I let my head fall back against the headboard. "I'm going to have to call her and deny it."

"And that's fine," Maisy said. "It's public comments we need to avoid. If I put out a press release to deny it, every media outlet not paying attention will sit up and take notice. We need to avoid making it a story and hope it fades on its own."

I sighed, running a hand through my hair as dread filled my stomach. "Okay."

"Thanks," Nathan said, finally ending the call with a heavy sigh of his own. He turned to me, his brow furrowed with concern and his gaze searching. "Do you agree with it?"

"Does it matter if I don't?" My words came out sharper than intended.

"Yes. I'll do whatever you want me to."

I studied his earnest expression. "You really would, wouldn't you?"

Before he could answer, my phone rang. I glanced at the screen, pulse racing as Mike's name flashed across it. This was the moment I'd feared, when lies might crumble beneath scrutiny.

"Hello, Mike." I struggled to keep my voice steady. My mouth felt dry as ash.

"Is it true?" Mike asked bluntly. "Are you involved with Nathan Logan?"

"Of course not," I lied, ignoring the rush of guilt. I couldn't hesitate, or he'd see through the charade. "I saw the articles but the guy in the photos isn't even Nathan."

Mike sighed, a deafening sound that echoed my own anxiety.

"For a moment there, I was worried. You're right, it looks nothing like him. Damn vultures." Relief coated each word. "This is why I don't do entertainment cases."

I met Nathan's watchful gaze, unable to read his reaction from across the room. He sat motionless on the sofa as if afraid to breathe, to disturb this precarious moment.

"Yeah, I'm probably going to avoid another Hollywood project." My laugh felt hollow.

"I understand completely." There was a pause, then Mike cleared his throat. "Well, I'm glad that's not true. Keep up the good work and I'll see you after the holidays."

The line went dead before I could say goodbye, leaving bitter remorse in its wake.

I'd lied to my boss — a fact that left my stomach churning.

With a weary sigh, I tossed my phone aside and closed my eyes. Behind the lids, chaotic thoughts whirled and collided until exhaustion washed over. When I opened them again, Nathan was watching me, brows knit with concern.

"It's going to be okay," he said softly, crossing the room to sit beside me. The warmth of his arm brushing mine soothed ragged nerves.

I wanted desperately to believe those words, to cling to his steadfast reassurance. But doubt lingered, poisoning hope.

"I need to get back to the wedding." Nathan stood and paced away from me. "Do you want to come with me? It'll be a good distraction, and there's nothing more we can do on New Year's Eve."

My stomach churned at the thought of food, but it rumbled all the same. As hungry as I was, leaving the hotel with Nathan seemed like a terrible idea.

"Thanks, but I think I should stay here."

"You sure?" He tilted his head, studying me from across the room. "There's no room service here, and all the take-aways will be rammed tonight."

I sighed, acknowledging the truth in his words. "I know, I just… going out there again so soon seems unwise. If anyone recognises me from that photo—"

"They won't." He crossed the room again to kneel before me. "We have food, music and a few hundred guests to disappear into. A perfect place to hide in plain sight."

I searched his gaze, finding nothing but sincerity and a hint of pleading. How was I meant to refuse him anything when he looked at me that way?

"Please, Cat," he whispered. "Come with me. We'll tackle this mess together after some food and drink." His mouth quirked into an attempt at a smile, optimism undimmed.

"Okay," I agreed reluctantly.

With my hair in a messy bun, a lick of makeup and a fresh top, we made our way back to the wedding reception, fairy lights casting an ethereal glow over the elegantly decorated room.

As we approached the top table, they shuffled seats around to make room for me beside Nathan. Though touched by their acceptance, envy prickled — I craved connections like those he shared with lifelong friends. Their laughter was contagious, affection for one another evident.

"Thank you for making space for me," I said, taking my seat.

Nathan smiled, warmth in his voice. "Of course. You're welcome here."

CHAPTER FOURTEEN

CATRINA

"I'll take the sofa."

His brows rose. "You're volunteering to sleep on that tiny excuse for a sofa?"

"Better than making you do it."

"Thanks for the offer, but absolutely not." He shook his head, a lopsided grin playing on his lips. "Besides, you'll need a good night's sleep after the flight and all that dancing."

"Are you sure?"

"Positive," he answered, chuckling softly. "Now go on, get ready for bed."

"Alright, fine." I tried to keep the relief out of my voice. "You use the bathroom first."

"Deal."

Nathan ducked into the en suite, the water almost immediately turning on, while I changed into pyjamas, cursing my choice of silk shorts and camisole. They had seemed like a practical choice when I packed it, but now they felt too revealing.

The bathroom door opened, and Nathan emerged wearing only a pair of pyjama pants that revealed his toned, bare chest and abs. He ran a hand through his tousled hair, making it look even more dishevelled and undeniably sexy.

Just like he had after round two in my bed.

"Your turn," he said, flashing me a charming smile before heading towards the small sofa.

"Thanks," I muttered, my cheeks heating.

I gripped the sink edge as I stared at my reflection. What have I gotten myself into?

Less than a day ago, I was in LA, living in blissful denial, believing that I could get through New Year's and seal the deal on Starlight Studios.

Or more to the point... pretending my heart didn't race at the thought of Nathan's smile. Now here I was, worlds away and about to spend the night close enough to touch him.

Being with Nathan felt as natural as breathing, yet could ruin everything I'd built. No amount of deep breathing could slow my racing thoughts.

Sure my boss had bought my excuse for the picture, but I'd lied, hadn't I?

I wasn't in a relationship with Nathan, but…

He sent me occasionless gifts, brought me food on a late night and checked in on me regularly. We talked non-stop.

If pushed, could I seriously deny that we were involved? Even unofficially?

After tonight, I was thinking the answer would be no.

What was I thinking, getting on that plane?

My traitorous body still reacted to Nathan's presence after all these weeks, heart racing as I imagined exiting this room to find him waiting. I splashed cool water on my face, taking another calming breath.

Who would know if I gave in?

In just two weeks, there'd be nothing standing in our way and, in the meantime, who the hell would know? We were thousands of miles from home, locked in a private hotel room. If there were ever a safe time to give in to Nathan, now would be it.

If the press figured out we were sharing a hotel room, it would cause issues whether I gave in or not. So really, I'd only be torturing myself by continuing to hold on to my professionalism like a shield.

With that sobering thought, I patted my cheeks dry and checked my reflection. Cool, calm and collected — just as I should be.

A sharp knock at the bathroom door nearly made me jump out of my skin.

"Cat? Do you mind if I brush my teeth?"

Of course, he would choose now to be considerate. I steeled myself and opened the door.

"Come on in."

We stood side by side at the sink, diligently brushing in silence. Our eyes met in the mirror, heat building between us. Nathan flashed his playful grin, quickening my pulse.

The intimacy of sharing such a mundane routine felt uncomfortably natural. How many times had we lingered on the phone late into the night, texting details of each other's days? In those unguarded moments, the rules I clung to for self-preservation seemed unnecessary... like now, locked in a hotel room with him with no prying eyes or cameras.

I rinsed my toothbrush and met Nathan's gaze in the mirror, flashing a polite smile.

"Well, good night." I slipped past him out of the bathroom. A thrill went through me at our accidental touch in the narrow space.

I climbed into the bed and pulled the covers up to my chin. Nathan emerged a few minutes later, running a hand through tousled hair.

"Are you sure you're okay on that thing?" I asked, trying to keep my voice even, as he made his way over to the sofa.

"Absolutely." He grinned, though his eyes betrayed a hint of discomfort. "I've slept in worse places."

A pang of disappointment hit me as I watched him attempt to get comfortable on the tiny sofa. His long legs dangled over the edge.

The anticipation of sharing such close quarters with Nathan made my heart race. The man was intoxicating, and it took every ounce of my self-control not to demand he get into bed with me. Every time I thought about asking, my throat closed up. Something about throwing my interest out there, after months of pushing him away, made me nervous.

I turned my body away from him, trying to ignore the magnetic pull between us but failing miserably.

"Sweet dreams, Catrina," Nathan whispered, sending shivers cascading down my spine.

"Sweet dreams, Nathan." I desperately hoped that sleep would come quickly.

I lay there, my mind filled with thoughts of Nathan. His muscles, his captivating voice, the way he gazed at me in the reflection…

My body tensed every time he shuffled around, my ears straining while my heart hoped this would be the moment he gave up. At least half an hour ticked by, grinding my patience to nothing.

"Okay. Enough" I sat up in bed, fixing my determined stare on Nathan. "Get in. You can't sleep on that thing and I'm not going to be able to live with myself if you can't move tomorrow." I flipped the duvet back and patted the mattress.

"I don't want to make you uncomfortable." He sat up and dragged a hand through his already messed-up hair.

"Trust me, I'll be more uncomfortable knowing you're suffering over there." A mix of emotions coursed through me — relief, anticipation, and a growing sense of vulnerability.

"Are you sure?" His gaze searched mine.

I nodded, feigning confidence. "Just don't hog the covers."

"Deal." A playful smile tugged at Nathan's lips.

My heart skipped as he approached the bed, climbing in carefully while preserving distance between us. Laughable. His warmth was tempting, urging me to close the gap.

"Thanks," Nathan whispered, his voice barely audible as he settled in.

"No problem." Instead of turning over, like I should have, I slid closer. Not close enough to accidentally brush against each other, but all I had to do was reach out and—

"Goodnight again, Icy." His breath caressed my face before he rolled over.

The nickname filled me with a warm and fuzzy feeling.

"Goodnight, playboy."

I clenched my hand into a fist, stopping myself from reaching for him the way I desperately wanted to.

As the minutes ticked by, I found myself listening to the steady rhythm of his breath, finding comfort in the sound. His body radiated heat, my skin tingling in response.

"Are you alright?" he asked, keeping his voice low and tentative, as I climbed out of bed.

"Fine," I said finally, trying to sound confident despite the butterflies fluttering wildly in my stomach. "Just... a little warm, that's all."

A half-truth — the warmth was of my own making, but I had every intention of using the lie to my advantage.

I tugged the thin pyjama strap top over my head and shimmied out of the shorts, leaving me in just my panties. As bold moves went, this was my wildest. With nerves balling up in my throat, I slid back under the covers, shuffling even closer to Nathan.

"Want me to open a window?" he offered, already starting to move.

"No, stay." I reached out, my fingers finding his arm, firm yet yielding. "It's fine. Really. Just... stay where you are."

"Alright." He settled back onto the mattress. His arm was

inches away from brushing against my bare breast. The thought of it sent a jolt of electricity coursing through my veins.

I reached up, tracing the contours of his handsome face in the muted glow of the streetlights outside. His breath caught and he tensed, holding still as my fingers grazed from his strong jawline, the slight stubble that had grown since morning scratching my hand, to the fullness of his lips. Despite his reputation as a ladies' man, there was a vulnerability and sincerity that shone through in moments like these, making it impossible not to be drawn to him.

"Try to get some sleep." His warm breath tickled my skin as he shifted closer to me.

His hand slid down my hair, my arm to my waist. He held himself unnaturally still, and I barely managed to restrain my amusement. *Took you long enough.*

"Cat?" he asked, his tone hesitant.

"Yes?" I bit my lip, just barely suppressing my grin.

"Where did your clothes go?"

"I was hot."

He absorbed my blasé response, his fingers clenching and unclenching on my waist. I could just make out his furrowed brow and knew he was probably arguing with himself to release me.

I didn't want that.

"Nathan?" I shifted closer, until my chest brushed against his.

"Yeah?" he said on a sharp inhale.

My hands smoothed up his chest, nails grazing at just the right pressure for goose bumps to break out beneath my fingers.

I leaned forward and ran my nose along his jaw, lifting myself up so I could whisper in his ear.

"I want you to fuck me, Nathan."

His grip on my waist tightened. He turned his face into my

hair and groaned. "I thought you wanted to wait," he said, his voice strangled.

"No one can see us and I'm changing the rules."

I pressed little kisses to his jaw, working my way to his lips as he held stock still. Then something must have clicked, because the next thing I knew, I was on my back and Nathan's lips were fused to mine.

His kiss rendered all arguments obsolete. I was lost — and despite the warnings echoing through my mind, I couldn't bring myself to care. I had given in at last.

Moaning, I wrapped my arms around him and dug my heels into the mattress, revelling in the feel of his bulge pressing against my clit. He ground against me, each stroke sending tiny sparks of pleasure through my body. I wanted more.

I shifted my hips and reached between us, pushing down the fabric of his boxers to free his impressive cock. His breathing became shallow as I stroked my hand up and down the length of him.

He broke our kiss, grinning as he removed my hand.

"Did you forget, baby?" He pressed it to the pillow beside my head, hovering over me, his lips inches from mine but out of reach. "No touching until I say so."

I bit my lip and nodded, squirming against him as if it would make him move faster.

When I didn't try to touch him again, he smiled. "Good girl," he whispered as he pressed a quick chaste kiss to my lips.

Then he kissed down my body, his stubble grazing my sensitive skin and intensifying my squirming before his lips brushed once, twice, across my taut nipple, making me ache. His fingers teased the other, driving me mad until he suckled on the other. After that, all I could do was moan, tossing my head against the pillow. The warmth of his tongue and the hard grazing of his teeth sent shivers through my body.

Every nerve-ending in my body was alive with sensations I'd denied for months. *Why did I do that to myself?*

His mouth continued its exploration further south until he reached the apex of my thighs. He hooked his fingers into the waistband of my panties, sliding them down my legs, dragging his blunt nails against me as his tongue followed in their wake.

Then he reversed the direction, tracing up along my inner thigh until he reached the swollen lips of my core.

A gasp escaped me as his tongue lapped at me, exploring and teasing. His fingers pushed through my slick folds, circling my clit, and I cried out, arching up against him, begging for more.

Nathan chuckled in response before increasing the pressure and pace, his fingers joining in on the fun, building the slow crescendo. Every flick of his tongue was a spark of pleasure that surged through me, making me dizzy.

Nathan moaned in approval as he drove me closer to the edge. His hands gripped my hips tightly as he increased the intensity of his assault, alternating slow licks with hard sucks that sent me hurtling towards the edge.

The orgasm shuddered through me like an earthquake and I screamed his name, the pressure almost too much to bear before it dissipated into blissful pleasure.

Nathan didn't let up though; he kept licking and teasing until I came again. Only then did he let me fall back onto the bed.

He crawled up my body slowly and kissed me thoroughly, his lips tender yet demanding on mine before pulling away. I opened my eyes and found him smiling down at me, a mix of satisfaction and hunger written across his face.

"Ready?" he asked hoarsely, already pulling away from me to find a condom.

"More than you know." I nodded eagerly, wanting nothing more than to feel him inside me again after months of fighting this need.

Nathan chuckled, ripped open the package, and rolled on the condom. He kneeled between my legs, his thick cock drawing all of my attention. He hooked his arm under one of my legs and leaned forward, grazing my entrance, teasing me like he had all the time in the world.

Which, okay, I didn't have anywhere I needed to be tomorrow, so maybe we did.

"Stop messing around." I tried to lift my hips, to rock against him, but he held me still with a hand on my thigh.

"Patience, baby," he said with a smile. "I don't want to hurt you."

He gently pressed inside me inch by inch until I was full of him and I gasped at the stretch of it. *Fuck, I missed this.* His thrusts were slow but deliberate as if savouring every second.

I pressed my foot into the mattress and rocked against him, urging him to go fast. He grabbed my hands and pinned them to either side of my head as he increased his pace. Each stroke went deeper and harder than the last. My breathing quickened as he lost control, his grip tightening.

"You feel so good," he whispered in between kisses. "I've missed this. Missed you."

I wanted to tell him how much it meant to me, that given the choice, I would have given him what he wanted months ago. But words were beyond my reach, and really, what good would they do? I arched into him instead, feeling the connection between us as each stroke tightened the coil inside of me.

My orgasm crashed over me like a wave, taking away all of my thoughts until there was nothing left but pure pleasure that rippled through my body like electricity. His movements became more urgent until, finally, he followed me over the edge.

Nathan collapsed beside me, our chests heaving in unison as he gathered me close. His fingers gently ran over my arm, his thumb mapping out circles against my wrist. We lay there in silence for what felt like hours until finally, he spoke.

"Thank you for giving us this chance, Cat."

With my ear pressed to his chest, I could hear the hammering of his heart, a solid sound that grounded me. While he smoothed circles on my back and pressed gentle kisses to my scalp, I closed my eyes and listened, savouring the moment, hoping that he wouldn't move on now that I'm no longer a challenge.

No matter how hard I tried, I couldn't fall asleep.

"Would it help if we talked about something?" Nathan asked

"What did you have in mind?"

Nathan's voice took on a wistful tone describing his English hometown, a world away from Hollywood yet forever part of him. Rolling green hills, wildflower fields and a tight-knit community shaped the boy with dreams too big for a village. Acting became his release and road to freedom.

I pictured the little Devon seaside village through his words, quaint yet confining. His path resonated with me, over-coming constraints through purpose and passion. Success in London then Hollywood — chasing a vision of creative freedom without compromise.

"And now you're working on opening your own studio."

"The next step," he said, his voice filled with pride and excitement. "I want to turn Starlight Studios into a space free of industry politics. That might be an unattainable aspiration, but I'm going to try."

"Wow." Sincerity rang clear in my voice. "I hope it works."

"Thank you." Nathan turned to his side to face me. His hand found mine, twining our fingers and eliciting delicious shivers. "Now, what about you? You mentioned growing up in a small town as well. What was that like?"

I hesitated for a moment, unsure if I wanted to reveal the more vulnerable parts of my past. But something about the intimacy of the moment, the shared confessions and the warmth of Nathan's presence gave me the courage to open up.

"Not easy. Everyone had their expectations for me, and my mother was no exception. She pushed me to excel at everything I did, never satisfied with anything less than perfection."

"Sounds tough."

"It was," I said. "But it also taught me the value of hard work and perseverance. And, in a way, it made me who I am today – someone who's not afraid to chase her dreams, even if others said they were impossible." My voice held notes of wistfulness and melancholy.

"You're an incredible woman." Conviction filled his words. "Don't forget that."

"I won't." Emotion swelled in my chest at this man who saw and believed in me. "Thanks."

"Anytime, Cat." He squeezed my hand. "We all have struggles and doubts, even those of us who seem to have it all together."

"Even the great Nathan Logan?" I teased.

He chuckled, the sound intimate in the shadows. "I have fears and flaws like anyone. I've just learned to hide them well."

"Maybe you don't have to hide them with me." The words left my lips before I could restrain them, a tentative offering to this kindred spirit.

"Maybe I don't," he agreed, his voice barely above a whisper.

He tucked a stray strand of hair behind my ear. The gentle touch sent shivers down my spine, but it also made me feel safe and cherished.

I sighed as my eyelids grew heavy and I allowed myself to sink into the warmth of his embrace. It felt so right, so natural to be this close to him, and I wished we could stay like this forever.

CHAPTER FIFTEEN

NATHAN

The next morning, my eyes opened to the sun filtering through sheer curtains. For a moment, I forgot where I was, caught in that hazy space between dreams and waking. Then I felt the warmth of Cat's naked body curled against mine, head nestled into the space between my shoulder and chest, and it all came rushing back.

Shaun's wedding, the roar of laughter and fiddles during the Ceilidh dances, spinning Cat across the floor of the grand ballroom until we were both breathless.

We'd only meant to spend one dance together, yet I couldn't let her out of my arms or my sight all evening. Her smile lit up the room brighter than the glittering chandeliers overhead. She charmed my friends effortlessly, like she'd always known them.

Then she'd surprised me in bed.

A grin tugged at my lips as I smoothed soft circles on her sleeping back.

When I'd left for Edinburgh, never in my wildest dreams

had I thought I'd get to taste Cat again. Never thought she'd be the one to come on to me.

And now here she was, curled against me.

I shifted slightly, careful not to disturb her as I took in the details of her delicate features. Strands of her golden-brown hair splayed across the pillow, framing her face like a halo. Her lips curved into the faintest of smiles, and I wondered what dreams put that cat-got-the-cream look on her face.

I reached out to brush an errant lock of hair behind her ear and she stirred. Her mesmerising green eyes blinked open while a sleepy smile curled her lips.

"Good morning," she mumbled as she shuffled away from me.

A jolt of heat shot through me at her smile.

She could bring me to my knees with a look, make me forget my own name with one kiss. If only she'd use that power more often. The fun we could have.

I'd been with countless women before, but none had ever made me feel this way, none had ever made me so much as think 'relationship.'

Since becoming a household name in the US, I'd steered clear of committed relationships. Especially after a perfectly normal woman snapped nudes pictures of me.

Cat believed this thing between us would burn out, but I knew better. As stubborn as she could be, I was worse. Our first night together had surprised me, shocked me out of my apathetic existence and I'd mourned the thought of never seeing her again.

In one night, she'd convinced me that there were still genuine people in the world. I left her apartment believing I could be myself with a woman.

Hollywood had a way of blinding you, convincing you that the universe revolved around who you knew, who you were fucking, and who you were screwing over.

Cat was a breath of fresh air.

Who knows what I would have done if I hadn't walked into her office on Monday morning?

She was a craving under my skin, in my every thought.

And after last night, I had no intention of giving her up.

"Did you sleep well?" I asked, trying to keep my tone light despite the storm of emotions churning inside me. "Considering I kept you up for most of the night?"

Her smile widened, and she stretched like a cat under the covers, her body pressing against mine. "It seems sharing a bed with you has its perks."

"Is that so?" I resisted the urge to pull her back against my chest and wrap my arms around her.

"Definitely." Her gaze locked onto mine and, for a moment, our unspoken feelings hung heavy in the air between us, creating an electric charge that threatened to ignite at any second.

"Care to elaborate on those perks?" I asked, needing to break the spell before I got lost in her eyes and kissed her.

Laughable really, considering how hard I'd pushed her up to now. Why exercise restraint anymore?

Because she had a choice before. She wasn't stuck sharing a room with me.

Her laughter filled the room, light and melodic, chasing away the shadows of uncertainty. "Well, for one, you're really warm. And two, I think your presence helped soothe my worries a little."

I chuckled, relieved that she wasn't regretting last night.

"And three?"

She pursued her lips, considering. "I can't think of a third." If not for the laughter shining in her eyes, I'd be hurt.

"So, I'm a human heater and a calming force. Good to know."

"You really know how to make a girl relax." Her fingers danced up my chest as she grinned. "I think I might need a little more…"

Before I could ask for clarification, Cat leaned forward and kissed me. It was hot and sensual, a kiss that could make me forget myself in an instant. I felt like I was melting into her, my body responding to the heat of her lips and tongue.

I wanted nothing more than to be consumed by this feeling but the morning was already getting away from me. Breaking the kiss, I leaned back, smoothing my fingers over her cheek and into her messy hair.

The hair I'd spent half the night gripping…

For a second, I let memories of last night override logic. I forgot I had somewhere to be and almost reached for her again.

"As much as I'd love to spend the entire day in bed with you…"

"Oh?" She shifted against me, her bare pussy dragging against my thigh.

I groaned. "I promised the guys I'd meet them for breakfast."

Cat stilled, her cheeks turning a delicious shade of red.

"Why don't you come to breakfast?"

Cat hesitated, eyebrows drawing together. "I don't want to intrude on your time with friends."

"You could never intrude." The words were out before I could stop them. I reached for her hand, threading our fingers and hoping she couldn't feel them trembling.

"But I'm not even meant to be here." She chewed her lip. "You should just ignore me and do what you would have without me crashing your trip."

"Cat, Cat, Cat," I tutted, locking my gaze onto hers, "I could never overlook you or forget about you. It's impossible." The words felt heavy and full of emotion, and I meant every one of them. I wanted her to know that she was important to me, even as I struggled to keep my growing feelings under wraps.

"Okay," she agreed. "Breakfast it is, then."

"Mona and Abi will be happy to see you again too. You could finish grilling them about me."

Cat chuckled. "Who said we didn't cover it all last night?"

"Knowing the pair of them, they have a million more questions." I grinned as I forced myself out of bed. It took serious willpower to not turn back around and bury myself in her. "I'll just take a quick shower, and we can leave in an hour."

CATRINA

I slipped into the ensuite bathroom, steam rising around me like a co-conspirator.

Through the fogged glass of the shower door, I could just make out Nathan's silhouette, water sluicing down the lean muscles of his back.

I undid the tie of my silk robe, letting it fall off my shoulders.

What was I still doing here? Once I knew they had the picture handled, I should have stayed at the airport, gotten the first flight back to LA this morning.

A sensible woman, one thinking straight and using all the intelligence that earned her a law degree, would have put much needed distance between herself and Nathan Logan as soon as possible.

Instead, I was going all in, throwing all reason aside for a man who threatened everything I'd worked for. A man I couldn't get out of my head. A man who'd made me orgasm five times last night.

The shower door creaked open. Nathan's silhouette emerged through the steam, all tanned muscle and sinew. My mouth went dry.

He froze when he saw me, water trickling down his chest. Then a slow, wicked grin spread across his face.

His gaze raked over me, intense and predatory, fixating on the exposed skin revealed by my pooling robe.

"Enjoying the view?" I teased, feeling a blush creep up my neck.

"I'd be lying if I said no." He made no attempt to hide his appreciation or cover himself.

Water pooled at his feet, cascading down his body in rivulets. The urge to chase each one with my tongue took me by surprise.

Nathan was fit — there was no denying that. His body showed the effects of countless hours in the gym, with strong defined pecs, a washboard stomach, and abs so tight they could cut glass.

The room felt charged with electricity as I let my gaze wander further south, where his hard cock was standing at attention, throbbing in anticipation. I licked my lips in anticipation.

Nathan's smirk deepened as he stepped closer, the heat from his body warming me even further. "It's not every day I get to see such a beautiful sight."

"Flattery will get you everywhere, Mr Logan," I said playfully.

"Is that so?" He took a step closer, his heated eyes clashing with mine. "I hope you have a good explanation ready for Shaun to explain why we're late." His thighs forced my legs wider as he stopped in front of me. He lowered his head, until his lips hovered inches from mine. "Well?"

My body took over, swaying towards him.

"So what's it going to be?" He grazed my lips with the lightest of kisses. "Are we going to breakfast or am I fucking you on the bathroom counter?"

"I like the sound of the second option."

"You're sure?" He traced circles on my thigh, pushing the robe higher and higher. His touch left a trail of fire in its wake.

"Yes, but first I have a proposition for you." Heat flooded my cheeks, but I held his gaze.

"What kind of proposition?"

"The kind where we don't leave the room for a week." I moistened my lips, watching his eyes darken.

Nathan's eyebrow inched up, a smile tugging at his lips.

"I could get on board with that." His fingers danced higher, skimming my bare hips, and I shivered.

I licked my lips, knees parting of their own accord as he moved closer. "So you're on board? We'll get it out of our systems, take the heat off. So when we go back to LA, we have enough patience to wait out the studio sale." I leaned in, mouth hovering just shy of his.

"I'd never say no to you, Cat." Nathan closed the last breath of distance between us. "But let's get one thing straight, there'll be no getting it out of our systems. You're it for me." He stared into my eyes, his focus unwavering and his determination shining through in his blue eyes.

"After breakfast..." I traced my fingers across his pecs, circling his nipples. He bit his lip, holding in a groan but he crowded closer. "We could come back here, order room service..." My touch dipped, my nails scraping against his taut stomach and running down his body to the trail of hair guiding me to his rock-solid cock. "And not leave the bed until we're satisfied."

Nathan's eyes gleamed. "I like the sound of that."

He crushed his mouth to mine, kissing me with a hunger that stole my breath. His arms wrapped around me, while he tugged me closer to the edge.

My body responded instantly, pressing against his as if we were two perfectly matched puzzle pieces finally clicking into place.

I melted into him, my hands roaming over his slick, heated

skin. He groaned, the sound vibrating against my lips, and deepened the kiss, his tongue expertly teasing mine.

My legs wrapped around his waist, pulling him tight against me. His hands slid under my robe, rough and calloused and pure sin.

"So we'll stay for a few days," he murmured against my lips, nipping at the sensitive skin. "Explore Edinburgh properly... explore each other."

A moan escaped me as his mouth trailed lower, teasing the pulse point at my throat. "Yes — anything. Just don't stop."

Nathan chuckled, a low rumble that did wicked things to my insides. "So commanding, counsellor. How can I refuse?"

He lifted me effortlessly from the counter and carried me into the adjoining room.

"Beautiful, perfect, Catrina," he sighed against my mouth, clearly struggling with the same whirlwind of emotions that had taken hold of me. "Every time I look at you, I feel like I'm losing control."

"Me too," I admitted, my voice barely audible as I ran my fingers through his damp hair, feeling the heat radiating off his skin.

"Right now, all I care about is you." He pulled back, his eyes locked onto mine with a fierce intensity that made my heart skip a beat. "Just for this moment, let's forget about everything else."

He lay me down on the unmade bed and I shrugged my robe from my shoulders. His eyes devoured every inch of newly bared skin. I should have felt exposed under such scrutiny, yet I only craved more — to be consumed by this man who knew me too well, who tempted me beyond reason.

Weaving my hands through his tousled locks, I pulled him closer, our mouths meeting in a feverish dance. He followed me down to the bed and a hiss escaped me at the feel of his naked body covering mine again. No barriers left between us.

We were a tangle of limbs grasping and pulling each other

nearer, two people who had fought this for far too long and were now drowning in it.

There was a raw, undeniable power in the way Nathan kissed me – a desperate longing that made me feel as if I were his lifeline, and he was mine.

CHAPTER SIXTEEN

CATRINA

*N*athan and I walked into the cafe, the smell of coffee and pastries greeting us. His friends — Shaun, Finn, Jackson, Mona, Isla, Abi and Ros — were already there, taking up a large table near the window, their plates filled with delicious treats.

They looked up as the bell rang above the door. Grins spread across their faces, clearly amused at our tardiness.

"About time!" Shaun said, his Welsh accent thick. "Thought you'd gotten lost."

"Or distracted." Finn winked.

"We were just…" my cheeks flushed, "taking in the sights." My gaze met Nathan's, and I could see a hint of amusement dancing in his eyes.

He smiled. "Edinburgh is beautiful. But the company's even better."

I chuckled. Smooth as ever.

"Aw, Nathan, you're such a charmer," Abi chimed in, her

New York drawl dripping with sarcasm. Her wavy red hair was piled on top of her head. "But really, we're just glad you're here. It wouldn't be the same without you two."

"Yes, we were hoping for an update," Mona said, her bubbly Scottish personality radiating warmth. Mona sat next to Shaun, her manicured hand resting on his arm and her nails painted a bubble gum pink to match her bobbed hair.

Ros grinned, her punk rock aesthetic making her Mona and Abi's complete opposite with her pixie cut raven black hair. She leaned forward with a conspiratorial glint in her eye. "Anything you'd like to share with the group?"

Abi swatted her. "Ros!"

Mona's eyes widened and she pressed her lips together, delight lighting up her expression.

"Nothing to tell," I said, trying to keep my voice steady. "We're just… friends."

Mona and Ros rolled their eyes.

"Uh-huh," Jackson muttered under his breath, smirking into his coffee. "Just friends," he drawled, his thick Scottish accent doing nothing to hide his amusement.

Nathan and I exchanged nervous glances as we took our seats at the table, trying our best to appear casual. It was one thing for us to know we'd given in, adding others to the mix could make it… messy.

The warm scent of freshly baked pastries filled the air while laughter and conversation buzzed around us. Beneath the surface, however, a current of electric attraction pulsed between Nathan and me.

Nathan's fingers grazed my thigh beneath the table, sending a thrill up my spine and making my sore core clench with need. He caught my eye, a knowing glint in the blue depths that told me he wanted to do much worse.

"Running late today?" Finn asked. He grinned. "Not judging— Abi and I understand quickies."

Abi blushed. "Finn!"

"Apologies, love," Finn chuckled, casting a wink in her direction. "But seriously, it's more than worth it, am I right?"

My face burned and I glanced down at the menu in front of me, trying to hide my blush.

Nathan's hand caught mine beneath the table, weaving our fingers together in my lap. He squeezed it, silently questioning if I were okay. Barely suppressing my smile, I tipped my chin, trying to be inconspicuous. A wasted effort with seven pairs of eyes scrutinising your every movement.

Our connection had intensified in a way we couldn't deny, no matter how casually we acted. I mean, really, we'd have to be dreaming to think Nathan's closest friends wouldn't be able to see the changes in him: the way he sat so close his shoulder brushed mine or the way his torso kept twisting towards me.

"Actually, we went for a walk up to the Mile," Nathan said. "It's hard not to get caught up in the magic of this city."

"Sure, sure," Finn teased, clearly unconvinced. "Admiring the architecture, eh? Well, whatever gets your blood pumping in the morning."

"Enough, Finn." Abi placed a hand on his arm. She shot him a wide-eyed look, though that didn't stop her lips from twitching as she fought a smile. "Let them enjoy their breakfast in peace."

"If you say so." Finn pouted but raised his hands in mock surrender. "Let's eat."

"Come on, you two." Ros leaned forward, placing her elbows on the table and propping her head up on her hands. "No need to hide it. We're all friends!"

"There's nothing—"

"Pity." Ros sighed. "I'd love to be able to wear that post-orgasm glow as naturally as you two seem to."

Nathan choked on his coffee, stifling a laugh.

"Okay, how about we give them a break?" Abi glanced at Ros, her brows raised. "What was your favourite Edinburgh experience, Ros?"

"I love this city," Ros said, her eyes sparkling with excitement. "The other day, I stumbled across this hidden gem of a bookstore tucked away in an alley. You know how much I adore old books, and this place was so cute."

As Ros described her discoveries we relaxed. Enjoying our meal, the secret between us forgotten for now.

But Nathan's grip on my hand didn't loosen up. In fact, the teasing man pushed our joined hands lower, forcing my legs wider until he could rest his fingers against my mound. At some point, I must have stopped breathing because how I held in my surprise, I had no clue.

He grazed his finger up and down the seam of my jeans, teasing me but also torturing me because I could barely feel it.

"Did you try the scones at that little bakery near the hotel?" Abi asked, getting caught up in Ros' enthusiasm. "They are absolutely incredible — I swear they must use some sort of magic in their recipe."

A second finger joined the first, pressing firmer and focusing instead on the denim at either side of the seam. Delicious sparks of pleasure shot through me. I bit my check, stifling a groan as I struggled to keep up with the conversation.

"No, but adding to my list!" Ros said. "Always up for good sweets."

Listening to them, I glanced at Nathan, engaged in conversation, laughing easily. The picture of perfect attention. None of them had any clue what his hand was doing to me.

But even as my mind grew foggy with pleasure, for a moment, in a little bistro in a foreign city where no one knew us, I could pretend that the deal had been signed and he was all mine.

I leaned into him. Nathan glanced down at me, a sweet smile curling his lips while his blue eyes burned with a need that made my chest ache.

I need this.

NATHAN

While the rest of us ate, Jackson only had eyes for Ros. She just kept talking, oblivious to the poor sod hanging on her every word. None of them had noticed Cat, slowly relaxing into my side, her eyelids growing heavy at my teasing, so I guess it was plausible that she'd just missed all of his hints.

Ros chattered on, describing a quirky vintage shop she's stumbled across and I swear he almost offered to buy her the shop. He'd pulled his phone out to note it down at least.

Jackson never put so much effort into picking a woman up. He also would never agree to do things he hated.

Whenever I teased him, Jackson insisted they were "just friends." Before I could take the piss out of his odd behaviour, Shaun clinked a knife against his water glass, reducing us all to silence.

"We've decided to leave for our honeymoon right away," Shaun said, grinning from ear to ear.

Finn's fork halted mid-air. "Today?"

"Yes!" Mona flushed, thrilled. "We've waited so long. Why wait any longer?"

I shook my head at the lovebirds. "No patience, you two."

Shaun laughed and pulled Mona close. "We've got the jet on standby."

Joy radiated from them. It was contagious. Our table erupted into congratulations and well-wishes. Even amidst the chaos of our lives, it was heartening to see two people so in love and excited for their future together.

"Don't worry, there's plenty of time for it to pick you up at the end of the week," Shaun said, his tone reassuring. As if it would have crossed any of our minds to quibble over something like that.

"Where are you guys headed?" Abi asked, her eyes sparkling with curiosity.

"Thailand." Mona smiled. "Bangkok, then an island resort."

"Sounds absolutely heavenly," Isla, Mona's sister, said with genuine warmth. "You deserve it."

"Thank you, Iz." Mona's eyes shone with emotion.

Shaun caught Mona's gaze, lifting her hand to brush his lips against her knuckles. "However long the honeymoon lasts, it won't be long enough."

Watching them, joy radiated through me. The future was messy and unclear, but somehow, against all odds, they'd stumbled into forever.

"Leave it to you two to make the rest of us swoon." Ros' smile held a touch of wistfulness.

Shaun's grin only broadened at our teasing. "What can I say? I'm a lucky man." He kissed Mona's temple, drawing her close.

A familiar ache rose within me, longing for the connection they shared. Could Cat ever love me like Mona did Shaun?

The thought rushed in, impossible to escape. However complicated we were, the pull was undeniable.

For now I forced my gaze away, joining the cheers. "To the happy couple!"

Glasses clinked as I pushed aside fears of a future without Cat at my side.

Mona met my eyes with a knowing look. "Someday, Nathan."

I shook my head, raising my glass once more. "To love without bloody limits!"

Ros snorted. "Since when did you become such a romantic?"

"Must be these two." I gestured at Shaun and Mona, wrapped up in each other. "They're a bad influence."

My friends laughed, their brows climbing in a way that called bullshit. Shaun tore his attention from his bride just long enough to meet my eye. His smile softened in understanding.

I turned to Jackson. "Do you still have that cottage in St. Andrews?"

Jackson's brows shot up. "I do... Why do you ask?" A knowing grin spread across his face when I didn't immediately answer. "Oh, I see. You two are looking for some alone time away from prying eyes?"

Cat ducked her head, cheeks flaming.

Jackson chuckled. "Of course, you can use the cottage. I'll give you the keys and the alarm code."

"Thanks, mate." I clapped him on the back gratefully. "I owe you one."

"You can thank me by naming a lot after me," Jackson teased.

I laughed, ignoring the curious looks from our other friends. Jackson immediately started typing on his phone. Mine pinged as he put his away.

"You've got the code for the alarm and the lockbox with the keys." He smirked. "Try not to break anything."

I shook my head at him, but chose not to indulge him. Instead, I glanced at Cat, tilting my head towards the door.

"Thanks for understanding." I stood and Cat followed. "We're going to check out the Christmas Market before it gets too crowded."

Cat nodded and gathered her things. "It was lovely to meet you all again."

Finn grinned. "Sweet of you to think you've escaped us."

Before she could reply, I steered her out of the bistro, waving to the catcalls and whistles behind us.

"Subtle, aren't they?" Cat laughed.

"About as subtle as a sledgehammer." I smiled, leading her into the cool Edinburgh air.

Alone with Cat at last, the teasing faded. Her hand found mine; I laced our fingers and brought them to my lips.

"This alright?" I searched her eyes.

Cat smiled, leaning into me. "More than."

The future was messy, unclear— but with Cat by my side, exploring the cobblestone streets of Edinburgh, I had all I needed. My friends could speculate and tease, but what lay between us was ours alone. And for now, that was enough.

CHAPTER SEVENTEEN

CATRINA

*N*athan steered the car down a winding gravel drive, massive pine trees hugging us close on either side. I breathed a sigh of relief at the seclusion they provided.

A sprawling two-storey house came into view as we surfaced from the tree line, glowing in the fading sunset. The light bounced through its countless windows.

The rhythmic crashing of waves reached me through the closed car windows, soothing me even from a distance. A perfect place to spend a week undisturbed.

"It's stunning," I muttered as we parked.

"Wait until you see the inside." Nathan grinned. "Jackson's always had a knack for finding hidden gems. He found my house after all."

"You're joking."

Nathan nodded before throwing open his door. I turned my attention back to the beast of a house pretending to be a cottage. For a second, I stared at it.

Three days ago, I'd been holed up in my cramped LA

apartment that was in desperate need of an upgrade and now I got to spend a week in that? "Pinch me, I must be dreaming."

Then my car door opened and I blinked against the sunlight shining behind Nathan's silhouette, blond hair glowing like a halo, holding out his hand with an easy grin. "Welcome to our retreat, Miss Sinclair."

I smiled at his exaggerated gallantry. "You call this a cottage?"

"Take it up with Jackson." He chuckled.

Nathan grabbed our bags and led me up the steps to the front door. At the front door, he fished a key from the lockbox and swung it open with a flourish.

"After you."

The interior was cosy yet spacious, filled with comfortable leather furniture, a massive stone fireplace, and windows overlooking the sea.

"Wow."

"Jackson doesn't do anything halfway." He set our bags down at the bottom of the stairs. "I'll give you the grand tour."

He led me through the massive living area with two groupings of sofas. I immediately noted the bookshelves surrounding one couch and the open fireplace set before the second. I'll be the first to admit that I judged Jackson wrong. The man's appearance screamed laid back surfer, happy to let the world revolve around him. But this? There had to be secret layers to him.

"If this is roughing it, sign me up," I muttered, wandering into the kitchen.

The kitchen was state of the art, with granite countertops and stainless steel appliances that gleamed under the recessed lighting.

"Very fancy. Jackson didn't skimp on a thing, did he?"

I might have caressed the handle to the double dishwasher

a little too long, but who could blame me? I didn't even have an old ratchety one, but Jackson put it in a house he barely used. Celebrities: more money than sense.

All the same, surrounded by top-of-the-line appliances, with a beautiful view out of every single window, I could see myself actually learning to cook decent food in a space like this.

Nathan wrapped his arms around my waist from behind, pulling me back against his chest. His body radiated warmth, enveloping me completely. I sighed, relaxing into his embrace, loving that for the first time I could enjoy his touch without having to worry about anyone seeing us.

"I'm glad you like it here. Because you're stuck with me for a week."

I leaned back into his embrace. "However will I survive?"

"I have ideas." His stubble grazed my neck, as he nibbled at my pulse point, eliciting a squeal.

For months I had agonised over every stolen moment, worried constantly about ethics and lines being crossed. But here, secluded in our own private world, I was free simply to be with Nathan. No more professional codes of conduct keeping us apart or demanding I resist his affections. Just us, unrestrained, finally giving in to what we both so desperately wanted.

His playful nip sent warmth pooling low in my belly, a smile curving my lips. This was the man I'd come to know in our brief time together — playful, passionate, tender. The side of him hidden from colleagues and work responsibilities, reserved only for me when we were alone.

I turned in his arms, looping my own around his neck. His eyes shone bright with laughter and promise of mischief, sending my heart racing. "A whole week alone… however will I handle you?" I arched an eyebrow, hinting at the futile battle I'd waged to maintain professionalism.

Nathan's grin widened, crinkling the corners of his eyes. "I have a few ideas." He nuzzled into my hair, breath warm against my ear. "But I suppose that depends on whether my girl really is ready to stop fighting…"

His girl. The phrase filled me with warmth, assurance that this was as real for him as for me. I clung to his words, to the heat and strength of his body pressed so close — tangible reminders this man I had been forbidden to have was here, was mine. For one week we could be simply Cat and Nathan, leaving behind rules and restrictions in favour of what felt right.

When his hands wandered, moving down my back to cup my ass. He tugged me tight against him and a spark of need shot through me at the feel of him hardening against me.

I stopped his downward descent, lifting his grip back to my waist, laughing. "Down boy. You promised me a tour first."

Nathan sighed. "Cruel woman, revving a man up like that." Then he slapped my ass before quickly dancing away, grinning like a boy caught doing something he shouldn't. The reverb travelled straight to my clit, forcing me to bite my lip against a moan.

He held his hand out to me and I took it, letting him lead me from the kitchen.

The ground floor had a den, bathroom, and conservatory opening onto the deck. The sound of the nearby waves hitting the beach reached me, though the dunes obscured the view.

Hard not to fall for such beauty.

After so much stress and worry, the peace of this place felt like a much-needed reprieve.

On the deck, he wrapped his arms around me again, lips at my ear. "See anything you like?"

"Hmm." I covered his arms, tightening his hold. "A few things are catching my eye."

With Nathan's hands at my waist, his chest warm against my back, contentment flooded through me. The ups and downs of the past months fell away, leaving behind only this quiet joy at simply being with him, no more stolen moments or longing looks across a room. Here we had the luxury of time, to talk and laugh without reservation.

Nathan groaned into my neck. "You're killing me. Any more of your teasing and we won't make it to dinner." He kissed my cheek and released me, giving me a playful swat. "Go on, explore upstairs while I scrounge up some dinner. I need a cold shower before I ravish you on the countertop."

I laughed at his exaggerated expression but didn't immediately follow his suggestion.

"You sure?" I followed him back inside. "I could help."

Nathan smirked, steering me from the kitchen. "Not happening. I owe you after today."

I hesitated for all of a second before racing up the stairs. They led me to a wide hallway with rooms on either side. I bypassed them all, heading for a set of double doors at the end.

My jaw dropped. This wasn't a bedroom —it was a work of art. And the view from the balcony left me speechless.

I could have stayed out on the balcony for hours, but eventually, the rumbling of my stomach couldn't be ignored. I made my way back downstairs, following the sounds and scents wafting from the kitchen.

Nathan looked up from the stove as I entered, flashing me a grin. "There you are. I was about to send out a search party."

"Something smells amazing." I peered over his shoulder at the pans sizzling on the cooktop. "What are you making?"

"Linguine with lemon and asparagus. I found the ingredients in the fridge and pantry."

My mouth watered. "Can I help with anything?"

Nathan snorted. "Not unless you want to be responsible for burning down Jackson's house on the first night." He shooed me away from the stove. "You can keep me company from over there while I work my magic."

"If you insist, chef." I perched on one of the stools lining the kitchen island and reached for the open bottle of white wine to fill up our glasses.

We chatted and laughed as Nathan cooked, the tensions from the previous afternoon fading away. Being here like this, engaged in such a simple domestic moment, felt so natural. I never wanted it to end.

"Why does Jackson need such an enormous beach house when he barely spends any time in the UK?" I asked, sipping my wine.

Nathan chuckled. "You've met the man. Subtle and understated aren't in his vocabulary." He tossed the asparagus in olive oil and lemon juice before adding it to the pan. "But in all seriousness, I think he finds the place soothing. When the pressures of fame get too much, he escapes here. And he likes to rent it out to friends the rest of the time."

"Lucky us then." I gazed out at the sea and the dunes. "I can see why he finds it soothing. It's so peaceful."

"That it is." Nathan flashed me a smile over his shoulder. "Though with you around, peace is the last thing on my mind." Nathan drained the linguine and plated up two bowls with a flourish. "There. My masterpiece is complete."

He placed one of the steaming bowls in front of me. I breathed in the scents of lemon and herbs and my mouth watered.

"This looks and smells incredible." I picked up my fork, twisting linguine around it. "Aren't you going to join me?"

"Patience." Nathan grabbed his own bowl and took the stool beside me.

We ate in contented silence for a few minutes, both enjoying our meal too much for conversation. I couldn't remember the last time I'd eaten something so delicious.

"You've been holding out on me." I pointed at him with my fork. "I didn't know you could cook like this."

"There's a lot you still don't know about me, Icy." Nathan

bit his lip. "And I look forward to exploring all of them with you this week."

A slow smile crept across my face. This week would reveal what months of professionalism had kept locked away. After denying ourselves for so long, being with Nathan felt like gulping fresh air. I expected more than a few skipped dinners in favour of activities requiring far less… conversation.

Still, part of me looked forward to the simple things — lazy mornings without meetings on the schedule, bad jokes from hours of pointless conversation, enjoying the pleasure of sitting together with nowhere else to be. Our relationship had never left much room for ordinary coupley things. But this week at least, that would change.

"That was amazing," I said eventually, pushing my empty bowl away with a happy sigh.

"Glad you enjoyed it." Nathan's gaze turned heated as he bumped his shoulder against mine. "Now, since I fed you, I think you owe me dessert."

My pulse leapt. "Is that so?"

Nathan rose from his stool and came to stand before me, grasping my hands to pull me up against him.

"Yes, and lucky for you, I have something sweet in mind."

His lips claimed mine, slow and sensual. I melted into his embrace, ready to savour his attention.

When he broke the kiss, he cradled my face, our foreheads touching as we caught our breath. I smiled, overcome with affection for this infuriating, charming man.

Nathan pressed another swift kiss to my lips before releasing me. "I've been thinking about doing that for hours."

"I'm glad you finally did," I whispered.

"Sorry to have kept you waiting." His eyes lit with mischief. "Fancy a moonlit stroll along the beach?"

I hesitated, not keen to venture outside even in the seclusion of darkness, especially not when all I wanted to do was tear his clothes off. But the way Nathan's eyes lit up at the suggestion melted my resolve.

"Okay, if you promise we won't encounter any fans."

Nathan laughed. "The beach stretches for miles, Icy, and this cottage is in a private cove. I think we're safe."

He laced his fingers through mine and led me outside, down the steps of the back deck and through a gap in the shrubs. Within seconds, we were stepping onto the sand. The night sky was clear, stars twinkling brightly overhead, and a crescent moon cast a silver glow across the rippling sea.

The deserted beach stretched for miles in each direction, making me feel for just a moment like we were the only two people in the world. I'd never felt so free.

NATHAN

Cat's laughter rang out, sweet and melodic, as we strolled along the beach. I gazed down at her, struck by how the moonlight lit her smile. Utterly captivating.

"You're impossible," she said, shaking her head after I'd teased her about her competitive streak.

"And yet you put up with me." I flashed a grin, giving her hand a squeeze where it was nestled in my grip.

I could barely believe my luck. After months scheming to get Cat all to myself, here she was — walking the beach with me, not an objection left between us. Free at last to show her just how hard she made me fall, body and soul.

Gone were the excuses she clung to. In their place, a playful warmth I'd only dreamed of experiencing. Being together felt too good to be real. A whole week of her company, no rules to drive a wedge between us — just time to enjoy each other's company.

"Someone has to keep that ego of yours in check, Playboy."

I sniggered. "Still with the playboy?"

"It suits you." Cat's eyes sparkled with mischief. "You're Hollywood's precious playboy, are you not?"

"Only because the producers want me to be. You should know the film industry spins illusions, Icy." I lifted her hand to my lips, pressing a kiss to her knuckles. Despite her jokes, she saw far more than the image the industry built for me. She always had. "With you, I can just be Nathan."

Cat sighed, gazing up at the stars. "If only it were that simple."

I followed her gaze, wishing I could pluck a star from the sky to make her smile again.

"We have this week, at least." When Cat's eyes met mine once more, I gave her my most roguish grin. "And I intend to make the most of every moment with you."

She laughed, the tension melting from her expression. "Will you never change?"

"Not where you're concerned." I wrapped an arm around Cat's waist, pulling her close as we walked. "Admit it, you'd be disappointed if I did."

"I'd miss these verbal sparring matches of ours." Cat's lips quirked upward, a teasing glint in her eyes. "But I suppose your over-inflated ego needs deflating on occasion."

"By all means, have at it." I chuckled, leaning down to whisper in her ear. "Though I can suggest far more pleasurable ways for you to torment me tonight."

Cat's breath caught, a shiver running through her. "Promises, promises. You're all talk, movie star."

I grinned at the challenge in her voice, already plotting ways to make her eat those words. My girl was in for a long night of sweet torment if I had my way. And by the time I was finished with her, there'd be no doubt left in her mind as to whether I was all talk or not.

I flashed Cat a wicked grin, leaning in close to whisper in her ear once more. "Careful, Icy, or I may just have to sweep you off your feet like some cliché prince charming."

Cat snorted. "As if you could." But her eyes gleamed with a teasing light.

I chuckled. "Is that a challenge?" I swept a bow, clutching my hands dramatically over my heart. "Your wish is my command, my lady."

Cat smirked. "Maybe in the movies. But this is real life, movie star. It'll take more than charm and pretty words to win me over like one of your adoring fans."

I grasped her hand, bringing it to my lips for a kiss. "Good thing I don't intend to treat you like a silver screen damsel." I smiled. "Say the word, I'll show you just what swooning over me really looks like."

She sucked in a breath, pulse racing under my fingertips. I had her now, caught between desire and stubbornness. I loved her indecision.

She shook her head, torn between exasperation and longing. "You flirt."

I laughed, wrapping my arms around her waist and pulling her close once more. "So I've been told. But you wouldn't have me any other way, admit it."

Cat sighed, a reluctant smile curving her lips as she gazed up at me with a gleam of mischief. "You know, I was looking forward to sweeping you off your feet for a change."

I quirked a brow, intrigued. "And just how did you intend to do that?"

She'd already swept me off my feet, that first night in the bar.

"Oh, I have my ways." She smirked.

Before I could react, she stuck out her foot, catching my ankle.

I cursed as I tumbled gracelessly onto the sand. Unfortunately for Cat, her arm was locked in mine. A giggling shriek escaped her as she followed me down, landing on my chest with an 'oof.'.

For a moment we stared at each other, breaths mingling, her body pressed deliciously against mine.

Then I threw back my head and laughed.

She hit my chest, fighting back her own smile. "What's so funny?"

"You." I grinned up at her, brushing an errant strand of hair off her cheek. "Always full of surprises."

Cat snorted. "You deserved that, you arrogant charmer." But her lips quirked upward, and she made no move to stand.

"Maybe I did." I threaded my fingers through her silken hair, gazing up into her eyes. "Though if this is how you plan on punishing me, I might need to tease you more often."

Her breath caught, her bravado faltering under the intensity of my stare. "You're terrible," she muttered, amusement warming her voice.

"So I've been told." I smirked, pulling her down until her lips hovered just above my own. "But you love me for it, admit it."

As much as I joked, I wanted nothing more than to hear her say the words. After months of flirting and fighting, tearing down her walls piece by piece, I was ready to throw all caution to the wind just to know if she felt the same. Cat had gotten under my skin from the moment we met, infuriating and intoxicating in equal measure.

When she sighed, her breath mingling with my own, I couldn't resist. I captured her lips in a searing kiss, swallowing her half-hearted protests.

She melted into the kiss for a breathless moment before pulling back with a gasp. "Someone might come!"

I grinned up at her, brushing my thumb over her kiss-swollen bottom lip. "It's a private beach, Icy. No one for miles."

To prove my point, I threaded my fingers through her hair and guided her lips back to mine once more.

Cat sighed into the kiss, her protests fading as I explored her mouth at a deliciously unhurried pace. I lost myself in her taste, the feel of her in my arms, wishing I could capture this moment and make it last forever.

I groaned as she ground her pussy against my stiffening cock. My hands tightened on her hips, pressing her harder, rocking her faster.

Her eyes flew open. A gasp replaced her moan. "Oh god," she muttered, cheeks reddening with embarrassment. "I'm so sorry."

She tried to stand, but I tightened my grip on her hips, urging her to stay. *Fuck, did I need her.*

"Don't apologise," I murmured against her lips. "Keep going."

Cat hesitated, her gaze filled with uncertainty as she glanced around again at the deserted private beach. I smiled reassuringly and pulled her face back down to me so I could distract her with teasing kisses.

After a few hesitant moments, she leaned into me with a sigh of surrender. Her fingers tangled in my hair as our kiss deepened, heat radiating off our bodies like a furnace.

She melted against me, sighing, her fingers threading through my hair. I kissed her as if my life depended on it, unwilling to waste a single second we had together. I wanted to brand myself onto her skin, her soul, make it so she could never forget these moments we'd shared beneath a sea of stars with the crash of waves our only soundtrack.

I explored her mouth hungrily, feeling every inch of her body pressed against mine. The freezing cold air bit at our exposed skin making me glad for our coats even if I desperately wished we were naked.

CHAPTER EIGHTEEN

CATRINA

My coat went flying across the kitchen and Nathan immediately reached for my t-shirt. He dragged it up and over my head, exposing my bra before I could register the heat of the kitchen.

"Remind me to fuck you *before* we go on any more beach strolls," he said before capturing my lips in a searing kiss.

The kiss went on for what felt like an eternity, the heat between us consuming me completely. He tasted of salt and sweetness and I wanted more. We clung to each other, hands wandering, tearing clothing off each other in a mad rush. His t-shirt joined my coat, decorating the plant in the corner, while his sweatpants hit the floor.

"Hmm, I can get on board with that rule," I mumbled against his cheek.

I squeaked as Nathan lifted me, resting my bare ass on the cold marble of the kitchen island. My legs instinctively wrapped around his waist as he kissed down my neck and collarbone. Sparks skittered across my skin everywhere his lips touched, making me gasp with pleasure as he explored further down my body.

His hands cupped my breasts as he teased them before trailing lower to unbutton my jeans with skilled fingers. I squirmed beneath him, wanting more and unable to contain the desire coursing through me.

The jeans finally slipped off my body onto the floor, and Nathan stepped back to look at me. I felt my cheeks flush under his gaze, and I bit my lip as he ran his hands down my thighs and calves. His fingers expertly traced circles around the sensitive skin of my inner thighs, making me shiver.

He smiled at my reaction before his fingers moved higher. I gasped as he dragged a finger through my folds before slipping it inside me. This time, I didn't even try to bite back my moan.

"So ready for me," he murmured, his voice so low it turned me on even more.

He fingered me with slow, gentle strokes, pushing me higher and higher until I was panting. My hips bucked against him in a desperate plea for more, begging him to take me the rest of the way there.

Nathan smiled, his eyes dancing with desire as he watched me move against his hand. His free hand grabbed my hip and held me still as he moved his fingers faster.

"Please," I gasped, my voice barely above a whisper. "Please Nathan, fuck me."

He grinned at me, his eyes twinkling with mischief as his fingers stilled. Instead of giving in to my plea, he withdrew his hand and stepped back, putting nearly two feet between us.

"If you want me so badly then show me," he said, a challenge in his voice.

For a second, I froze, a shyness I'd never felt before sweeping over me. But this was Nathan. I trusted him with my body, and the thought of making him pant for me the way I did for him, did delicious things to me.

I slowly slid off the counter and moved closer to him. My hands trailed over his chest and along his arms as I circled around him.

He groaned as I pulled him close, rising up on my tiptoes to capture his lips in a heated kiss. I ground my stomach against his hardening length. The feeling of him pressed against me drove me wild with desire.

His tongue tangled with mine as our kiss grew hungrier and more passionate. My fingers curled into the waistband of his boxers and I dragged them down his body, freeing him.

Nathan gasped as my hands curled around his shaft, my grip tight and sure. I moved my hand up and down in a slow rhythm, marvelling at how he felt beneath my fingers. His mouth moved to my neck, sucking and biting. His moans of pleasure only served to drive me higher, and my movements grew more frantic.

Then he broke my hold, capturing my hands and placing them around his neck. "Any more of that, and I won't be able to take you on the kitchen island like I want," he murmured against my neck.

His hands snaked around to grip my hips, guiding me backwards until my back hit the edge of the counter. He gently lifted me back onto the cold marble surface and climbed up to join me.

"On your knees."

I did as he said. Thank fuck for stupidly big islands. *Maybe I should send Jackson a thank you card...*

Nathan caught my hips, steadying me before he forced my knees wider.

His breath was hot on my neck as he positioned himself behind me. I shivered in anticipation, biting my lip hard enough to draw blood as his tip teased my entrance.

"Are you ready for me, Catrina?" he asked, his voice low and urgent.

"More than ready."

He thrust forward, filling me inch by slow inch. I gasped, my fingers clawing at the marble surface beneath me as he adjusted to my size. His hips rolled in a mesmerising rhythm that had me panting and moaning within minutes.

Then he stilled.

"No, don't stop." Instead of answering, he pressed his face into my neck and groaned. "Nathan?"

Was he in pain? Did he need to stop? *Please don't stop.*

"I forgot the bloody condom."

Oh. "I'm on the pill."

I held my breath, waiting for his response, desperately wanting to tell him to hurry up and ruin me already, but also concerned it might be a step too far for him.

"And you're okay with going bare?" he asked, his tone carefully devoid of emotion.

"Yes." More than okay.

"Thank fuck," he muttered on a relieved sigh.

He started to move again, his thrusts becoming more frenzied with each passing second. So frenzied that I started to slide across the counter. His grip tightened on my hips, holding me firmly in place as he pounded into me.

The kitchen echoed with our moans and the sound of flesh meeting. One of his hands moved from my hips to my breast, kneading and teasing it until I was panting and begging for more.

"Needy today, aren't we?"

He chuckled in response before pinching a sensitive nub, sending shivers straight to my core. I cried out, arching my back as he increased the pace of his thrusts, pushing him even deeper inside of me. My head spun and my body trembled. I was so close, almost there...

"Nathan," I gasped, my voice hoarse with need. "Don't stop."

He groaned in response, slamming into me again and again. His hand left my breast, tracing a ragged line down my stomach before delving between my legs. I gasped as he started to rub his thumb against my swollen nub at the same time, teasing me yet tightening the coil inside of me so fast I forgot how to hold myself up.

My arms slid out from under me and I collapsed onto my elbows.

"Oh fuck," I muttered as the altered position made Nathan feel five times bigger inside of me yet.

Heat rippled through me in waves as his thumb continued to work its magic between my legs. My breathing was ragged, my body desperate for release.

"Keep doing that." My voice barely coherent.

His reply was a guttural moan as he thrust deeper, faster. His fingers dug into my skin and I cried out with pleasure as he increased the intensity of his movements. I pushed back against him, met each thrust with an eager roll of my own, pushing us closer to the edge with every motion.

"Oh god." My whole body shook with anticipation.

"Come for me," Nathan demanded. "Now, Catrina."

The coil snapped inside of me and I was lost to an orgasm so intense that all my muscles went rigid. I clung to the edge of the counter, unable to move as my core clamped down on Nathan's cock.

He slammed into me one last time.

It felt like a million tiny explosions going off inside me. Every muscle trembled with delight as he slowly pulled out.

I collapsed onto the counter, uncaring of the cold stone beneath me. Through heavy lids, I watched as Nathan joined me, shifting so he could lie on his side next to me.

His hand moved up my back, tracing circles over my skin

and sending shivers through my body even though I was still twitching from the aftershocks of my orgasm.

My breath came out in little sighs and I melted into him completely as sleep began to overtake me. Never thought I'd fall asleep on a kitchen island. *Never thought I'd let someone fuck me senseless on one, either, but here we were.*

Just before I drifted off completely, Nathan spoke softly into my ear.

"I love you."

CHAPTER NINETEEN

NATHAN

"Time to wake up, sleepyhead." I shook Cat's shoulder gently.

Cat lay sprawled out on her front, her hands tucked under the pillow and her face buried in it. Her golden-brown hair lay in a mussed state against her pillow. The duvet had slipped down to her waist, making me itch to smooth my hand along her back and lower.

She grumbled, batting my hand away. "Go away. I'm sleeping."

I chuckled, shaking harder. "Not anymore. We've got places to be, things to see. Up and at 'em!"

She cracked one eye open to glare at me. "Nathan, I swear to god, if you don't leave me alone…" Her empty threat ended in a yawn.

Christ, she was gorgeous. Even yawning and glaring at me.

"You'll what?" I asked, grinning. "You're losing your edge, Cat. Gone soft on me already?"

"One more hour." She turned away, burying her face in the pillow.

Somehow, when I'd imagined what a relaxed morning would be like with Cat, it wasn't sleeping until twelve. After our one-night stand, she'd kicked me out the door at seven on the dot. And that had been a Saturday.

Grinning, I pressed myself against her back and wrapped an arm around her waist, my lips finding the curve of her neck.

"Nathan." She groaned, but pushed back against me, teasing. "It's too early."

"It's 10 AM, and I've got plans for the day."

I squeezed her, desire simmering in my veins at the feel of her body against mine. I wanted nothing more than to stay here all day, exploring each delicious curve and hollow, but I refused to spend a week hidden away like we were ashamed of each other.

Cat peeked open one eye. "Can't we stay in bed?"

"Afraid not, gorgeous. My plans don't involve being horizontal."

I rolled her onto her back. She huffed at first, but her protests quickly died as I kissed her. She responded instantly, her body arching into mine, her hands grazing up my bare back and into my hair. Mine roamed over her soft curves, teasing those secret spots that made her ache for me.

When we finally broke for air, her eyes remained closed. "Okay, you win. We can stay in bed a bit longer."

I chuckled, trailing kisses along her jaw and down her neck. "Nice try, but we really need to get moving." I nipped at the sensitive spot below her ear, enjoying her soft gasp. "Or else we might not leave this bed today."

"I'm good with that," she muttered as she turned away and buried her face in the pillow again.

I slid out of bed and stretched, glancing at the clock.

"Tempting, I'll give you that, but I have things I want to show you, so move."

"We'll go later," she mumbled.

"Last chance…" I let the threat hang.

Cat peeked at me over her shoulder, eyes still heavy with sleep. "Dare try and make me move, Nathan. See how that goes."

I grinned. "Okay, don't say I didn't warn you." I walked over to her side of the bed.

Her eyes widened as I bundled her up in the duvet and then lifted her into my arms, firefighter-style.

"Put me down right now!" She squirmed in protest, but her scowl wavered as I strode toward the bathroom. "I mean it, Nathan!"

She clung to the duvet as I set her on her feet in the bathroom, scowling at me. "I was sleeping. You didn't need to manhandle me like a bloody Viking."

Her gaze tracked from my blond scruff to my muscular chest. A hazy look entered her eyes, and I grinned.

"See something you like?" I whispered, stepping closer.

Cat bit her lip and hummed, desire flickering across her face.

"I promised you an unforgettable week, didn't I?" I stole a quick kiss, distracting her. She hummed again, only this time in agreement. "I can't do that if we lose the day. It's half gone already."

"It's only ten" she mumbled against my lips.

I nodded. "And the sun rose hours ago."

Seeing my moment, I tugged at the duvet and stepped back. She caught it, gripping it tight so that it still covered her gloriously naked body.

Her eyes gleamed with amusement while her lips pinched together. "You may live to regret that promise."

But she released the duvet into my waiting hands.

"I do love your threats."

I tossed it aside and pulled her close. Desire simmered as I nuzzled her neck, hands roaming over her curves.

Cat laughed as I walked her backwards. "You're a stubborn ass."

Her fingers slid into my hair, drawing my lips back to hers. I groaned against her mouth, thoughts scattering.

By the time her back met tile, water streamed over us as she moulded herself to me. I deepened the kiss, pulse hammering at the feel of her body against mine.

When we came up for air, she gazed up at me through damp lashes, her green eyes dark with desire. "Well, you have me here." Her fingers trailed down my chest in challenge. "Now what do you intend to do about it?"

*A*n hour later, we climbed over sand dunes to a hidden cove, waves crashing louder with each step. Gulls screeched overhead in a cloudless blue sky — shocking for January in Scotland.

I'd definitely picked the best day for the trip, but had I lost my mind forcing Cat to experience the Scottish winter on a good day? Maybe.

Was I going to turn around at the first blast of wind? Fuck no. That's what coats, hats, scarves and gloves were for. And we were bundled tight.

When we crested the dune, Cat gasped. She gazed at the glittering water, eyes wide. "This place is incredible."

"I found it a couple of years ago when we all had a random break in filming." I set the picnic basket down on the sand and popped the lid. "It's my escape."

I spread out a blanket, weighing the edges with rocks.

"Were you all filming in the UK?" Cat asked as she took my hand and lowered herself to the blanket.

"Nah. All over Europe." I glanced around the secluded

and empty inlet. "It fit our craving at the time I think." I joined her on the blanket.

Cat nodded. "That makes sense, but do you always meet up between jobs?"

"Hell yes." I cracked open the picnic basket again and pulled out two bottles of water, handing one to her. "They're family to me, so when we're not all with our actual families, we're together. Whether in LA, elsewhere or on video calls."

My real family was an ocean away, so I rarely got to see them. But Finn, Shaun, and Jackson had seen me through more over the years than anyone. They knew all my tells, my bad habits and deepest secrets — and stuck around anyway.

I chuckled. "We're always up in each other's business."

Because they were the nosy, interfering lot a guy couldn't live without. The ones dragging you out to celebrate your wins as hard as they'd commiserate on your worst days. No matter how far apart work might scatter us at times, when we landed in the same place again it always felt like coming home.

She grinned. "What I'm hearing is you're nosy and a gossip."

"Maybe."

Cat laughed. The sea breeze carried it off. "You're terrible. Though I guess that level of closeness comes with the territory in your line of work."

"It does." I gazed out at the waves, the familiar ache of missing them catching me off guard. "Spending that much time together, you get to know each other's irritating habits and secrets whether you want to or not."

"Must be difficult being away during filming."

I shrugged. "Comes with the job. We stay in touch when we can." I forced a grin. "And gives us lots to catch up on when filming wraps."

"Still, it's not quite the same, is it?" Her fingers slid over mine, the warmth of her touch easing the ache. "Being able to see them whenever you want, I mean."

I sighed. "No, it's not." I clasped her hand. "But we make the most of the time we have." I cleared my throat, shifting to lighter topics. "How about you though? Any close friends or family around still?"

She looked away, gaze drawn to the wheeling gulls. "No, I'm pretty much alone." She gave my hand a quick squeeze. "But I keep busy with work, and California's offered opportunities I never would have found in Canada."

"Running from something or towards something new?" The words slipped out before I could catch them.

Cat sighed, eyes distant. "A bit of both, I suppose." She looked down at our joined hands, brow furrowed. "My mother and I don't speak anymore. Haven't since my first year of law school." She dashed at her eyes. "She never approved of me studying law. Or anything that took me away from home, really. Expected I'd fail and come running back home."

No wonder her work meant everything. If Cat lost her job now, after fighting so hard to build this life for herself...it would be like proving her mother right after all.

I slid closer, wrapping an arm around her shoulders. She leaned into me, trembling.

"The further I got, the worse she got." Her voice cracked. "I just couldn't take it anymore."

I pressed a kiss to her temple, heart aching for her pain. "I'm so sorry. That must have been incredibly difficult to deal with."

She gave a weak laugh. "Difficult is putting it mildly." Cat tilted her face to me, eyes gleaming. "But I refused to prove her right. I worked my ass off, finished top of my class." She smiled sadly. "Not that she cared to know that."

I brushed stray tears from her cheeks. "Her loss then. Because you're amazing."

Her smile deepened the lines around her eyes. "Thank you." She traced my jaw. "For listening and for saying that."

I clasped her hand over my heart. "Any time." I sighed.

"Life takes us in unexpected directions. But the people who truly matter are the ones who support us, scars and all."

"My mother wasn't always that way." Cat leaned into me again. "But after my father left, she just spiralled. The pressure of small town gossip and judgement."

I wrapped both arms around her, holding her close. "I'm so sorry you went through that alone." I pressed my lips to her hair. "But you're not alone anymore."

She tilted her face up, eyes searching mine. I cupped her cheek and then her lips brushed mine, soft as a sigh.

I deepened the kiss, hoping to convey without words that I was here — and wasn't going anywhere. She moulded herself against me, fingers sliding into my hair.

When we finally broke for air, she gazed at me through damp lashes.

"Thank you," she whispered. I smiled, leaning in to kiss her again.

We stayed wrapped in each other for a little while, just watching the waves and the sea birds. The peace of it made me ache to spend more time with Cat like that. No distractions, no fear of a man with a camera hidden in the bushes, or fans drawing attention to us.

"Have you ever gone cold water swimming?"

"Are you seriously asking a Canadian if she's done a polar bear swim? " She leaned back until she could see my confused face, her brows raised. "Oh my god, you are." She laughed, the sound easing the lingering ache in my chest. "I grew up with frigid winters, Nathan. A little seawater won't shock me."

I grinned. "Then you won't mind if we go for a dip?"

Her eyes widened. "Now? We don't have swimsuits or towels."

"Minor details." I stood and offered her my hand. "Live dangerously, Icy."

Cat bit her lip, eyes dancing with mirth. "You're mad." But she still placed her hand in mine.

I helped her up. "Certifiable, according to some."

Before she could protest further, I tugged off my coat and then my jumper. I kicked off my shoes and started folding items of clothing.

Her breath caught as I unbuttoned my jeans, her gaze locked on me.

"Your turn." I raised a brow in challenge.

She shook her head at my antics but her fingers stilled mine, helping me shed the last of my clothes. I returned the favour, fingers grazing over soft, heated skin until we stood breathless under clear winter skies, laid bare in more ways than one.

Hand in hand, we raced toward the waiting sea, crashing through icy waves. Catrina shrieked at the cold, trying in vain to splash me. I caught her body against mine and sank into the waves, my lips fused to hers, drinking in her kiss and the tang of salt on our lips.

I could get used to this.

CHAPTER TWENTY

CATRINA

The coffee maker gurgled as I squinted at its maze of buttons. Mornings weren't meant for operating complex machinery. At least, not without a steady infusion of caffeine first.

"Need help?" Nathan strolled into the kitchen, dressed and disgustingly alert.

"I've got it." I pressed another button, and sighed as the gurgling turned to sputtering. I jabbed at it again, frustration getting the better of me. "What's wrong with a good old-fashioned pour-over or a French press?"

Nathan chuckled. "Jackson's a coffee snob, babe. No chance of less than the best in his house."

I groaned but kept pushing buttons. Something had to work.

"Let me, before you scald yourself." Nathan bumped me aside and started turning dials at a speed I couldn't follow.

He handed me a steaming cup of black coffee and I stared

at it in shock. I'd spent a good thirty minutes trying to work the damn machine out and he got it in seconds? Not fair.

"Hungry?"

Rubbing sleep from my eyes, I shrugged. "If you're cooking."

He smirked. "Actually, I thought we'd make pancakes together." He shot me a teasing grin. "Could be fun."

My eyes narrowed. "The last time I tried to make pancakes, I set off the fire alarm and ruined a pan."

"Impressive, but relax." Nathan took my cup of black nectar before I'd even braved a sip. After placing it on the counter, he pulled me into his arms. "I'll supervise the entire time. Will you at least give it a shot?"

I peered up at him, unconvinced. His confidence I wouldn't send breakfast up in flames was endearing but unlikely.

Was this one of those moments where he said one thing, and secretly hoped for another?

Don't be stupid. He's not your mother and he's not setting you up to fail.

"Only if you swear we have a fire extinguisher handy. And you'll call the fire department at the first hint of smoke."

"We have an extinguisher." Nathan dropped a smacking kiss on my cheek. "And I wouldn't let anything happen to you. Come on. Live dangerously."

"Famous last words." But the laughter dancing in his eyes crumbled what remained of my resolve. How could I say no when he asked like that? "Fine. But don't say I didn't warn you!"

Nathan's face lit up. "That's the spirit. Pancakes, here we come!"

While he went to gather ingredients, I picked up my mug and smothered a smile behind it. His eternal optimism might get us both into trouble yet. When it came to my cooking, anyway. But with Nathan guiding me, flipping pancakes seemed more entertaining than an impending disaster.

Nathan rattled off measurements while I scrambled to keep up. I grabbed the bag of flour and attempted to scoop some into the cup. The bag slipped, puffing a cloud of white all over the counter.

"Oops." I grimaced, bracing for Nathan's reaction.

Instead, his deep chuckle filled the kitchen. "Could be worse. At least it's not in our hair."

I bit my lip as I glanced up at him, expecting to see some form of disappointment. But the laughter lighting his eyes was free of judgement. Only warmth that both soothed and excited me in ways I couldn't begin to explain.

He brushed a smudge of flour from my cheek, the gentle slide of his thumb igniting sparks beneath my skin.

My mother would have blown up, but not Nathan. He seemed to take it in his stride, smiling like I hadn't just covered him in flour too. *What did I do to deserve him?*

"No harm done. Here, let me help.

He sidled up behind me, his solid chest flush against my back. Guiding my hands, his breath caressed my neck and sent shivers down my spine as we poured and measured.

"Now we mix while I distract you."

His arms wrapped around me, the brush of lips on my shoulder pure sweet torture. His hands covered mine, prompting me through the motions. I surrendered to the feel of him, my pulse racing at the hard strength of his body fitted against mine.

"Distract away. But if I mess up the pancakes, I'm blaming your 'help' entirely."

"You can try." He laughed. "Wet ingredients next. Pour the milk."

His grip guided my hands through the motions, his touch threatening to unravel me completely. His murmured instructions in my ear sent a thrill coursing through me that had nothing to do with following the recipe.

If not for the counter, my knees might have given out. But I couldn't care.

Nathan slid the bowl of pancake batter across the counter. "Your turn. Do the honours?"

I stared at the bowl like it might bite. "Me?"

"You've got this." He winked. "I'll be right here if you need me."

He stepped back, giving me space. I glanced between him and the stove, heart pounding. His belief in me was sweet torture, especially given my history of kitchen disasters.

"I don't know…" I grimaced, lifting the bowl with shaky hands. The batter sloshed dangerously close to the rim.

"Easy. Take your time." Nathan kept his tone light, but I sensed him poised to intervene if needed. "You'll never know unless you try, right?"

I exhaled, steadying myself. "If the smoke alarms go off, I warned you."

He grinned. "They won't."

I poured a tiny amount of batter into the pan, biting my lip as it spread into a circle. Maybe I could do this after all. At least with his guidance.

After a few seconds, I steeled myself, spatula ready to attempt the flip. "Here goes nothing…"

The pancake sailed up and over, landing neatly back on the pan. I blinked, stunned it had worked.

Glancing up, I found him watching with carefree joy. I laughed, giddy at my small success.

"Told you so." He pulled me close for a quick kiss. "My little chef. Ready to make this a proper breakfast for two now?"

"With you here?" I smiled up at him, heart overflowing. "Absolutely. And no smoke alarms yet, see?"

Nathan chuckled as he pressed a kiss to my neck. "I always had faith in you, baby."

How such an innocent statement could gut me, I didn't know. For a second, it winded me. I'd always worried that my flaws outweighed the good — all courtesy of my mother and countless failed dates — but he didn't care about them. He embraced every imperfection.

Maybe he really did love me.

We cooked the rest of the batter, laughter filling the kitchen.

When the bowl was empty and a massive stack of pancakes sat on the plate, I turned off the heat, stunned. Not a single smoke alarm sounded and they were all golden brown.

I'd done that.

Nathan carried the plate to the tiny table by the window, shrouded in weak winter sunlight. I grabbed plates and fixings before joining him.

I sank into the chair opposite, shaking my head at the feast we'd created. "I still can't believe we did this."

"Better get used to it." Nathan grinned. "Now that I've discovered your hidden talents, we'll be cooking up a storm."

"Don't get ahead of yourself." I laughed. "It'll take more than one success to convince me this wasn't beginner's luck!"

Nathan reached across the table, tangling his fingers with mine. "Then we'll practise. A lot." His eyes gleamed with mischief and promise, heart skipping in response. "Don't worry, you're in safe hands with Chef Nathan."

I sniggered. "Chef? Now your ego's talking."

"Hardly." He loaded pancakes onto his plate, his expression perfectly serious. "I trained."

"You trained to be a chef?" My brows climbed.

In all my research about him, that had not come up.

"Well, technically it was for a romantic comedy—"

"That doesn't count."

"Semantics. I studied hours of cooking videos for that role. Same difference." His eyes gleamed with mischief and promise, my heart skipping in response.

I shook my head at his ridiculousness but let it lie. Everything he'd cooked for me so far had been delicious. Maybe he had learnt a thing or two.

"I don't get to use the skills much at home." He explained. "Have to stay in 'drool-worthy condition' for roles, you know. Nothing but cardboard protein and powdered supplements for this action hero."

"Drool-worthy condition?" I snorted. "I think your ego's talking again."

Nathan chuckled. "Jealous I get paid to work out? Comes with the territory, babe. All part of being America's action hero sweetheart."

"More like action hero pain in my—"

"Careful!" He pointed his fork at me, eyes dancing. "Or I won't kiss you for the rest of the day.

I shook my head but laughed. "You wouldn't last an hour."

"Try me." He winked, loading his plate with an obscene amount of pancakes and toppings.

I laughed, dragging the stack toward me. "Don't worry, I'll be too busy eating these to miss your kisses."

Nathan clutched his chest in mock offence. "And leave none for me?" His eyes gleamed even as he protested. "At least save me a few. A man's gotta eat!"

I lifted the platter, holding it teasingly out of his reach. "Have to protect your drool-worthy bod. That means more for me!"

Nathan chuckled, catching my hand to guide the platter back to the table. "Give a guy a break, will you? It's Christmas and I gave myself weeks off from the boring diet!" He pointed at the pancakes with his fork. "It'll be our little secret. If you don't tell my trainer."

"Wow. Two whole weeks of not worrying about calories or carbs." I shook my head. "There's something really sad about that, but I'll agree if you never tell anyone how many nanaimo bars I pack away each year?"

Nathan grinned, attacking his own stack of pancakes. "There she is — the girl who's more excited about extra dessert than an extra hour at the gym." He squeezed my hand, eyes gleaming. "I knew she was in there somewhere."

"Damn straight." I popped a piece of pancake into my mouth and moaned. "I want to marry these pancakes."

"Slow down." Nathan held out his hand, amusement creasing his eyes. "They're not even the best we can do."

My brows climbed. "That ego really is something. This was a fluke, don't expect me to master anything else."

"It's not ego if it's true." He grinned. "I can teach you how to cook anything, Icy, and it'll be delicious."

"Don't start planning culinary school just yet." I rolled my eyes at him, my pulse racing at the thought of more mornings like this. "I'll need to make it through round two first. If there is one."

"There will be." Nathan lifted my hand, brushing a kiss over my fingers. "However many times it takes for you to see what I already know."

"That you're destined for a career change into food styling?" I teased.

He chuckled. "Funny. No, that you can do anything you set your mind to." He peered up at me, expression soft but serious. "With the right motivation and support, anyway. And I intend to keep motivating and supporting you if you'll let me."

His promise left me breathless...

I blinked back tears. "You're stuck motivating and supporting me now, Chef Nathan." I winked to show I was teasing. "But don't say I didn't warn you when we end up with burnt scones or soggy bread!"

"I'm more than ready." Nathan laughed.

We enjoyed our pancake feast, laughing over stories of Nathan's romantic comedy role and my past kitchen disasters. By the time we finished, my sides ached from giggling and I couldn't remember why I'd resisted this. Why I'd resisted him for so long.

Nathan eyed the single leftover pancake and snatched it up. But instead of eating it, he tore it in half.

"Open wide." He held out a piece, syrup dripping.

I raised a brow. "Seriously?"

"Come on, Cat. You trust me, don't you?' His eyes gleamed, laughter chasing any reluctance from my thoughts.

I leaned forward, taking a bite of the offered pancake. Sweetness burst over my tongue, but not from the syrup. The care and playfulness Nathan lavished on me were sweeter by far.

As I chewed, he popped the other half into his own mouth. Then he leaned across the table and stole a syrup-sweet kiss, whispering against my lips, "I never doubted you for a second."

I stared at him, struck speechless. He had known me a little more than a month, yet had more faith in me than my own mother ever possessed.

Overcome, I blinked back tears. With Nathan, I could be more than the failure my family expected. I could be the woman he somehow already saw — clever, playful, daring... and able to craft more than edible pancakes when given the chance.

Flashes of what life might hold with Nathan after the studio sale danced through my thoughts, more golden than any sunrise. Lazy Sunday mornings making breakfast together. Discovering hidden talents and passions I'd long suppressed. Endless laughter and support.

I wanted that badly.

"You did so well, I feel like I should reward you," Nathan said once we'd washed up.

"Reward me how?"

He bit his lip as he considered me. His blue eyes burned with desire and the way his gaze roamed my body, it made me ache in the best way.

"How do you feel about roleplay?"

CHAPTER TWENTY-ONE

NATHAN

"We shouldn't do this..." Her protest was half-hearted, her desire bleeding through.

I drew back just enough to meet her gaze. "No one has to know. The door's locked. If you keep quiet, it'll be our secret." My pulse roared in my ears, enjoying our make believe far more than I thought I would.

Cat sat next to me in Jackson's massive leather office chair. His heavy mahogany desk sat in front of us, and after this trip, I had no intention of telling him that I'd christened his desk. Didn't even feel a grain of guilt about it either.

Especially not when I'd barely touched Cat before she started panting. My girl loved the thought of being bent over a desk and giving up control. Oh what a departure from the first night we met.

She swallowed hard, eyes drifting closed as I nuzzled into her neck. "This is crazy. We can't..."

I nipped at her collarbone, a soft gasp escaping her. She

shivered at my touch but didn't push me away, lost to temptation.

Wordlessly, she turned, capturing my mouth. The next thing I knew, my careful attorney was straddling me, her chest pressed tight to mine and her lips devouring me. Her hands slid under my t-shirt, her nails raking across my back. I groaned at the sensation, my fingers digging into her hips, urging her to grind harder against me and take what she needed.

"What are we doing?" Cat groaned against my lips, breathless. "We'll get caught."

I rested my forehead against hers, struggling to think with her in my arms. Her feverish eyes fixed on me and a small smile curled her lips.

"Then we'll have to be quick and quiet, won't we?"

Her breath caught as I slid my hand up her thigh, dragging her skirt higher and higher.

"What do you say, Icy?" I whispered, my voice hoarse. "Are you in?"

I drew circles on her inner thigh, teasing her with barely-there touches. She swallowed, her focus fixed on the skin-on-skin contact.

When she met my gaze again, her eyes darkened with need, and she nodded.

"I'm going to need you to say it, beautiful." I leaned forward, capturing her swollen lips in a quick kiss. "Do I stop and you can imagine the things I would have done to you on this desk? Or do you want to know?"

"I want to know," she said with zero hesitation.

"Good girl."

I teased her through the silk and lace of her panties. Her hands speared into my hair, pulling my mouth back to hers. Our kiss grew heated, desperate, feral.

My fingers grazed her clit through the silk and she jolted. I groaned against her neck as she squirmed in my lap. Continuing my teasing movements, I slid my fingers up and down, around and over her panties, anywhere but where she wanted me. Her hips rocked up into me and she moaned against my lips.

"Nathan," she said, my name lost to a breathy sigh. "Stop teasing me."

I smirked against her lips. "What do you need, baby?"

Her head fell back, a faint sheen blanketing her skin. "Let me come."

"Patience."

I let my fingers dip beneath the fabric, grazing her ever-growing heat repeatedly, feeling how slick she was becoming for me. Anticipation vibrated through me as my fingertips drew ever closer to where she wanted me most.

Cat gasped against my mouth as I thrust a finger inside of her. I could feel the wetness pool around my fingers as I caressed her walls.

Unable to bear it anymore, I stood, taking her with me. She squeaked as I lifted her, setting her on the desk.

"I've imagined fucking you like this so many times," I murmured.

True. If she'd given me the right look, I would have had her over it the first day I saw her in her office. Instead, I'd have to make this everything we'd both dreamed about.

My hands slipped up her inner thighs, hiking her skirt up. She blushed but didn't protest as I slid her panties off.

"Me too," she whispered, peeking up at me through her lashes.

Fuck. If law ever fails her, she'd make a great actress.

"Yeah?"

At her nod, I tugged her forward to the edge of the desk, forcing her legs wide, putting her pussy on display for me as I settled back into Jackson's chair. "What did you imagine?"

I moved forward to press my face against the soft heat between her legs, drawing in a deep breath of her arousal as I licked her eager bud. She shuddered and moaned, her fingers tangling into my hair.

Then I lifted my head and met her feverish gaze with raised brows. "Well?"

She swallowed. "I imagine you teasing me before you take me... like you are." She bit her lip. "Laying me down and eating me out."

I pressed a firm hand to her stomach, forcing her down onto her back. Papers slid off the desk, fluttering across the room.

"What else?"

"After..." Her voice shook as I captured her clit between my lips, sucking hard.

She squirmed and I grabbed her hips, holding her where I wanted her.

"After?"

"I wanted you to bend me over and fuck me from behind," she said in one rushed puff of air.

I smirked against her. When Cat had fallen into my arms in The Noir Bar, I never imagined I'd found myself a little vixen.

"That can be arranged."

I dragged my tongue through her folds, circling her clit as my fingers thrust in and out of her tight pussy. Her fingers gripped my hair, tugging to the point of pain as if she had any control.

Chuckling, I pulled back and she released a breathy groan.

"Does it make you feel dirty knowing people are just outside the door while I have my mouth on you in here?"

Even pretend, it fucking did something to me, that was for sure.

"Yes," she hissed as my lips returned to her and my fingers crooked inside of her.

Her feet found purchase on the chair arms and she thrust against me, her restless body reaching for more and more.

Her back bowed off the desk and her hips bucked wildly. "Oh god, Nathan," she whispered, "I'm going to come."

My name sounded like a prayer on her lips and I worked an extra finger inside of her as a reward, driving deeper, licking harder. She covered her mouth stifling her moans as if someone could actually overhear her. Her pussy convulsed and her body tensed, her orgasm rushing through her.

"Will you think about me when you're sitting here late into the night?" I circled her clit with my thumb while my fingers continued to milk her orgasm. "Will it make you wet?"

"Yes," she whispered, the single word strangled.

I pulled back, releasing the stranglehold I had on her hips to slide my fingers from her pussy, trailing them up her stomach to her breasts. I cupped them through her shirt, rubbing my thumbs over her nipples until they were hard peaks,

"Do you want me to bend you over your desk now?" I asked, unable to conceal the intense need burning through me.

She nodded, and that was all the confirmation I needed in my desperation to get inside of her again.

CATRINA

Nathan had my panties, blouse and bra off in seconds. He pulled me onto my feet, kissed me hard, pressing my naked body to his fully clothed chest. I shivered at the mental image it created.

If we'd done this in my office, I'd have never gotten through the day without thinking about him.

As if you did anyway.

He pulled me back and I felt something entirely new, a building anticipation as he guided me to the desk. He bent my body over the hard surface and placed my hands on the polished wooden surface. My heart raced as Nathan hiked my skirt up, until it turned into a belt around my waist, the only remaining piece of clothing on me.

My breath came in short gasps and my heart pounded as his hands trailed down my sides and waist, pressing against me firmly.

"Are you sure you want this, baby?" His warm breath hit the back of my neck and I closed my eyes, savouring every sensation his touch sent through me.

I nodded and moaned softly as he teased my entrance with a single finger.

Nathan groaned. "Always so wet for me."

Then his touch completely vanished, leaving me straining to figure out what he was doing behind me. The sound of his zipper mingled with my soft pants.

I jumped at the first drag of his broad cock head through my folds.

Nathan was all business as he pressed into me, his hard length sliding over my wetness, spreading me wide.

I barely had time to process the sensation when he withdrew and slammed into me, rocking my body forward.

"Fuck," he moaned into my ear. "You're so tight."

I panted, holding my body up with shaky arms and trembling legs.

"Do you have any idea how good you feel?" he asked, his voice gravelly.

He began to move faster and harder, pushing me further over my desk until I was lying flat on it, my head off the edge. I gasped for air as he pounded into me, each thrust making me cry out louder and louder.

His movements slowed as he leaned over me, his lips dragging against my neck. "Shh, you don't want anyone to walk in on us, do you?" he whispered in my ear.

"N-no," I stuttered, struggling to breath as his hips rocked against me in short, sharp bursts.

"I think you're lying." His deep voice made me shiver. "You want someone to walk in on us, don't you?"

"No." I tried to shake my head but with the desk pressed against my cheek it was impossible.

Nathan straightened up, pulsing in and out of me until my head spun.

"Oh my God, yes, Nathan," I whispered.

He slapped my ass hard, then again.

"Oh!" I gasped, shocked, my eyes wide. He hadn't spanked me hard, but the sharp sting had been unexpected. It surprisingly sent sparks of need to my core, making me squirm against the desk.

"Don't lie to me, Catrina." He leaned over me again, gathering my hair in hand. He pressed his lips to my ear, nibbling my earlobe. "You want to be found."

"Yes," I moaned, unable to deny it any longer. I was desperate for him to take me, and the thought of someone walking in on us made my heart race and my body tremble with anticipation.

"Good girl."

The edge of the desk bit into my thighs but I could barely feel it through the coiling pleasure.

His thrusts picked up speed again, pushing me further into the desk. He tugged on the handful of hair in his hands, the slight bite only adding to the need spiralling inside of me. He leaned over me then, kissing me roughly. I gasped as his lips travelled to my ear.

"You're so fucking hot, spread out on your desk like this," he groaned, his thrusts growing fast and rough. "At my absolute mercy. I'm going to come inside you, baby."

My pussy clenched as he spoke and I moaned loudly, his words turning me on more than I'd ever imagined.

Nathan increased his thrusts, his breathing getting heavier

as he neared his climax. Every muscle in my body tensed up, the pleasure mounting until I couldn't hold it off any longer.

"Yes! Nathan!" I screamed, my body shaking as my orgasm rushed through me.

He growled low in his throat and increased his pace. His hands grasped at me tighter, holding me still against the desk as he pounded into me until the orgasm ripped through us both.

My body quivered in pleasure, every nerve ending firing off sparks of electricity as Nathan collapsed over me. After a couple of minutes of heavy breathing, he pulled out and gathered me in his arms. He collapsed into Jackson's office chair, cradling me to his chest.

"Well, it's official," Nathan said, amusement tinging his voice. "If we'd had sex in your office the entire world would know about us."

I laughed. He wasn't wrong.

CHAPTER TWENTY-TWO

NATHAN

Cat and I lay curled together on the blanket, stargazing in our thick coats and gloves. We huddled for warmth under the blankets, her body pressed against mine. After weeks of stolen moments, whisking her away felt like a dream.

"You're quiet." I held her hand to my chest, drawing circles through her glove.

"Just thinking how perfect this is... you and me, together at last." She sighed, rolling to face me. The blanket slipped, and I reached to tuck it back around her shoulders. "Even though it has to end for a little while."

"It's not going to end at all," I murmured. "Just a couple of days pretending I haven't seen you naked." I grinned. "Easy."

Cat swatted my chest in faux-outrage but she pressed her face into my shoulder, laughing.

The sound melted the last of the tension from my bones. I relaxed into her embrace, staring up at the sea of stars stretching endlessly above.

"Look at them all," I murmured. "So many stories in a single glance."

When I gestured to a cluster of stars in the night sky and said, "Do you know the story of Andromeda and Perseus?"

She shook her head. "I don't think so."

"Andromeda's father forbade her to be with Perseus. But when she was sacrificed to a sea monster, Perseus slew the beast and saved Andromeda. He overcame every obstacle and won her heart. Their love was eternal... just like the stars." I brushed a wind-tousled lock of hair from her cheek. "Remind you of any two fools you know?"

"Real subtle, playboy." She trailed her fingers down the line of buttons on my coat. "Mm, no. That story couldn't possibly remind me of us." Her lips brushed my jaw, the barest whisper of a kiss. "After all, you and your attorney know nothing about breaking rules or throwing caution to the wind, right?"

I turned my head, capturing her lips and kissing her softly. She smiled against mine, her hands sliding up my chest to the back of my neck, fingers threading through my hair as she held me close. I tightened my arm around her. Cradling her close, I traced her jaw.

"Is that so?" I asked when we finally parted, resting my forehead against hers.

We both knew the rules shattered long ago.

She trailed her fingers down the line of buttons on my coat. A comfortable silence fell between us, broken only by the crash of distant waves. I held her, treasuring the feeling of her in my arms.

A flash lit the sky, over in an instant.

She gasped. "Did you see that? A shooting star!"

"Make a wish," I whispered, nuzzling her cheek.

Cat's eyes shone as she gazed up at the sky. Her lips moved in a silent wish, heartfelt and earnest. I wondered what dreams still lived inside her, waiting to be caught.

After a moment, she sighed, leaning into me. "Your turn, playboy. See any stars left to wish on?"

I pressed a kiss to her temple, murmuring against her skin. "I don't need to wish on stars. I already have everything I could dream of right here."

She tilted her head to glance up at me, a soft smile curving her lips. She shook her head, even as a blush coloured her cheeks. "Always the charmer."

"It's easy to be charming when I speak the truth." I stroked her cheek with the back of my fingers. Her skin was cold against my touch. "You're shivering. Here, sit up — I'll add another log to the fire."

Cat reluctantly sat up, wrapping her arms around herself for warmth as I coaxed the fire back to crackling life. The additional logs finally ignited, bathing our private retreat in a golden glow. I settled back onto the blanket beside her, wrapping her in my embrace once more.

For a time we lay together silently watching the flames dance, lost in the peace of solitude and the warmth of shared body heat. She nestled against me, her head coming to rest on my chest once more. I breathed in the lavender scent of her hair, my arms wrapped securely around her as she relaxed into my embrace.

"Tired?" I asked, my lips dragging against her hair, the strands catching in my stubble.

She shook her head, stifling a yawn I felt more than heard. "No, just... comfortable. I don't want this week to end."

There was an ache in her words that echoed in my bones. "I know." My arms tightened around her instinctively, as if I could shield her through will alone...

Cat sighed, gazing up at the sea of stars glittering above. "I used to stargaze all the time as a girl. Me and my friends would pile into the back of old pickup trucks and drive out to the fields to get away from the lights of town." A wistful smile curved her lips. "We'd wrap up in blankets, drink hot cocoa and search the sky for hours hoping to spot a shooting star. Each time we did, we'd make the silliest wishes."

"Sounds like a great night."

Her smile faded, eyes clouding with memories. "Wishes to escape that suffocating little town. To find purpose... freedom." She gave a humourless chuckle. "I guess in the end my wish came true. I got out."

There was an old ache in her words I longed to soothe.

"We'd stay out for hours. My mom would get so angry, afraid I'd catch cold... or get into trouble." A wistful smile flickered across her lips. "Little did she know I was already dreaming of life far beyond that little town's borders."

Her smile faded. "After my dad left, she just got so... clingy. Smothering. She never wanted me out of her sight." Cat shrugged. "I guess she thought she was protecting me. But she didn't understand — I had to get out. I was suffocating."

My arms tightened around her and I pressed a kiss into her hair. "If my mom had been that smothering, I probably would have hopped on the first bus out of town myself."

She snorted. "We'd spot a shooting star and make silly wishes to get the hell out of that one-stoplight town. Not every night, just whenever life felt too small."

I stroked her hair. "Can't blame you. A brain like yours would've gone to waste in a place like that."

Cat sighed. "Sometimes I wonder if working so hard to escape, I missed out on living an actual life. My nose was always in a book, chasing the next goal." She gave a rueful chuckle. "Not much time for friends or fun, always trying to prove myself."

I tilted her chin up, meeting her gaze. "You've time enough yet to live for yourself. But you'll make partner. Anyone with sense can see what a brilliant lawyer you are."

She leaned into me. "Always talking me up. Even when I'm full of doubts."

I pressed a kiss to her forehead. "Because I see who you

are, Catrina Sinclair. Beyond the doubt, beyond the drive. And you are bloody brilliant."

A soft smile curved her lips as she relaxed into my embrace. We lay together in comfortable silence, gazing up at the sea of stars stretching endlessly above.

The need to share my every dream, explain every step I'd ever taken following logic and gut instinct. But most of all, I wanted her to see me as more than the pretty face they had always cast me as.

The words stuck in my throat. Old fears and doubts. Would she think I was daft, chasing purpose beyond the flash of cameras?

Showbiz had been my whole life. Producers saw a face they could sell, casting me as the action guy or romance lead. I was sick of those hollow roles. I wanted to show the world, and myself, I could do more.

Cat saw beyond the hype and fantasy. With her, maybe I didn't have to keep proving myself. Maybe, just this once, I'd be enough.

If there was one person I could trust with the truth, it was her. She knew me, wounds and all.

I took a deep breath and spat the words out quickly, before I chickened out. "The studio isn't just an investment. It's where I met Jackson, Shaun, and Finn. We were young and daft, dreaming of changing the world through stories. For years we've talked about starting our own company, to make the films we believe in."

Cat tilted her head, brows knitting together. "You've never mentioned that before."

"I know." I sighed, gazing up at the stars. "When I first arrived in LA, just off the plane from London, I was a fish out of water. Young, naive... and hungry to prove myself."

Cat rested her chin on my chest, gazing at me with soft, patient eyes.

"The industry moves fast. Everyone wants to use you,

mould you into whatever the latest trend demands. It's easy to get caught up chasing the flash and fame, losing yourself along the way." I threaded my fingers through her hair, anchoring myself in her warmth.

"Then I met Jackson, Shaun and Finn on the set. We were all cast as soldiers, stuck in that damn trench for weeks on end while cameras rolled. During breaks, we'd talk about the scripts we wished we were filming instead. Stories that meant something." I smiled at the memory. "They became my anchors in that world of smoke and mirrors. The only ones I could be fully myself around. Dreaming up an indie studio felt like what we were always meant to do."

Cat smiled, leaning up to brush her lips against mine. "I'm glad you found good friends in that madness."

"They supported me for years, chasing this dream of the studio. Now it's finally happening, thanks to you." I brushed a soft kiss over her lips.

Her eyes shone. "Not much longer now until the deal is done."

"And I can at last drag you away as my captive, with no studio business standing in my way." I nuzzled her cheek.

Cat laughed, but then she sat up, turning onto her front to face me. She searched my gaze, chewing her lip. "Do you mean that?"

"With all my heart."

She smiled and pressed her palm to my jaw. "Thank you."

Her lips found mine in a soft, slow kiss. I lost myself in her taste, her warmth, wrapping my arms around her and holding her close.

When we finally parted, breathless, I rested my forehead against hers. "These past weeks have been torture, stealing moments with you only to part again."

Cat sighed, her breath misting the air between us. "I know." She traced the line of my jaw with a gloved finger. "But it will all be worth it soon."

I nodded, turning to press a kiss into her palm. "One more week. Just seven more days of pretending I'm not constantly thinking about your lips, then you're mine."

She laughed at that, shaking her head even as a blush coloured her cheeks. "You're incorrigible."

"When it comes to you, absolutely." I stole another soft kiss, revelling in the warmth of her in my arms. "Part of me still can't believe this is real. That you're here, that this mad plan of ours is actually working."

Cat's eyes shone as she gazed up at me. "We make a good team, you and I." She traced the line of buttons on my coat with one gloved finger. "Even if we did go about this whole thing a bit backwards."

"No regrets?" I searched her eyes, brushing an errant lock of hair back from her cheek.

She smiled, leaning up to brush her lips against mine in a feather-light kiss. "Not a one."

CHAPTER TWENTY-THREE

CATRINA

I wandered into the kitchen the next evening, drawn by the aroma of garlic and onions sizzling on the stove. Nathan stood at the counter, knife flying over a cutting board piled high with vegetables.

"Something smells incredible in here," I said, leaning against the counter. "What's on the menu?"

Before arriving in St Andrews, I'd never thought so much about food. With limited distractions, our days were structured around it and, honestly, the simplicity was glorious.

No emails. No people to please. Just the two of us.

He glanced up with a smile. "Thought I'd make you my fancy mac and cheese."

For a second, I just stared at him, shocked. He remembered my favourite meal? Then a smile spread across my face.

"That sounds perfect." Going up on my toes, I pressed a quick kiss to his cheek. "Thank you."

"I'm here to please." He grinned. "But I might also expect a reward in return."

I chuckled. "Naturally." As I grabbed a bottle of Riesling from the fridge, I asked, "And what will it be this time?"

Nathan hummed, tilting his head from side to side as if considering his options. "I haven't decided yet."

Shaking my head, I uncorked the wine and poured two glasses.

He dumped shredded cheese into the pot, stirring frequently as it melted into a creamy sauce. The kitchen filled with the smells of childhood before everything changed, a familiarity I hadn't realised I missed and craved.

"How was the new script?" I asked, handing him a glass of wine. He took a sip and turned back to the stove.

"Really good, actually. It's a great concept, with lots of complexity. I think you'd love the story too." He glanced over with a grin. "Maybe I'll let you have an exclusive sneak peek before I sign it."

I laughed. "Oh, I see, using your girlfriend as a test audience. How convenient."

My mind stalled, fixated on that word. *What else would you be, idiot?*

Yeah, I know. I should have realised. Still it sent an unexpected thrill through me, one that made me want to grin uncontrollably and tell everyone I passed in the street.

Nathan mixed in breadcrumbs, totally oblivious to my mini-revelation. "Of course. Your opinion means the most to me. And the rewards of making you laugh are too good to pass up."

He knew how to lift my mood and make me smile no matter the circumstance. The playful camaraderie felt comforting, a warmth like the bubbling cheese sauce itself. I took a seat at the table, rubbing my hands together for the cheesy goodness in my immediate future.

Nathan filled two bowls with the pasta and handed me one. "Comfort food for my best girl. Hope it hits the spot!"

I tapped my glass to his. "To cosy nights together."

His eyes shone with warmth and affection. "The cosiest nights of all."

After nearly a week tucked away from the world, the beach house felt like home. I never wanted to leave.

Jackson would just have to accept me as a squatter.

Nathan's phone rang, the harsh buzz cutting through the quiet. His brows rose as he glanced at the caller ID.

He answered on the second ring. "Maisy. What can I do for you?"

He listened without a change in expression and I braced myself, tension coiling in my veins.

"Understood. You'll handle it?"

My shoulders relaxed at his calm tone. *Maybe it's not bad news.*

"Thank you, Maisy. Keep me posted."

He ended the call and his gaze met mine, his stoic expression shifting to grim as he grimaced.

"What was that about?" My voice wavered and my stomach clenched with worry.

"More photos hit the internet today."

My heart dropped like a stone. I closed my eyes, shaking my head. "Oh god. They're clear photos this time, aren't they?"

"I'm afraid so." Nathan reached over to squeeze my hand, voice filled with regret. "There's no denying it's us. I'm so sorry, Cat."

I took a shaky breath, dread pooling in my stomach. "How bad are they?"

Nathan sighed, rubbing his thumb over my knuckles. "Maisy said our faces are clear in all of them. They're one or two of us holding hands."

My anxiety spiked, thoughts racing, trying to pinpoint a time where I'd let my guard down in public with Nathan, sure no one would recognise us outside of LA.

Why the hell would I think that?

How naive.

But no moments sprung to mind.

"Where was it?" Horror trickled into my voice, but inside, I berated myself.

I knew better.

Even though you don't know where it happened?

Yes. I knew better than to ever get comfortable with Nathan in public.

"They're from breakfast," Nathan said, stopping my internal attack in its tracks.

"How?" My brow furrowed as I tried to recall any cameras near us.

"Maisy thinks they were taken from outside."

"What does that mean?"

"They were waiting for us." He bit his lip, hesitating for a second while he studied me. "Some of the shots were through the glass of the bistro windows."

The look he gave me said that was an important piece of information, but I couldn't make sense of it. Thankfully, he took pity on me.

"They didn't come from some passing fan."

He stared at me, almost willing the pieces to click.

If they didn't come from a fan, then that meant… we were tailed?

"A photographer must have been following us in Edinburgh," he said.

One sentence and my stomach dropped like lead.

"Does that mean we were followed here?" I shot to my feet, my hands dragging through my hair as I paced around the kitchen island. "We practically mauled each other rolling around in the sand on multiple occasions." My eyes widened and I stopped. "We went skinny dipping on the beach."

"They didn't follow us here," Nathan said, his voice perfectly calm.

"How do you know that?"

He stood, edging towards me with considered steps. "If they had better than a reflection-marred image, they would have released it."

"That doesn't mean they won't."

Nathan grabbed my hands and tugged them down to my side. He stared into my panicked gaze, holding me still while my mind raced.

"Trust me, baby, they would have released them already."

Something about his serious yet serene expression calmed my racing heart.

"How many photos went up?"

"Maisy didn't specify the exact number." He gazed at me with concern etched into every line of his face. "She's already working to contain the spread and draft a statement. Try not to worry, Cat."

Don't worry?

"Draft a statement?"

Last time they were all for silent denial.

He nodded. "We can't hide from this one."

"What will it say?"

"I don't know. Maisy's spinning options at the moment." He rubbed his hands up and down my arms, trying to sooth me. "They'll send over some press releases for us to choose from soon and we'll figure it out together, okay?"

I collapsed back into my chair, pulse pounding in my ears. Easy for him to say, the news wouldn't really impact him.

My boss was already suspicious thanks to the last leak. How could I face him after this?

I studied Nathan. He'd worked hard to toe the line between professional and suitor. I might have made a show of resisting him, but I couldn't deny that I'd enjoyed his every attempt to break my resistance.

I'd agreed to a date after the deal was done.

I didn't have to let him kiss me, didn't have to let him go down on me in my office or fuck him again.

We might not have been dating, but we were definitely involved.

You just called yourself his girlfriend.

So I had, in fact, lied to Mike.

I pressed the heels of my hands to my eyes, taking a steadying breath. Every week new gossip flew around the office about someone breaking the firm's rules. This was no different from that and none of them lost their positions. My job would be fine.

It had to be.

Nathan crouched beside me, gently prying my hands away from my face. "Talk to me, Cat. What are you thinking?"

I opened my eyes to find his filled with remorse. "I'm thinking how unfair it is that I can lose everything thanks to a few photos, while your life goes on unchanged." The words slipped out before I could bite them back.

Nathan flinched.

"What if it ruins everything?"

My phone rang, Mike's name flashing across the screen and my career flashed before my eyes. I tensed, pulse spiking. Mike never called unless it was urgent.

Swallowing hard, I answered on the second ring. "Good morning, Mike."

"Catrina, do you have a moment to chat?" Mike's tone was clipped, professional. My anxiety ratcheted up another notch.

"Of course, what can I do for you?" I kept my own voice measured, as if this were any other work call.

As if I didn't already know why he was ringing.

"You promised me there was nothing happening between you and Nathan. And now I see images of the two of you clearly together in Edinburgh. What are you even doing in Scotland?" He sighed and my stomach dropped. "Not the point. The partners feel you were dishonest and have lost faith in your judgement."

"I didn't lie to you. When we last spoke, Nathan and I were just friends."

Friends who occasionally had sex and kissed.

"But you're not anymore?"

I glanced at Nathan, patiently watching me from across the table. There would be little point in lying. If the pictures showed us holding hands, it would be obvious. Especially when, in a week's time, we signed the deal and started dating for real.

Plus I'm tired of fighting.

"It happened so fast, events just got away from us. I never meant to mislead you or break my word." The confession burned.

"I'm afraid it's too late. The partners have made their decision. Catrina, I have no choice but to terminate your position effective immediately. All your current casework will be handed over to Theo."

"Theo? The guy who cheated on his wife with his assistant and was caught on camera?" Bitterness and resentment rose like bile in my throat.

Mike's voice softened. "I argued to give you another chance but was overruled. Given the firm's strict policy against fraternisation with clients, I'm not surprised. I'm sorry."

The words slammed into me like a kick to the chest. I struggled to breathe, to process what Mike was saying through the rushing in my ears.

"Catrina? Did you hear me?"

I fought back tears, clutching the phone tight. "To say there's a strict policy against dating clients is a bit of a joke, don't you think?"

Mike cleared his throat. "The partners feel this situation reflects poorly on the firm's reputation and judgement. I wish the outcome could be different." He sighed. "But policy is policy."

My voice shook, raw with anger and betrayal. "Ever wish

you worked at a firm that judged women based on their work rather than who they date?" I choked on a bitter laugh. "Guess all that talk about nurturing female talent was just lip service."

Mike was silent. That said enough.

I squeezed my eyes shut, tears spilling free. The call ended, phone slipping from my fingers onto the table. My career, my livelihood, everything I had worked and sacrificed for, gone with a few innocent photos. The unfairness of it choked me, tears burning in my eyes.

Nathan reached over to grasp my hand. "What happened?"

I turned to him, the carefully constructed walls around my heart crumbling at the concern in his eyes.

"That was Mike. He fired me, effective immediately."

Nathan paled. "No, that can't be right. On what grounds?"

"Fraternising with clients." I gave a bitter laugh.

"That's outrageous." Nathan's jaw clenched, anger darkening his eyes. "They had no right—"

"They had every right." I shook my head, swiping at my cheeks. "I knew the policy and the risks. And now my idiocy has cost me everything I worked for, a career that,"—my voice broke— "meant more to me than anything."

Nathan reached for me but I shrank from his touch, the wound too raw. I rose to my feet, feeling unmoored and adrift. "I need—some air. Excuse me."

Before Nathan could protest, I fled outside, a sob catching in my throat. The cold hit me as I stepped outside, but I barely felt it. I walked down to the beach on autopilot, my thoughts churning.

The beach house no longer felt like a shelter or escape, but a gilded cage of my own making. The consequences of following my heart had finally caught up to me, and now there was nowhere left to run.

Just last night Nathan and I had rolled around in the sand here, sharing secrets, opening our hearts. Laughter echoing across the empty shore. Now those memories seemed to belong to different people, a past already slipping away.

I sank down onto the damp sand, drawing my knees to my chest. The beach looked different in daylight— less magical, more ordinary.

I dropped my head into my hands, angry tears welling up.

You knew the risks and consequences, but you chose to ignore them.

And for what? A pair of stunning blue eyes and sweet promises in the dark? I gave a bitter laugh, the sound swallowed by the crash of waves. I had played with fire, and now could only watch as the life I knew went up in smoke and ashes.

I said all along that something like this would happen. But no, he had to push. If Nathan had listened to me just once, I wouldn't be in this mess. I wouldn't be jobless and facing deportation. My stomach wouldn't be twisting itself in knots with the uncomfortable knowledge that my mother had been right.

Why couldn't he just do as I said?

CHAPTER TWENTY-FOUR

NATHAN

I paced the length of Jackson's beach house patio, phone pressed tightly to my ear. My steps and my heart quickened as Maisy updated me.

"Alright, it's settled then," I said, trying to contain my excitement. "Thank you so much."

I hung up, my fist clenching around the phone and the need to tell Cat buzzing through me. She'd been gone for half an hour, and yes, for a couple of minutes I'd worried about her out in the cold without even a jumper.

But I had a solution!

The effects wouldn't be instant, but I had one.

The sliding glass door opened, and there she was, her face red from the cold and her eyes puffy from tears. My heart twisted.

"It's going to be alright." I hurried over and gathered her hands between mine, rubbing furiously to get some heat back into her. "I've figured everything out."

Cat blinked up at me, confusion mingling with the sadness in her eyes. "What are you talking about?"

"Your job, the photos, all of it." I beamed at her, confident my plan was fool proof. "Don't worry, in a few weeks this will all be behind us."

Cat pulled her hands from mine, anger flashing across her face. "A few weeks? Have you lost your mind?"

She walked out of the kitchen without a second look. I followed.

"My entire world has just fallen apart, and you think you've solved it in a phone call?" She collapsed onto the sofa and dropped her head into her hands.

I hesitated, my smile fading. Clearly I had misjudged the situation. I sat down beside her, reaching out to rub her back.

"I'm just trying to make things right so we can finally stop hiding."

Cat turned to me, eyes blazing. "By doing what, exactly?"

"Remember when Miranda thought I was at that strip club, and it turned out to be my lookalike?" I could see the gears turning in her head as she recalled the incident. "Well, I've found him."

Her head tilted to the side, her eyes narrowed.

She doesn't need your cryptic shit right now, idiot.

"I've hired him to pose as your boyfriend for a few weeks. This way, everyone will think we're not together, and you can get your job back."

Cat blinked at me, lips trembling. "That's your solution? Have someone pretend to be my boyfriend so everyone thinks we're not together?"

*H*ow *could she think so little of me, after everything we had shared?* I slammed a fist into the floor, frustration and self-loathing churning in my gut.

Because you gave her reason to. You failed to understand how much her career meant to her. Your foolish scheme only proved you saw her pain as an obstacle to overcome rather than a battle she had invited you to fight at her side.

In my desperation to fix things I had broken whatever trust remained between us. Cat had opened herself to me in a way she never had with another man. And I had betrayed that vulnerability with callous disregard for her feelings or pride.

I grabbed my phone and scrambled to my feet, hitting dialled on Jackson's number. I paced as it rang.

"This better be important," he growled. "I was in the middle of something."

"I need the code for your wall safe. And I need to borrow something from it. It's urgent."

There was a pause. "You're off yer head. I'm not giving you the code to my safe. What's going on, Nathan?"

I squeezed my eyes shut, guilt and panic warring within me. *I have to make this right.*

"I've made a mistake and I have to make things right before it's too late. Please, Jackson. I'm begging you, as your best friend. Let me borrow the ring."

"The ring..." His sharp inhale told me he understood. "Are you out of your mind? That bleedin' ring is cursed!"

"I have to try. I love her, man. Lending me that ring might just give me a shot at fixing this."

There was a heavy silence. Then a resigned sigh. "You're a fucking numpty. Don't blame me when this all goes to hell!"

Relief washed over me. "Thank you. I owe you one."

I hung up and raced into Jackson's study. I flipped a wall of books back and reached for the safe keypad. My fingers shook as I inputted the code.

The door swung open on silent hinges. The little blue satin box sat tucked into the corner. I grabbed it, heart pounding.

This is madness. I can't propose to fix my mistakes. She'll never accept, not after I hurt her like this.

I started to put the ring back. But something made me hesitate.

You have a chance to prove your love and commitment. Isn't that what she deserves?

My hand closed over the box again. Before I could second-guess myself further, I slipped it into my pocket. I headed upstairs, pulse racing, ready to lay it all on the line and hoping she wouldn't slam the door in my face again.

"Cat? It's me," I called out as I knocked on the bedroom door. "Please, just give me a chance to explain."

My mouth went dry as I waited for her response. There was a pause, and for a second, I worried she'd just ignore me. Then the door flew open.

"What?" Cat snapped.

She stared at me with fire in her reddened eyes. The bed behind her was stripped bare, blankets and pillows in a tangled heap on the floor.

"Are you okay?" I asked, my voice hoarse.

Her gaze drifted over my shoulder as she shrugged, lip trembling. The urge to pull her into my arms was almost more than I could bear.

"I know I hurt you, and I'm so sorry. I never meant for that to happen. You have to believe me, Cat— you're the most important thing in my life. I was just trying to fix things but it was the wrong way."

"Then what's the right way?" she whispered.

I took a deep breath, pulse hammering in my throat, and reached for her hands. "The right way is facing this together, side by side. I want to be there for you every step of the way. I want us to make these decisions together like partners should."

"Is that really what you want?" She blinked, tears shining in her eyes.

I brushed a tear from her cheek. "You're all I want. I can prove that to you, if you'll let me."

I sank down on one knee, gazing up at her with all the love and sincerity in my heart.

"Catrina Sinclair, will you marry me?"

CHAPTER TWENTY-FIVE

CATRINA

"Cat, please say something." Nathan searched my face, brows knitted together.

I stared at him kneeling before me, a riot of emotions warring inside of me. I couldn't process it. Marriage? Now? After everything that had just happened?

It stung, realising this was just another attempt to fix things, as if I were some broken trinket he could patch up.

How dare he?

After everything, how dare he think a ring could make things right!

The pink diamond glinted between his fingers, drawing my attention.

I hate pink.

I swallowed the lump in my throat. "Get up."

He blinked. "What?"

"Get. Up." I bit out each word, ire simmering beneath my skin.

Nathan rose slowly to his feet. "I don't want your money, or a green card, or anything else you're offering to fix me."

"Cat, no, that's not what I—"

"I'm not some doll for you to play with and discard when I become inconvenient!" I shouted. "I had a career, a life of my own. And you took that away without a second thought."

"I know, I—"

"Do you?" I whirled around, rage bubbling over. "Do you have any idea what you've cost me?"

He swallowed hard. "Cat, I never meant—"

"My career!" I shouted, fists clenched at my sides. "Everything I've worked for, gone because of you and your stupidly recognisable face." A pang of guilt stung me, but I forced it away. "Because you care more about your reputation and this damned studio deal than you do about me."

Nathan paled, clearly stunned by my outburst. Good. Let him feel a fraction of the hurt and betrayal raging within me.

"I want my dreams back, Nathan. Not a ring, not empty promises. But you can't give me that, can you?" I drew a shuddering breath, fighting back the sting of tears. "So take your grand gestures and hollow words and leave me alone. We're done here."

"I can fix this. I can give you those things back."

His gaze never left mine. Once it had made me feel cherished. He could have had his pick of women desperate for his attention and he'd wanted me instead.

He chased me.

That had thrilled me once. Now it just made me want to cry that something so wonderful had been reduced to empty gestures.

The fight went out of me and I sagged against the doorframe. "Just go," I whispered.

❄

The next morning, I woke to sunlight filtering through the curtains and the remnants of a headache pounding at my temples. For a few blissful seconds, I couldn't remember why I felt so wretched.

Then it all came flooding back — the photos, losing my job, Nathan's misguided proposal and my fury at having my life torn apart for the sake of his reputation.

I groaned, pulling a pillow over my face. What a mess. I never should have let things get this far. I should have listened to the warnings about actors and their empty promises. Remembered who Nathan really was — just another Hollywood playboy tossing money at his problems.

How could I have been so foolish to believe we shared something real? That this was more than just another role for him to play, more lines to deliver with his charming smile and earnest gaze?

The door creaked open and I sat up, rubbing my temples.

"Cat?" Nathan's voice was soft, cautious. "Can we talk?"

I didn't respond. Couldn't. My throat felt tight, raw from shouting and tears I didn't remember shedding.

The floorboards groaned as he took a step closer. "I know I made a mistake last night." He grimaced. "More than one mistake. But what we have is real. I'm not giving up that easily."

"There's nothing left to give up on. This — us — it was all a fantasy." I clenched my hands into fists, nails biting into my palms. "I got caught up in your charm and lies, let myself believe things that could never be."

Silence. The mattress dipped as he sat down, reaching to gently pry the pillow from my hands. I kept my gaze averted, focused on the rumpled sheets.

"That's not true," Nathan said. "What we shared was real. I have never lied to you about how I feel."

I rubbed my face, headache building behind my eyes.

"You're an actor, Nathan. Lying is what you do. I was just another role for you to play. Did you really think I wouldn't eventually realise the truth?"

He caught my hands in his, ducking his head to meet my eye. "You know that's not how I see you. I know I'm not perfect but you... you're the one thing that makes sense in all this madness. My love for you is the truest, most real part of who I am. I'm begging you not to throw this away because of a mistake."

I shook my head, heart racing as I struggled to ignore the warmth and familiarity of his touch. "It's too late. I'm not going to marry a man who can't respect me or my wishes. I deserve better than that."

"I know you do. But I'm not that guy, I promise you that. I want to build a real future with you by my side. You're it for me, the one I want to wake up next to each morning. I need you to believe in me... in us. "

His eyes searched mine, raw sincerity etched into the lines of his face. I swallowed hard, nausea churning in my gut. *How many times had that same earnest gaze made me trust in dreams that could never come true?*

The damage was done. I steeled myself against the longing building inside and pulled my hands away, wrapping my arms around my knees.

"I can't do this anymore. I want you to leave."

Nathan reeled back as if struck. "Cat, please—"

"Just go!" My voice broke on the words.

He rose slowly to his feet but didn't move to leave, hands clenching at his sides. I refused to look up, fighting to hold onto my resolve as the silence stretched between us, fraught with words left unsaid that might haunt me for lifetimes to come.

❄

I sank into an uncomfortable chair at the gate, avoiding the curious glances of strangers as they passed by. My eyes felt raw and puffy from crying. Anyone who looked closely enough would recognise the signs of grief etched into my features.

How long before someone placed where they had seen my face before, connecting it to the photos of Nathan and I splashed across every gossip site just days ago?

My pulse raced as I glanced around at the crowds milling nearby, waiting to board their flights. Any one of them might at any second make the connection and approach me, eager for details about my sudden break from Hollywood's most eligible bachelor.

I sank lower in my seat, longing for the days of anonymity before charming smiles in low lit cocktail bars had swept me into a world where I never truly belonged.

Escape would be impossible — in LA I would always be defined by the shadow of all of this.

My phone buzzed with an incoming text and I glanced at the screen, grimacing at the name. Sam.

SAM

Hey! Want to grab lunch at the deli next week, catch up on our first day back? I feel like it's been ages.

I sighed, fingers hovering over the keyboard. How could I tell Sam the truth — that there would be no returning to familiar routines or gossiping over sandwiches at our usual table?

CAT

I can't, I'm sorry. I should have called sooner. I'm not coming back to work.

The phone rang in my hands before I could slip it back

into my pocket. I wiped my eyes, sniffling as I answered. "Hello?"

"What's going on? What do you mean you're not coming back?"

"They fired me." The words stuck in my throat, raw as the lingering ache that had become my constant companion. "The partners decided my position was no longer viable after..."

I trailed off, uncertain how to explain the rest without breaking down completely. The line was silent for a beat before Sam responded.

"After what? Don't tell me this is because of those photos with Nathan?"

I couldn't say the words but my silence spoke volumes.

"Those hypocritical bastards. "

Her outrage echoed my own simmering beneath the surface. I blinked back tears, clutching the phone like a lifeline as I struggled to respond.

I sighed, fresh tears welling in my eyes. "I don't know. I guess I should have been more careful but... it's done now. No point arguing about the unfairness of it all."

"Cat, this is unacceptable. You're the best associate they have. They'll be begging you to come back within weeks." She sighed. "Are you at least okay? What are you going to do now?"

I pressed my lips together, struggling to find the words. "I don't know. I hadn't thought that far ahead."

My breath hitched on a sob I couldn't contain and I heard Sam's sharp intake of breath.

"Talk to me. You know I'm always here for you." Her voice softened, filled with concern.

"Everything's just fallen apart." I dashed tears from my cheeks with the back of my hand. "Nathan and I... we had a fight after those photos leaked. I said such awful things, and now I've stranded him in Scotland and taken his rental car..."

I broke down, releasing all the anguish and uncertainty I had bottled up since leaving St Andrews. She listened without judgement, murmuring words of comfort as I poured my heart out to the one person who had always understood me best.

"I feel so lost. My whole world has crumbled around me, and I have no idea where to even start picking up the pieces." I sighed, sagging back into the seat as the tears finally slowed.

"Listen to me," Sam said, voice firm. "You're one of the strongest, smartest women I know. Whatever happens with Nathan, you will get through this. Take some time for yourself, go home and relax. The rest will work itself out, I promise you that."

I clutched the phone tighter. "But what if it doesn't?"

"You can't think like that. Focus on today, on putting one foot in front of the other. The future will still be there waiting when you're ready, and you'll come back stronger and wiser for this. "

I smiled faintly, tension easing from my shoulders. "Thank you, Sam. For always knowing exactly what I need to hear."

"Anytime. Now go catch your flight, go home and get some rest. The world can wait — you need to take care of yourself right now." Then she chuckled. "And you know I'm more than ready to drink the bar dry with you."

I smiled as the line went dead. The ache hadn't cleared, but I could breathe a little for now.

Glancing up at the board, I blinked. Final boarding call for my flight. *Shit.*

CHAPTER TWENTY-SIX

CATRINA

My bedside clock glared at me when I finally dragged myself out of bed. I'd glare too at the sight of me, hair a tangled mess and eyes swollen from another night of tears. A week had passed since returning from Scotland, yet still the ache in my chest refused to fade.

I shuffled into the kitchen and switched on the coffee maker, the familiar gurgling and hiss of brewing java the only sound disturbing the oppressive silence blanketing my apartment. *When did the space I once found cosy become so suffocating?*

A knock at the door startled me from my thoughts. I peeked through the peephole, sighing in relief as Sam's smiling face came into view. At least there was one person left I could still count on.

I unlatched the door and Sam swept inside, wrinkling her nose at the stale air. "When was the last time you opened a window? It smells like heartbreak and despair in here."

"Well you barged in here without calling first," I muttered, irritation warring with gratitude.

Sam shook her head but said nothing.

Instead, she grabbed my coffee mug from the counter and emptied the contents down the sink.

"Hey! I was drinking that."

"Nope. No more wallowing. We're going for a walk."

"I can't go outside looking like this." I pointed at my greasy, tangled hair and blotchy skin.

My protests barely slowed her down. She flung open the curtains and started tidying up my living room. She picked up a leftover container of Chinese food, her nose wrinkling before she dumped it in the bin.

"Wash, dress, now. You've got ten minutes." Sam shoved me toward the bedroom. "You need sunlight and fresh air, stat."

I knew better than to argue when she used that tone. Twenty minutes later, we were strolling through the park near my building, takeout coffees in hand, as she preached the restorative power of vitamin D for emotional angst.

The sun felt warm against my face, lifting my spirits after days of solitude.

Sam squeezed my arm. "That's better, see? Fresh air does wonders for a broken heart."

I took a sip of coffee, still clinging to the remnants of my resistance. "Easy for you to say. You've never had your heart shattered into a million pieces."

"Maybe not, but I know sitting alone in the dark won't fix it. Trust me, sweetie, in situations like these vitamin D is just as important as a tub of ice cream and a bottle of wine."

I couldn't help smiling at her conviction. "So you're prescribing sunshine and positive thinking?"

"Absolutely. The more you isolate yourself the worse you'll feel." Sam steered us onto a walking path lined with bare trees. "Keep your head up. Your life isn't over. There are better things waiting, you just have to open yourself up to finding them."

Her words struck a chord. I sighed, gazing up at the sunlight dappling the path ahead. "I know you're right. It's just hard. It feels like my whole world has been turned upside down."

"I know. But it won't always hurt this much. The pain will fade, and when it does, you'll see there's so much possibility waiting." Sam wrapped an arm around my shoulders in a half hug as we walked. "The future's still unwritten. All you need is the courage to start the next chapter on your own terms."

"Easy for you to say," I muttered from behind my take-away coffee cup. I took a deep drink, draining it.

It felt like my entire world had been turned upside down, leaving me feeling unsteady and unsure about my future.

Sam nudged my arm. "Come on, don't be like that. You know I'm right."

I crumpled the empty cup in my hands. "Do I? Because from where I'm standing my life resembles the inside of this cup — empty, crushed and utterly devoid of hope."

"Cat, stop it." Sam's voice was stern. "Your life isn't over, it's just beginning! So Nathan turned out to be a jerk, so what? There are —"

My heart hurt at her calling Nathan a jerk. Objectively, I knew it hadn't all been his fault and it would be unfair of me to blame him for my life imploding. But I wasn't ready to deal with those thoughts, not yet.

"If you say plenty more fish in the sea," I shrugged her off and stepped away, pointing at her in warning, "I swear to god, I'm leaving."

Sam smirked. I rolled my eyes and crossed my arms, continuing to walk along the path.

She sighed as she followed, linking our arms again. "I know it's hard to imagine now, but this pain won't last forever. You have so many wonderful possibilities awaiting you, if you'd only take those first steps forward."

"My rent needs paying before I can think too much about those possibilities."

Sam shook her head. "Don't change the subject. We're talking about your love life, not your finances."

I hung my head back, gazing up at the cloudless sky like someone up there might be able to save me from myself. Or Sam. Either would work.

"What love life? In case you've forgotten, I no longer have a job or a boyfriend. My so-called possibilities seem rather limited at the moment."

"That's quitter talk." She nudged me, a grin curling her lips. "The Cat I know never lets life's little setbacks keep her down for long. You'll land on your feet, you always do. In the meantime, let's focus on more enjoyable pursuits — like finding you a rebound romance or two."

She winked, eliciting another eye roll from me.

"You're terrible, you know that?"

"I try my best." Sam laughed. "But seriously, promise me you'll start living again? Do something fun this weekend, let your hair down a little. A few carefree flings might be just what the doctor ordered to help mend that broken heart of yours."

I swatted her arm, torn between laughter and exasperation. "The last carefree fling landed me in this mess."

Sam bit her lip, barely containing her amusement. "Yes, that was unfortunate. I clearly need to teach you the meaning of a one-night fling."

I scoffed. "Because your track record with men is so stellar?"

"Ouch." She placed a hand over her heart in mock offence. "Low blow, Cat. My one night fuckups pale in comparison to your Scottish disaster of doom."

"Don't remind me." I sighed, gazing up at the clouds drifting across the vivid blue sky. "I wish I'd never gone rushing off to Edinburgh like an idiot."

Sam squeezed my arm. "Don't beat yourself up. You panicked. We all do stupid things when we panic. The point is you survived."

I grimaced. "Barely. A few tears, public humiliation and the loss of my career won't soon fade from my memory."

"No, but the bruises will heal in time." She steered us to an empty park bench, sitting beside me. "You can't let one relationship disaster convince you to give up on love forever. That's not living, Cat, that's hiding from life!"

I threw up my hands in frustration. "Well what do you suggest I do? Leap straight into the arms of another fling?"

"Of course not." She placed her arm on the back of the bench and leaned back. "All I'm saying is don't close yourself off. Take time to heal, learn from your mistakes, then try again when you've regained perspective. Staying holed up alone will only make you feel worse."

But would it make me feel worse? Would it really? Staying in meant no chance of some stranger, or worse, a photographer, recognising me on the street.

"Let yourself scab over first, but promise me you won't lose hope. There are still amazing times ahead for you, even after this mess, if you'll pick yourself back up and keep moving forward."

"I'll do my best." Despite my misgivings, I appreciated her attempt to pull me out of my funk. I smiled. "As long as I have you to bully me out of any sulking, how could I possibly stay down for long?"

Sam grinned. "You're damn right. Call if you need anything, and remember what I said. This too shall pass. The story's not over yet."

I shook my head at her. "I'll try to keep that in mind."

She chewed her lip, studying me like she had a secret she was ashamed of keeping.

"What is it?"

"If you could find out who took the photos, would you want to know?"

Did I really want to know who had started all this? Whoever had captured those stolen moments had set into motion the chain of events leading to the loss of everything I'd worked so hard to achieve.

"Logically, I should say no. I couldn't do anything with the information, so what would be the point?" I pursed my lips. For a second, I hoped they were suffering as much as I was.

But what good did it do me? Revenge wouldn't change what had happened. It wouldn't fix the past or win back the life I'd had.

Yet curiosity still one out.

"But I'm a masochist, so yeah, I'd want to know."

"It was the intern." My mouth dropped open and Sam nodded. "That was exactly my reaction. The kid seemed so normal, but she didn't turn up for work in January and the office grapevine says she got a payout for the picture."

The intern. Of course, it was. Delivering packages that normally would have waited at the front desk for me. All those compliments and giggles over the flowers and dress Nathan sent, she must have been fishing for details. Watching and waiting for the chance to catch me off guard. How could I have missed the signs?

Sam sighed. "Who turns on the people they work with like that? You just can't tell what's going on in some people's heads."

No, you really couldn't. Not that the reasons behind her betrayal mattered now. The damage was long done, and knowing her name didn't change a thing. She was out of my life as quickly as she'd entered.

Sam's phone buzzed and she frowned at the screen. "Sorry, I have to run. Forgot I made plans." She gave me an apologetic smile. "Will you be okay?"

I waved off her concern. "Of course. Thank you for dragging me out, even if just for a little while."

"Anytime." Sam pulled me into another fierce hug. "Keep your head up!"

With a grin and a wave, she hurried off down the path and out of sight. I took a deep breath of the fresh spring air, feeling lighter than I had in days.

The ache was still there, lurking beneath the surface, but Sam had been right. The wounds would heal.

*T*he next morning, my phone buzzed on the nightstand, Maisy's name flashing on the screen.

My stomach dropped at the sight of her name, a torrent of worries flooding my mind.

What now?

I swiped to answer, pulse quickening.

"Morning, Cat! How're you holding up, hon?" Her warm voice sounded concerned.

I clutched the sheets, throat tightening. "Doing okay, I guess."

A lie, but she didn't need to know that.

"Good to hear. Listen, I've got something important I want to discuss with you. Do you have a minute?"

I sat up, apprehension mingling with curiosity. "Of course, go ahead."

"So here's the thing. My agency's expanding like crazy and we're looking for fresh talent. I immediately thought of you." She paused. "How would you feel about training to become a talent agent?"

I blinked, stunned. "I'm sorry, did you say agent?"

Maisy laughed. "I know, it's out of left field! But hear me out. You've got a razor-sharp mind for business and a way with people. Repping talent isn't so different from legal work.

I'd train you myself, show you the ropes. The job's yours if you want it."

My head spun at the offer, impossibly well-timed. This had Nathan written all over it.

"I'm beyond flattered, but I have to be honest, I don't know the first thing about being a talent agent or working in Hollywood. I don't even pay attention to the gossip unless forced. The industry's a foreign world. I wouldn't know where to begin."

"That's the beauty of it! You'd bring a fresh outlook, and I'd be with you every step. Think about it, okay?" Maisy's tone softened. "This could be exactly the change of pace you need right now. Promise you'll consider it?"

"I don't know what to say." I clenched the phone, panicked at the thought. An agent? Me? "I'm flattered you thought of me, but being an agent... that's just so far outside my realm of experience. I was a lawyer. I have no idea how to even begin navigating entertainment law or wooing clients."

"I know it's a big change, sweetheart, but that's why I'd mentor you so closely." Her voice softened. "You've got a gift for this work, even if you can't see it yet. I've been impressed with you from day one. The way you handled PR for Nathan's last deal, keeping everything on track even under pressure... that's the mark of someone with talent for this business."

Could I really be praised for keeping the deal on track when my lack of self-control had tanked the entire thing?

Still, I sucked in a breath, stunned that the idea appealed to me. But surely it was too good to be real — it had to be Nathan pulling the strings.

"Please don't take this the wrong way, but did Nathan put you up to this?"

She sighed. "I know how it looks, and why you'd be suspicious. But I'm seriously offering you a job and it has nothing to do with Nathan. "

I bit my lip, torn between hope and doubt. "It's a generous

offer, truly. I just need time. My life's been turned inside out and I have to be realistic. I'm not in any state to make major decisions right now." I took a shaky breath. "Could we revisit this in a few weeks?"

"Of course, I understand." Her tone softened. "Take all the time you need. The position will still be here when you're ready."

I squeezed my eyes shut in relief. "Thank you. I appreciate your patience, and the opportunity. I just..."

"You need to make sure it's the right move. I get it." She sighed. "Well you know where to find me when you've regained your footing. And Cat?"

"Yes?"

"Keep your head up, hon. The pain fades, and there are brighter days ahead. Just remember that."

CHAPTER TWENTY-SEVEN

NATHAN

The pounding on my front door echoed through the silent house, rattling my skull. I peered out from under the duvet, wincing at the sunlight streaming through the open curtains. *How long had I been in this bloody bed?*

I didn't want to think about it.

For the first couple of days, my phone had rung non-stop. My agent. My friends. The blasted attorney they'd assigned to replace Cat. *As if anyone ever could.*

When the screen finally went dark, I was relieved.

Blissful silence consumed my house. Just me and my razor sharp thoughts. Exactly what I deserved.

The banging continued, accompanied by Jackson's voice. "Nathan, open this door before I kick it down!"

Groaning, I dragged myself out of bed and down the hallway, dawdling as much as I could. When I opened the front door, Jackson and Finn brushed past me, arms laden with cases of beer.

"Next time you decide to go off the rails, how's about you

give us a key?" Finn shouted over his shoulder as he made his way into the living room. "It's only fair. You've got keys to all of our houses."

Jackson clapped me on the shoulder, a grim expression on his face. "You look like hell."

What state did he expect to find me?

I scowled at him. "Thanks. I'll get right on fixing that."

He shook his head, but amusement shone in his grey eyes. "Glad to see you've still got some bite left in you."

"What the hell is that supposed to mean?" I asked as Jackson guided me into the living room.

Jackson ignored me and joined Finn in staring at the tip my living room had turned into. My carefully controlled diet went out the window within hours of getting home. Really, it never came back. Takeaway containers and empty beer bottles covered every surface. Clothes lay strewn across the sofa.

They wrinkled their noses at the mess and, honestly, I couldn't blame them.

"When's the last time you cleaned in here?" Finn asked. "Or showered, for that matter?"

"We brought supplies, but this is going to need an army to fix." Jackson set the beer on the counter. "We'll call in reinforcements."

"Jesus, you stink." Finn pulled out his phone as he eyed me with something akin to horror. "Was I this bad when Abi left me?"

Jackson and I stared at Finn, our expression hardening. "Yes," we muttered together.

"Christ." Finn winced. "Go get cleaned up. I can't look at you without seeing my weak ass in your place."

Bemused, I turned away from them and trudged down the corridor, awed by the first glimmer of happiness I'd felt in a week. I sunk into a pit of numb despair before we'd even gotten on the plane back to LA.

By the time I returned, my friends had forced open the curtains, thrown the clothes off the sofa and were sprawled on the sofa.

Jackson shoved a beer at me. "Sit down before you fall down."

I sank into a chair and chugged half the bottle. They had spent hours comforting my sorry ass on that flight home. They deserved sainthood for still being here. Not that I said much in return.

Finn studied me, shaking his head. "You have to stop this. We're not leaving you to waste away."

"I hate seeing you like this." Jackson's gaze roamed down my now crease free clothing, but evidently fresh clothes couldn't hide the pain eating at my insides.

"Then you shouldn't have come, should you?" The words came out harsher than intended. I raked a hand through my damp hair with a sigh. "Look, I know you mean well. But I just... I need time. "

Jackson leaned forward, clutching his beer. "What happened with Cat? You've barely said two words since Scotland."

I scrubbed a hand over my face and sighed. "I made a mess of everything, as usual."

"How?" Jackson's brows furrowed. "By proposing? I told you that fucking ring was cursed, but would you listen? Of course not."

"It wasn't the ring. How I went about it…" A harsh laugh escaped me. "Fuck, it was all wrong. Those photos leaked, she lost her job... I panicked." I covered my face, groaning into my hands. "I don't know, I thought if I could find a solution to take the heat off her, it would help."

"What did you do, Nate?" Finn asked, his tone wary.

I dropped my hands and stared at him. Not even six months ago, our positions had been reversed. At the time, I thought he'd overreacted. How could he possibly fall in love with a woman he'd been forced to marry for a TV show and in such a short period of time?

Yet, here I sat. I'd given her my heart almost instantly, and I would have married her. All she had to do was ask, and I would have given her absolutely anything she wanted.

"I hired a lookalike to pretend he was in the photo with her."

Jackson and Finn stared at me, identical looks of horror spreading across their faces.

"Yeah, that's how she reacted too." I shook my head. "When she found out... she hated the idea. Then when I saw it all going wrong, I thought proposing might make it right." My laugh sounded wrong, hollow. "You can imagine how that went."

"No wonder she's upset," Finn muttered.

"Upset is an understatement." I stared into my beer. "She lost her job. She's probably going to be deported." Saying the words aloud made the reality hit home.

"You have to talk to her, mate," Jackson said, his tone surprisingly earnest for the true playboy of the group. "Apologise, do whatever it takes. Tell her you'll make this right."

I scrubbed a hand through my hair. "I hurt her... how the bloody hell do I come back from that? An apology won't stop her deportation or get her job back."

"At least she'll know you're sincere," Finn said. "That you realise your mistake."

I sighed. "What difference will that make? The damage is already done."

My friends fell silent, unable to argue. They were only trying to help, but unlike with Finn's fuck up, this wasn't about communication. I'd made my feelings for Cat perfectly clear. They didn't stop me fucking up.

As we worked our way through the case of beer, I recounted everything that happened in Scotland. With each word the ache inside me grew, the fear cementing that too much damage had been done.

"Right. Stop. Enough dwelling," Finn interrupted me, his head falling back against the sofa. "We'll figure out a way to get her back, but nothing's instant, and you can't waste away locked in this house."

Jackson nodded, but winced. "Finn's right, and you know how much I hate to admit that shit."

"I don't know why you'd hate to admit it, I'm always right." Finn frowned at him before fixing me with stubborn eyes. "You need to stop acting like a right eejit and focus on business."

I raised a brow. "And how exactly do you propose I do that?"

"Starting that production company we've always talked about," Jackson said. "So what if the Starlight Studio deal fell apart? I don't know why you were wasting your time buying it in the first place." Jackson held up his hand. "Of course, I know *why*, but it doesn't matter. It's history, Nate. A relic of our past. We never talked about preserving history, we talked about changing it."

"What Jackson's trying to say is we should get our production company up and running." Finn shrugged. "Give you something else to focus on and take your mind off this mess."

I snorted. "A new business venture is your solution?"

"Why not?" Finn asked. "I assume buying the studio was meant to be the first step."

"If he'd talked to us before he started, we'd be a lot further along," Jackson grumbled.

Finn shot him a hard look and Jackson snapped his mouth shut.

"We've been talking about it for years," Finn continued, getting more excited with each second. "I know you were already drawing up ideas for projects. There's no reason we can't bring that to life with our own production company. It'll be a hell of a lot easier to get off the ground than a studio anyway. It's the perfect distraction."

I stared at my beer, turmoil warring inside me. They weren't wrong. The idea had always energised me... until now. We had dreamed of having our own studio, making the kinds of films we wanted without some executive interfering.

"You need to do this." Finn pressed. "Sitting here dwelling on what you can't change won't help. But launching our company — that's productive. Do something to get your mind off everything else."

I sighed. "Easier said than done. My head's not in the right place for business deals."

"More reason this is exactly what you need," Jackson said. "Focus on the details, the planning. It'll shift your mind from other things, give you a sense of purpose for a little while."

Jackson's words echoed my own thoughts. A new project, something tangible to work towards, might provide the distraction I needed from the wreckage of my personal life.

And a studio had been a dream we had shared for years over pints at the pub.

"Alright," I said after a long moment. "Let's do it."

My friends exchanged a glance, then broad grins broke out.

"Now you're talking!" Finn lifted his beer in salute. "To new beginnings."

"To chasing dreams at last," Jackson added.

I managed a smile, lifting my bottle to join the toast. Their enthusiasm was contagious, awakening a spark of anticipation after days filled with dread.

We launched into a discussion of logistics, from funding to equipment to possible projects. Familiar banter filled the room as options and ideas were debated, each outlandish suggestion eliciting laughter. Pursuing this new path was the right choice, a chance to fulfil a dream.

Why should you get to live your dreams when you've killed Cat's?

The question rattled through my mind as Finn and Jackson discussed logistics, their enthusiasm awakening a spark of anticipation. But doubt lingered, a sense of betrayal I could not shake. Cat's own dreams had been shattered because of me, and now I dared pursue my own?

"Earth to Nathan." Fingers clicked in front of my eyes. "Are you listening or what?" Jackson asked. His concerned face hovered inches from mine.

"I'm fine." I pushed him away and slouched down in my seat.

"I'm glad you're fine, but I'm more pleased that you're on board with our first project being a risqué adaptation of The Great Gatsby." Jackson smirked as he backed away.

"A what?"

"So that's a no to listening." Finn chuckled. "He's joking, jackass. Pay attention."

I stared over Finn's shoulder, my gaze fixed on the entryway where I had kissed Cat breathless just a few weeks ago. A hollow ache filled my chest at the thought of never feeling the brush of her soft lips against mine.

The guys sighed when I didn't respond.

"You're thinking about Cat again, aren't you?" Finn asked, rubbing at his eyes. "I can't stop thinking about it." I dragged a hand through my hair. "I fucked up and I don't know how to fix it, how to make it up to her, how to help her. It's all a mess and I miss her."

Finn leaned forward, understanding blanketing his face. "I know you do. But you can't change the past. You can only learn from it and try to make things right going forward."

"You need to prove you're not the playboy she accused you of being." Jackson leaned forward, elbows on his knees.

"And how do you propose I do that?" I asked. "I haven't a bloody clue where to even start."

"For starters, stop with the self-pity." Finn shook his empty beer bottle, frowning at it. As he got up, he continued,

"Remember the man she fell for. Not the one we had to peel off the tarmac a week ago."

"Remember what you told us about her?" Jackson asked. "How she saw through your shit, kept you on your toes?"

"What will remembering that do to help me?" I dragged a hand across my face, barely biting back my irritation. "She's gone and she definitely won't care about her effect on me."

"Only if you give up." Finn said, handing me another beer. "That's not the Nathan I know. You go after what you want and you don't stop until it's yours. So stop reacting without thinking and make a plan!"

I stared at the unopened beer bottle, wishing it were that simple.

"She'll never forgive me."

"How will you know unless you try?" Jackson asked. "At least remind her of the man who pursued her even when it wasn't easy."

"An apology won't be enough." I sighed. "How do I fix what I did? Make her see I understand why she's so angry?"

"Do you actually understand?" Jackson asked.

I stared at him. Of course I understood. How could I not? I'd witnessed Cat's devastation first-hand.

"Fucking hell. When did I become the woman whisperer?" Jackson shook his head.

"What are you talking about?"

Both of them stared at me, mouths a jar.

"This specimen in a cage game is getting old real fast." I shoved myself out of the chair. "What the fuck are you two trying to say?"

"For one, stop talking about fixing it," Finn muttered, shaking his head at me. "That's what got you here to begin with."

"Then what do you suggest?" I paced around the sofa, hands in my hair. "I could get her a new job, cover her rent until she's back on her feet. Hell, I could probably fix her visa issues too, but she won't care about any of that."

"Of course, she won't," Jackson muttered. "Your usual tricks won't help. You need to show her through actions — meaningful ones— that you understand why she left and you're genuinely remorseful."

I scrubbed a hand over my face, shoulders slumping. "Great. But I don't know how to do that."

"You could always try bleeding listening." Finn leaned forward, elbows on his knees. "If I steamrolled over Abi the way you did Cat, I'd have been served divorce papers by now. You need to understand her needs and priorities rather than what you think they should be."

I winced. "Now you're getting it." Jackson leaned back on the sofa, tipping his bottle in salute. "This won't be won with grand gestures."

I let out a long breath, steadied by the certainty in their voices. How had I been so bloody blind for so long? I didn't know if I could ever get Cat back. But for her — for us — I had to try.

"She needs to know I understand." I stared at the table, guilt and fear warring inside me. "Why she left, why she was so angry. How I took away the one thing she loved."

Finn studied me. "And how will you show her that?"

The answer was simple, though the work would be hard. I lifted my gaze to meet theirs.

"By being the man she deserved all along."

A smile tugged at Jackson's lips. "There's the Nathan we know."

CHAPTER TWENTY-EIGHT

CATRINA

No matter how many resumes I sent out or how many contacts I harassed, I couldn't get an interview for another associate position. With limited options and rent due, I lasted two weeks before I caved and accepted Maisy's offer.

With February right around the corner, life was starting to feel more in my control. I hadn't cried myself to sleep in a week or got lost daydreaming about what might have been had I held strong and waited until the Starlight Studio deal finalised.

I could almost pretend the hollow feeling in my chest didn't exist.

Then I made the mistake of turning on the TV.

Nathan's smiling face stared back at me through a collection of stills and live footage.

He looked as handsome as ever, on the red carpet of some award show, dressed in an expensive tuxedo with his hair perfectly styled.

Business as usual.

"This has to be a first, Michael. Nathan Logan never walks the carpet alone."

"That's true. He's usually got his arm wrapped around some lucky lady, but not tonight."

The camera zoomed in on Nathan as he waved to a group of photographers and began walking up the stairs.

"Any idea why he's not bringing along a plus one this year?"

No way was he actually alone.

The shot changed and my gaze remained riveted to the TV. A glutton for punishment.

Nathan stopped next to a red-haired reporter with a big branded microphone. His typical charming smile remained firmly in place even as she brushed against him.

"Nathan, everyone's surprised to see you flying solo tonight." The redhead batted her lashes at him, a coy smile curving her lips.

The sight of her cosying up to Nathan inexplicably irritated me.

He's not yours.

I knew that, but it didn't stop the acidic feeling in my stomach.

"I'm just trying something a little different, Myka."

"Oh really?" she asked, dragging the words out while excitement flickered across her expression. "Do you have a special lady to share with us?"

Nathan shrugged, flashing that wicked smile of his. "There's someone I'm hoping to reconcile with, if she'll have me."

"I hate to speculate," she said and I couldn't help but snort.

All people like her did was speculate. The entire bloody entertainment industry thrived on gossip.

"That wouldn't be the woman you were pictured with in Edinburgh, would it?"

Nathan stared at her, his lips firmly pressed together.

"You two did look rather cosy."

Nathan's jaw tensed. "My personal life is private."

Myka held up her hands in surrender, though her grin said she was enjoying provoking him. "Message received. Well, we'll all be watching closely to see if this mystery woman makes another appearance by your side."

"I'd expect nothing less." Nathan stared directly into the camera for a beat too long before striding off without another word.

For a second, I sat frozen, staring at the TV, questioning whether I'd imagined it. Then my cell rang jarring me. I scrambled for the device and answered immediately after seeing Maisy's name.

"Well?" Maisy prompted. "Anything you want to confess?"

I groaned. "Why did he have to do that? Now the entire world will be speculating about his 'mystery woman'."

"You have to admit, it was a clever way to get your attention." I could hear the smile in Maisy's voice.

"It's a publicity stunt, and you know it." Even as I said the words, they rang hollow.

"Honey, I orchestrate all of his publicity stunts. That wasn't one of them."

The next morning, I choked on my coffee over the entertainment headlines.

Nathan Logan Launches Production Company, Adapting Indie Romance Novel.

My eyes flew down the page — the novel in question was none other than my favourite, *Beautiful Lies*.

I jabbed at the screen, hoping I was seeing things, that it was a misprint. Anything but what it appeared to be.

Picking your favourite book isn't a coincidence.

"Fucking sneaky men and their ulterior bloody motives."

I scrambled out of my chair and rushed down the corridor, muttering to myself all the while as I scrolled.

"Have you seen this?" I asked Maisy as I barged into her office. Stopping in my tracks, my eyes narrowed on her. "What am I saying? You're his agent. Of course you knew"

Maisy tilted her head, eying me with barely concealed amusement. "I'm going to need you to elaborate."

"Did you know about this?" I showed her the headline, practically throwing myself over her desk. "It's a joke, right? He's not really adapting *Beautiful Lies*?"

It had to be.

"It's not a joke," Maisy said, slamming the lid on that barely inflated hope.

I sank into the chair opposite her, staring at the headline in disbelief. "Why that book? Why now?"

Maisy shrugged. "You'll have to ask Nathan."

I shook my head vehemently. "There's no way I'm asking him anything. This is just another stunt to provoke a reaction, and I refuse to give him the satisfaction."

Maisy sighed. "I know you want to believe that, but do you really think it's true?" She nodded at the black-screened device in my hand. "Nathan could have chosen any well-known property for his first adaptation. Picking your favourite, *obscure*, romance novel seems an odd choice for a publicity stunt, don't you think?"

I frowned, scrambling for a rational explanation that wouldn't come. As much as I hated to admit it, Maisy had a point.

"Maybe this is another of his attempts to get your attention?" Maisy suggested gently. "To show you he remembers the little details?"

I shook my head, though her words struck a chord deep within me. "He's hurt me before. I can't go through that again."

"I know." Maisy smiled. "And no one would blame you for walking away. But it seems to me Nathan is at least trying to make things right, in his own way. Whether or not you give him another chance is up to you."

A few weeks later, I stumbled upon the casting announcements for *Beautiful Lies* plastered across entertainment sites and tabloids alike. Nathan had taken major risks, casting virtual unknowns in lead roles and bringing in revered West End theatre actors not typically seen on screen. He was making good on his promise to chase meaningful stories and talent outside the usual Hollywood fare.

I smiled, remembering his passion as he spoke about the project that night on the beach. This adaptation of *Beautiful Lies* was a labour of love for him, not just another blockbuster vehicle. And from these casting choices, it seemed he was intent on doing Paula Dombrowiak's story justice.

Of course, the tabloids cared little for Nathan's artistic vision. They were fixated on why he seemed perpetually alone at events, citing a "special someone" he longed to win back.

A few even dug up old photos of us in Edinburgh, proclaiming I was the mystery woman who still held his heart.

Old Flame in Scotland Still On Logan's Mind?

"More speculation about you and Nathan, I see."

Maisy watched me, two coffees in hand. She set one on my desk and nodded at the gossip sites open on my screen.

I shrugged, feigning nonchalance. "You know how they are. Always chasing stories where there are none."

She made a sceptical noise, seating herself across from me. "Yet Nathan remains alone, keeps refusing offers of strategic pairings, and the press keep noticing. A coincidence, I'm sure."

I bit my lip, staring into my coffee. She was right — if Nathan wanted to be seen with someone new, he easily could. His continuing solitariness spoke volumes, whether I wanted to admit it or not.

"He's trying, you know." Maisy sighed. "I've never seen Nathan work so hard on a project. This film means everything to him because the story means everything to you."

I shook my head vehemently. "A film doesn't change anything, Mais. It doesn't undo the past or give me back what I lost."

"No, it doesn't." She chewed her lip as she studied me. "But the effort and care behind it should mean something, Cat. Nathan loves you. Anyone with eyes can see that."

I scoffed, even as my traitorous heart skipped a beat. "Loves me so much he didn't even bother asking me what I wanted, and steamrolled over me in an attempt to protect himself, you mean?"

"You don't still believe that, do you?"

When I just stared at her, my lips firmly sealed, she sighed.

"People make mistakes and they learn from them." Maisy reached over and squeezed my hand. "How will you know if he's learned if you don't talk to him?"

I sighed, shaking my head. "I don't know if that's a good idea."

She frowned. "I understand your hesitation, Cat. But avoiding Nathan won't provide closure, and living with regret is difficult. Perhaps starting with a conversation, in person or on the phone, might help give you clarity."

Her words resonated within me, though my doubts remained. Did I really want clarity, if it meant reopening old wounds?

She squeezed my hand reassuringly. "Whatever you decide, I support you fully. But you deserve to find happiness again, Cat, however that may come about."

NATHAN

I'm still waiting.

*J*couldn't stop staring at those three simple words. They shouldn't have hit me with a pang of regret, but my throat closed up all the same, even a day after the text arrived.

Only last month, Maisy had put this persuasive idea in my head that things weren't as they seemed. I couldn't shake it. The thought that there were a multitude of actions behind one incident kept digging and digging until all I wanted to do was study my every moment with Nathan. Every gift, every softly spoken word, every careful touch.

For the last month every manner of solo picture had filled my feed. Nathan at galas, premieres, award shows, industry parties and more without a woman on his arm. With each interview, he pushed the speculation over his pining status harder and harder. He ate at my favourite restaurant, ice cream shop, coffee shop…. The list went on.

Each time, he took great care to ensure he'd be photographed. His media presence had exploded since St Andrews. A stark contrast to the man who'd done everything in his power to avoid being papped.

Why is he doing it?

"Everything okay?" Maisy paused by my desk, brows furrowed in concern.

I forced a sunny smile, tucking my phone away. "All good, thanks for checking."

She studied me for a second, seeing far more than I wanted. Her expression softened with understanding. "Want to go grab some lunch? There's a new place just opened down the street and they've got the best tacos."

"Sounds great." I nodded, grabbing my handbag.

Maisy looped her arm through mine as we made our way out of the building, her calm chatter soothing but no competition for the doubts swirling inside my mind.

I'd been with Maisy's agency for nearly two months now and the more I learnt the more I realised how unhappy I actually was at the firm. All I'd ever wanted was for someone to appreciate the effort I put into my work. To feel like we were a team. Instead, I got empty platitudes and constant competition.

With Maisy, things were different. She wanted me to succeed in all senses and not just because it reflected on her as my boss.

Maybe Nathan did you a favour…

The instinctive need to reject the idea jarred against the energised feeling I went home with each day. Our relationship had caused me a lot of devastation, but I could logically admit that my career change was no longer a part of that.

But did he actually mean it? Was he truly still waiting? I'd always thought someone like him would lose interest in me and move on. All of the press surrounding him belied that, and if I were to believe Maisy…

"Those must be some deep thoughts, Cat." She held the door for the restaurant open and flashed a smile that never failed to loosen my lips. "Want to talk about it?"

I sighed, following her into the bustling restaurant. "It's nothing. Just work stuff."

She gave me a knowing look as we slid into our seats. "I know that look. What's troubling you?"

I grimaced, avoiding her gaze. Her perception could be inconvenient at times. "Nathan texted again. I don't know what to make of it."

Maisy nodded, her expression kind. "This situation isn't easy, I know. But it seems he's trying to make things right. What's stopping you reaching out and asking him to explain himself?"

I shrugged, picking at the menu. "The last time we talked, it didn't end well. What if I don't like what I hear?"

"Would you rather spend your days guessing at his intentions?" Maisy countered gently. "The man knows how to do cryptic, honey. He can keep this up for months." She shook her head and picked up her menu. "You've come so far. Don't you owe it to yourself to gain closure once and for all?"

I sighed, staring out at the busy street. "I'm scared I guess."

"Of what?"

"Getting hurt again. Reading more into his hints than he intends." I chewed my lip as I scanned the taco offerings. "What if I give him a chance and we just end up repeating the same cycle again?"

Maisy smirked. "Well, we don't have any rules against you dating another agent's clients, so there'll be no secret relationship funny business and you won't have to worry about keeping it from me."

I chuckled at her joking tone, my shoulders easing. At least I wouldn't need to navigate that complication ever again.

Her expression softened. "You can't avoid risks forever. And, you know, there's one way to get answers to his cryptic hints."

"What's that?"

"Talking to him, really talking, might provide the clarity

you both need. If it goes well, wonderful. If not, at least you'll have answers."

I sighed, staring down at the table. "Do you really think he just wants to talk?"

"Knowing Nathan, definitely not." She chuckled. "But the man would be thrilled if you gave him ten minutes. He's not subtle and he's clearly not ready to move on."

I frowned. "What makes you say that?"

"Aside from all the hints?" Her brows rose and then she shrugged. "Call it intuition." A familiar mischievous glint lit her eyes. "He went solo to Finn's vow renewal, you know. He never goes to functions without a date."

"He went to Shaun's wedding alone."

Her brows rose as she fixed her severe gaze on me. "Why wouldn't he when in his mind he was dating you?"

I opened my mouth, then shut it again. No response I could summon seemed sufficient. After all this time, Nathan never gave up. He'd waited like it was just another bump in the road, sure I'd come back eventually.

While I got lost in my thoughts, we ordered our meals, deciding to share a mixed tray. No matter how I diced it, I couldn't argue with her logic, as much as I wanted to. Everything pointed to a man unwilling to let go, though whether from stubbornness or deeper feeling I couldn't be sure.

Maisy patted my hand, her expression kind but firm. "Stop hiding behind the past. You know as well as I do he's yours if you want him. Now it's up to you — will you close the door for good, or take a chance on happiness again?" Her expression hardened. "And for the love of god, choose fast. It may screw up sometimes but he doesn't deserve to be strung along."

Her words struck deep. As much as she supported me, she wouldn't coddle me or tell me what I wanted to hear. She saw the truth, even when I refused to face it.

I sighed, picking at my taco. "I don't know if I can trust

him again. So much has gone wrong, what if we've learnt nothing and just end up hurt all over again?"

"If he'd learnt nothing, honey, he would have made some grand gesture and tried to sweep the whole thing under the rug." Maisy canted her head considering me with far too much understanding. "He would have turned up at your door, old school boom box in hand and made a nuisance of himself. Don't tell me you haven't been on tenterhooks for months waiting for it. I won't believe you."

I grimaced, unable to deny it. "Maybe. But he didn't, did he?"

Maisy nodded, a knowing smile curving her lips. "Exactly. He's taking his time, letting you see he means it. This isn't some flash in the pan for him."

She had a point. Nathan didn't do half measures. I knew far too well that when he wanted something, he pursued it with a single-minded determination that knew no bounds. The fact he was keeping his distance, letting me come to terms with things in my own time, spoke volumes.

Maisy sighed, fixing me with a piercing look. "I know he hurt you, and it's not easy to forget. But people make mistakes. The question is, do you think what you share is worth fighting for?"

I stared down at the table, memories flickering through my mind.

We'd had something rare, a partnership and passion that couldn't be faked or replicated.

After a long moment, I met Maisy's patient gaze. "Yes, I think it is. But that doesn't make trusting him again any easier."

She nodded, expression kind. "Of course not. Love is never without risks. But you'll never know unless you try — and if you don't, you may live to regret walking away from something real."

CHAPTER TWENTY-NINE

NATHAN

*M*y phone buzzed just as Finn launched into another impassioned speech about lens filters. I glanced at the screen, heart skipping when I saw Cat's name.

"Sorry, got to take this." I stood, accepting the call immediately, not caring what they overheard. "Cat? Everything alright?"

There was a pause, and for a second I worried she might hang up. Then her voice came through, soft but steady. "Uh hi. I hope I'm not interrupting anything important."

I chuckled, running a hand through my hair. "Nothing that can't wait." The guys' brows shot up, their attention zeroing on me with a rabid focus. "How are you?" The question felt woefully inadequate, but I didn't know where else to start.

The fact she called was good. Right? I'd been dropping hints anywhere I possibly could, doing more interviews than ever before, getting "caught out" by the paps in the most mundane of places. It had been months since our fledgling relationship exploded in Scotland.

The longer I went without so much as a text from Cat, the more I questioned whether she'd seen any of it. I tried to get a firm grip on the hope fluttering in my chest while I waited for her response.

Walking to the massive windows running along the back of my open plan living space, I turned my back on my friends, leaving Finn and Jackson to their own devices, lounging on my sofas and eavesdropping like the gossips they pretended not to be.

"I'm doing okay, thanks." Another pause, and then she sighed. "Adjusting slowly to all the changes."

I smiled, relief washing through me that she'd landed on her feet. Guilt quickly chased it away. *You're the reason she had to land on her feet, dickhead.*

"How's working for Maisy going? She's not working you too hard I hope."

Cat's warm laugh came through the line, soothing the last of my worries. "Maisy's great actually. We've become good friends."

It made me happy that they'd developed a closer relation-ship, though it also solved a mystery that had plagued me for the last few months. When I first decided to work at winning Cat back, Maisy refused to offer any help or advice. At the time I couldn't understand why, but it all made sense now.

Of course, I'd known she'd taken Cat on as her new agent in training, but I thought she'd at least advise me like she always had before. Instead, she shut me down any time I tried to turn our catch up calls to Cat.

"Is that so? Well, you're working for the best."

"Uh huh. She's been really supportive through all the changes. I'm lucky to have her as a mentor." Cat's voice held a smile I could see perfectly in my mind.

An awkward silence descended, both of us grasping for

what to say next. I scrubbed a hand through my hair, clearing my throat. "So, how have you been otherwise? Keeping busy I expect, with the new job and all."

"Yeah, busy is an understatement." Cat sighed, a wry note entering her tone. "Learning the ropes of being an agent is challenging, but fulfilling. How's your new production company going? Have you started working on the first script yet?"

I rubbed the back of my neck, unable to keep the smile from my voice. "Going well. We just got the first draft of the script actually. Still a ways off from filming, but it's progress."

"That's great to hear. What's the first film you're adapting? Anything I might have read?"

I bit back a chuckle.

"No need to be coy. We both know I only have the rights to one story you care about seeing on the big screen. Do you really think I could forget your favourite book?"

Her sharp inhale echoed through the line, a silent concession that her game was up. "Why did you really choose that story, Nathan? The truth now, no more games."

I smiled, heart racing. The time for hints and evasions was over. She deserved the truth, and I could only pray she was ready to hear it.

"I optioned your favourite book hoping it would show you the truth: that every tiny detail of you matters to me. You've always been my heart, even after you walked away. I'm not the careless bastard you thought I was. I built this company to succeed on my own terms — but now I'm here to use every resource to fix what I lost."

"You really mean it, don't you? All those hints in the press…"

I smiled, a wave of relief washing over me at the confirmation that she had seen it all.

"I do. I know I have a hell of a long way to go to earn back your trust. The way I handled things that last day…

None of it was right. I was so desperate to fix my mistakes, I only made things worse."

"That's putting it mildly. Hiring someone to pretend to date me, Nathan? Seriously?"

I cringed, scrubbing a hand over my face. "I know. It was idiotic. I thought if the press saw you with my lookalike, they'd back off and your bosses would have had to keep you. But I didn't stop to consider how it might actually make you feel."

"No, you didn't." Cat sighed. "You never were very good at thinking things through." She hesitated, her voice softening. "But you meant well, misguided as it was. You were only trying to protect me, even if you went about it the wrong way."

I hated that she even needed to say something like that to me. I should have never gotten us into the situation to begin with. If I'd just been patient…

"The proposal was misguided. I thought putting a ring on your finger would solve everything, instead of actually supporting you through it."

"A ring doesn't replace trust. You didn't include me in big choices, just bossed me around when my life was falling apart." She hesitated, sniffling slightly on the other end of the line. "If we'd acted like a team… maybe it'd be different. But you always had to be in control."

"You're right. I was selfish and controlling, and it wrecked everything." I scrubbed a hand over my face. How ironic that we started with me calling her the control freak. "Give me one more shot, and I'll do better. No more going it alone. This time we're partners, win or lose." I hesitated, pulse racing. "If you'll have me."

The line went silent. Scared I'd blown it, I waited for her to speak.

"I just don't know, Nathan," she said eventually, her voice was barely a whisper. "So much has changed, and it still hurts like hell. You make big promises, but how do I know you'll follow through?"

My throat tightened at the doubt in her tone. "You're right, you can't know for sure. Not yet. I'm just asking for a chance to start making things right, for as long as it takes."

"I have to think about it. So much has happened…"

I scrubbed a hand over my face, my gaze fixed on the darkening skyline beyond my patio. "You need time, I understand. Take all that you need. I meant what I said — my heart's not going anywhere."

A shaky breath echoed down the line. "We should end this call. It's getting late, and tomorrow's a busy day."

My chest clenched at her words, even as I knew she was right. "Of course. Goodnight, Icy."

Her reply was soft, almost a whisper. "Goodnight, Nathan."

The line went dead, Cat's parting words hanging heavy in the silence. She hadn't refused me outright but hearing the doubt and distance in her tone, I knew I still had a battle ahead. Winning her trust and her heart wouldn't happen overnight. All I could do was use this chance I'd been given to show I meant every word.

I walked back to the guys and sank onto the sofa with a sigh, rubbing my watery eyes. When I looked up, my friends eyed me with concern. Probably expecting to see me break down again.

Finn cleared his throat. "You alright, mate?"

I offered a weak smile and a shrug. "Not sure yet. But she called, that's something, right?"

"It's a start," Shaun said. "The fact she's willing to talk is promising."

Their support buoyed my flagging spirits. I nodded, managing a wry grin. "Just have to pray I don't screw it up this time."

Finn clapped my shoulder with a chuckle. "Not a chance.

You're in too deep to mess this up again." His smile faded, gaze sobering. "You really love her, don't you?"

I sighed, nodding. "More than anything. I just have to show her that hasn't changed."

Jackson grinned. "And you will. Cat would be mad not to take you back after the media circus you've caused." The guys laughed, breaking the tension.

I laughed along with them, the tightness easing in my chest. Tomorrow everything could change, but just now, possibility hung in the air. Cat might never be mine again... or she might. And that uncertainty was enough to keep me fighting for the future I wanted.

CHAPTER THIRTY

CATRINA

hen I walked into work the next day, I was certain of one thing: I wanted Nathan back.

We were messy, our start had been complicated and I wasn't entirely sure our second go round wouldn't end in a train wreck. But after hearing him lay out his mistakes last night, I couldn't let fear hold me back.

He hadn't.

He'd thrown himself at the mercy of the press to get my attention. While words and gestures couldn't guarantee a smooth future for us, would I really want it to be plain sailing?

At some point, I had to face the fact that I'd fallen in love with an A-list actor and his celebrity status would follow us, whether I liked it or not.

We would be photographed unexpectedly. As much as we kept our private lives private, people would share our secrets with the world. Some weirdo may even steal my underwear — *God, I hope not.*

But after months without him, I couldn't let those things

or the fallout of a forbidden relationship we had both chosen to fall into, keep us apart.

So what did I intend to do about it?

"Maisy, I need your help." I walked into her office, puffing from a swift jog up the stairs.

She glanced up from her desk, her brows climbing but a smirk quickly curving her lips.

"Oh, this is going to be good."

NATHAN

The sedan glided to a stop and flashes immediately started popping outside my window.

"Just a minute," I said to the driver.

I stayed where I was, the din of the crowd muffled by the vehicle's walls. Three months I'd faced these circuses alone. I'd been to countless events like this one, but tonight... Talking to Cat last night and getting close again just reminded me how lonely I was without her.

The roar and energy of the crowd, the buzz I usually got walking the carpet evaporated at the thought of facing it without Cat tonight.

Eventually my driver would rap at the window, breaking into my thoughts to ask if I planned to make an appearance or needed a calendar reminder for why I was supposed to be here. The noise levels intensified. The vultures got impatient as they circled, hungry for a story, while I was starving for an escape from being the centre of attention.

A problem of my own making, I know.

I braced myself for the questions I didn't want to answer but couldn't avoid. "Alright, I'm ready," I told the driver.

He slipped out, closing the door behind him. I pasted a smile to my lips, slipping into a role I knew far too well.

A wall of sound unleashed as the door opened. Screams and shouts battered my ears but I soaked in the energy, enjoying the buzz and excitement around me.

Cameras flashed endlessly, pulses of light that came with the territory. Bodies jostled for position, questions lobbed from every direction.

A flash of green caught my eye and my body tensed as hope slammed into me.

Slowly I turned, breath catching. There she stood, golden brown waves tumbling over bare shoulders, green eyes finding mine through the chaos. The emerald green dress I'd bought her clung to slender curves. She looked radiant yet uncertain, stealing the breath from my lungs.

A dream I never thought would come true. She smiled at me, hesitant yet warm. I rushed to her, uncaring of the cameras trained on us or the questions that would follow as a result.

My hands slipped around her, pulling her close. Her familiar warmth and floral scent surrounded me.

"What are you doing here?" I shouted in her ear as I turned us, blocking her from the cameras.

She gazed up at me, a mix of nerves and warmth in her eyes. "I thought I was imagining it, all the signs that you still wanted me these past months. But talking to you last night, hearing you actually say the words... I realised I wanted it to be true more than anything."

Her admission stole my breath. I gripped her hands, pulse racing out of control. "You're all I've thought about. All I've wanted, every damn day we were apart."

She smiled, eyes glossy. "Once the anger faded, I just felt empty. It took me ages to realise the ache came from missing you. Missing us. Pretending I was fine without you was the hardest bloody thing I've ever done. I don't know why I put myself through that." She shook her head. "Stubbornness, I suppose. Wouldn't let myself get past some imaginary hurdle and forgive you."

"That stubbornness is infuriating and endearing in equal measure." I gently brushed a tear from her cheek. "The blame's mine. If I hadn't gotten us into that mess—"

She pressed a finger to my lips, silencing me with amusement dancing in her eyes.

Cat slipped into my arms. The familiar warmth and shape of her, pressed against my chest, overwhelmed my senses, something I thought I'd never feel again. The world faded away, questions and cameras forgotten. I had all I needed right here.

She gazed up at me, determination in her eyes. "This is where I belong, Nathan. Here with you. I know that now. I'll do anything you want."

Smiling, I brushed an errant curl behind her ear. "As tempted as I am to exploit that offer, I just want you back, Cat. That's all I've wanted every day since you walked away."

I captured her lips, kissing her until we were both breathless. Cat gripped me tight as if she'd never let go. Finally I pulled back enough to gaze into her eyes.

"I hope you meant all that, 'cause you're stuck with me now."

Cat laughed. "I meant it. You're it for me. I don't care about anything else." She shook her head. "Pretending I could just move on from that first night was a lie. I never stopped thinking about you."

I gripped her hand, never wanting to let go. "You were always on my mind too. Every damn day."

The noise of the crowd battered my ears but as Cat gazed up at me, everything else faded away.

"I love you, Nathan." Her words were quiet but sure.

Her eyes shone with a happiness that mirrored my own.

"Well don't leave me hanging."

I chuckled as I cradled her face in my hands. "I love you too. Always have."

EPILOGUE

 *ight months later...*

JACKSON

Lights blinded me as I stepped out of my limo. The crowd roared and I waved, smirking when the lasses along the front of the barrier screamed.

Just the way I like it.

Some actors hated to walk the red carpet. Something about the noise and the clamour of both fans and paparazzi set them on edge. Me? I fucking loved it.

I'd take a crowd of screaming lasses over my quiet house any day. Even the paparazzi shouting questions and demands didn't bother me. As long as they kept me focused and in the moment, I'd pose however they wanted.

Here, I couldn't hear my thoughts even if I wanted to.

Bliss. Pure fucking bliss.

Ahead of me walked Shaun and Finn, each of them holding their wives' hands as they worked their way down the press line. All of them done up to the nines and rightly so. This wasn't just another premiere.

Tonight, we launched the first film we'd ever created as Kings of Screen Productions.

Eleven months had flown by since Finn and I talked Nathan into ditching his plans to purchase a studio. Why he'd gone that route when we'd always talked about opening a production company none of us could understand, but we let it go and got on with the task at hand.

It had been a lot of work, some of it really bleeding miserable with Nathan moping over Cat, Finn stressing over his vow renewal ceremony and Shaun freaking out over becoming a dad. At times, I was the only voice of reason.

A weird situation I'd like to never repeat.

Thankfully, Nathan won Cat back, Shaun realised he was not his dad and wouldn't screw up his child — as if Mona would let him even try — and Finn's vow renewal went off without a hitch. We all returned from Bora Bora with a new determination to get shit done. No more distractions, we decided. Just *Beautiful Lies* and *Rogue Squad 5* for us.

We came home, hired the best team we could get our hands on and set them to work. I'd never spent so long poring over scripts and questioning every tiny decision. The process had been both fascinating and eye-opening. We'd disagreed at times, but we'd always found our way to a middle ground and the film was better for it. *Or so you believe.*

Nerves twisted in my gut, a foreign feeling these days and one I morbidly enjoyed. I'd thought I'd experienced everything I possibly could in this industry. It was nice to feel something new.

The crowd roared again while I worked my way down the carpet. I glanced over my shoulder as a new car pulled up at the entrance. Nathan's name filled the air like a chant. I stopped myself from rolling my eyes or shouting at them to focus their adoration on me. They didn't know how sickeningly serious Nathan and Cat were about each other.

Honestly, the pair of them were inseparable. Much like Finn and Shaun with Abi and Mona. Only more amusing.

After Nathan's failed proposal in Scotland, he'd been tiptoeing around the question for months. Anyone with half a brain cell could see through Cat's hints, but Nathan just kept second-guessing himself. *Serves him right, I fucking told him it would be a bad idea to propose with* that *ring.*

The driver rushed around the car, opening the door. Nathan stepped out, all smiles and windswept but styled in a tailored black suit. He nodded his head to the screaming fans before quickly turning back to help Cat out of the car.

She emerged, fitting right in among the glitz and glam of our Hollywood premiere in her sparkly dress. The screams intensified with hundreds of fans calling out her name. She smiled, hesitant at first, her grip on Nathan's hand tight. Then she stubbornly pushed her shoulders back and lifted her chin, waving with more confidence as she clung to his arm. Nathan whispered something in her ear and she laughed, the sound carrying over the roar of the crowd.

As much as I gave Nathan shit, I could appreciate the change in him. He'd worked his ass off to win Cat and she made him a stronger, better man. One actually capable of commitment. I smiled at the thought, giving him a nod as they started down the carpet.

Even so, sandwiched by happy couples was not a place I wanted to be. I could hear the reporters' questions already.

Jackson, how does it feel to be single when all of your friends are settling down with wives and babies?

I should have arrived late.

Not that I begrudged them their happiness. Not even slightly.

I loved the bastards. If the wife, two-point-five bairns, and the picket fence made them happy so be it. I just didn't need that in my life, and I really, really didn't want to spend my night fielding questions explaining my vehement determination to stay single.

Somebody has to keep the lasses of Hollywood entertained, and I volunteered as tribute.

Yeah, I couldn't see that answer going down well either, so instead, I'd either dodge the question or make up some bogus line about looking for Mrs Right.

Even though the first woman I thought was Mrs Right threw a ring in my face after cheating on me, and the second can't stand me, won't even agree to one date.

"Jackson! Over here! Sammy Miller claims you're the reason for her marriage breaking down. How do you respond to her claims that you're a homewrecker?" A pap shouted, breaking through my thoughts.

My smile froze in place. *What the fuck are they talking about? I'd never fuck a married woman.* I had always been extremely careful.

"She claims you promised to marry her if she left her husband," another shouted. "Were you involved with a married woman, Jackson?"

Who the fuck did I piss off enough to make up complete bullshit like this?

My jaw clenched as I forced another unaffected smile and kept moving. The second I got off the carpet, I'd call my agent, get him to track down the source and threaten legal action. *No, that might make me look guilty.*

Fuck, think. I needed to fix this without making it a bigger deal.

"Why were you involved with a married woman?"

I forced myself to keep moving down the line as I scanned the sea of reporters, trying to pinpoint the source of the accusations. *Who the fuck said that and why are they trying to stir shit up tonight of all nights?*

Tonight was supposed to be about the film, not some scandal. If it got enough traction it could derail all the good publicity.

Just keep walking, get to the end of this fucking carpet.

But if I didn't put it to rest, it would overshadow the entire launch.

"Do you make a habit of leading women on, Levi?"

A sharp stab of anger hit me. *I would never.*

"I don't know what you're talking about, pal, but I'm in a relationship, and it's not with a married woman," I said, somehow keeping the vehement disgust from my voice. Then my words caught up with my brain and my stomach hit the floor.

Why the fuck did you say that?

The paparazzi went crazy, the questions intensified as did the noise, all of them pushing and shoving to break their line and get closer to me.

"Who is she?"

"How long have you been together?"

"Why have you never been seen together?"

"Is she real?"

I scoffed. "Of course, she's bloody real."

"Then what's her name?"

My gaze tracked to Jimmy's white-faced assistant. I'm not sure my agent planned very well sending his brand new assistant to chaperone me down the carpet, but then who could have predicted this clusterfuck?

She stared at me, her eyes wide and silently begging me to fix it. But how? The words were out.

My eyes found Shaun and Finn up ahead, both of them looking back at me with furrowed brows and concerned frowns. Great, the last thing I need is them worrying about this shit right now.

I shook my head quickly, hoping they'd get the message to ignore it, then turned my attention to the reporters again.

"Her name is Roseline Butler and we've been together for the last six months."

I'm going to pay for this.

Ros had refused to even date me. How the fuck was I going to convince her to pretend to be my girlfriend?

Turn the page for a bonus scene with Nathan and Cat. I usually reserve this for my mailing list but this is easier in print. Plus, it's just nice to have it all together, right?

If you enjoyed *Acting Counsel*, please consider leaving a review on your preferred platform.

BONUS

NATHAN

"*N*athan! Cat! Over here!"

I couldn't stop grinning. I'd walked thousands of red carpets. None of them would ever compare to tonight. My nerves fizzled with excitement and my heart… fuck, I'd never felt this happy.

Glancing down at Cat in her glittering silver dress, her golden brown hair curled around her face, the feeling only intensified. She smiled at me, her green eyes glistening with the flash of cameras around us.

Eight months ago, I thought I'd lost her forever. Some days, it still felt like a dream.

She'd been instrumental in the launch of Kings of Screen Productions, working part time to help us get all the legal pieces in order. I'd planned to hire a team, but she'd insisted and, honestly, I craved the tiny thrill of our old forbidden romance.

Eventually, Cat had to step back once she started taking on clients. I mourned the loss of the extra spicy thrill of fucking my attorney again, but if I couldn't pretend we were doing something morally wrong then I had no business being an actor.

Unable to help myself, I leaned down, brushing my lips across Cat's cheek. "You look gorgeous, babe."

"You too." She flashed me a heated look. "I'll never get tired of you in a suit."

I smirked. "Does that smile mean I get to pull this pretty dress up around your waist and fuck you in the limo on the way home?"

Cat flushed and her gaze darted around us. "Someone will hear you," she hissed, turning her face towards me.

A good call; the news outlets had people on staff to read lips. The reminder should have made me stop, but I craved her feral heated looks.

I tucked her into my side, posing us for the next bunch of photographers. When they'd captured at least five hundred shots between them, I guided her away, ducking my head to whisper in her ear again.

"What about during the welcome cocktails?" I nuzzled my nose into her hair, my grip tightening around her waist. "I'm sure we could slip away for a minute or thirty."

Cat laughed. "You're incorrigible."

"You should have remembered that when you put this skintight dress on." I groaned as we stopped. "Watching you put it onwas pure fucking torture."

Cat smiled for the cameras, pretending she hadn't heard a word I'd said. But I could feel the way her body pressed against mine. If she could get away with holding my hand, her nails would have drawn blood by now.

"You didn't have to watch," she muttered from the corner of her mouth.

I shook my head, glancing down at her and projecting the image of a man utterly besotted with his girlfriend. It was true, of course. I just didn't need the cameras seeing how much I yearned to throw her over my shoulder and run away with her.

The weekend after we got back together, I forced her to move in with me. It was safer for her with the guarded gate and the… Alright so that was only half of it, but we'd been apart long enough. I couldn't wait any longer to wake up with her cuddled into my side, to experience every up and down of her new career or smother my amusement when she burnt anything she cooked unsupervised.

The mind-blowing sex was just a bonus… *Lies.*

You'd think I'd have had my fill after eight months, but the craving for her never waned. At this point, I hoped it never did.

"And miss the foreplay?" I bit my lip as I turned towards her, guiding her on. "Like fuck. I'm a masochist, Icy, not stupid."

Cat chuckled, but before she could throw out a retort that would only make me want her more, reporters started shouting Jackson's name further down the line. For a couple of seconds my friend froze up as the vultures fired question after question at him, shouting over each other in a mindless frenzy.

"Why were you involved with a married woman?"

"Did you know she was married?"

"What about her husband?"

"Do you make a habit of leading women on, Levi?"

What the ever loving fuck was going on?

He needed to keep walking. Mouth shut, shoulders back, head high, the paps don't exist.

What did the stupid fucker do? You guessed it. He opened his mouth. Not that I could hear a word of it from ten feet away, but the reaction was instantaneous.

"Who is she?"

"How long have you been together?"

"Why have you never been seen together?"

"Is she real?"

His agent's assistant paled as he responded. Jackson immediately tensed up. I resisted the urge to edge closer, wishing I could hear his responses. If I interfered, whatever he'd stumbled into would just get ten times bigger.

Finally, muscle memory snapped into place and he speed walked down the carpet, getting out of dodge as fast as possible.

"We can't follow him, right?" Cat asked, her disappointment clear.

"Right," I said. Tightening my grip on her before either of us got any ideas.

"What the hell did he just do?" she whispered as we moved up the line.

I had no idea, but it didn't look good.

"Nathan, did you know Jackson was dating a married woman?" A reporter asked as we stopped.

"Who's Roseline Butler?" Another asked.

"Is Jackson really dating this Roseline?"

How…? Oh shit.

I squeezed Cat, silently telling her not to say a word. I barely stopped my body from tensing up as the pieces clicked into place.

What the fuck did he do, and why did he involve Ros?

Over the summer, Ros had gone from open and chatty with Jackson to closed off and at times snappy. Every time we prodded him on it, he shrugged it off.

We made quick work of the remaining reporters, keeping our mouths firmly sealed unless the question related to the film and our premiere.

I'd never been so relieved to walk into a movie theatre. A crowd of people gathered in the foyer, all of them holding drinks and chatting like a scandal hadn't just blown up outside the doors.

"So I'm going to say that was unexpected," Cat said, her tone stunned.

"Understatement." I pulled her into the gathered crowd, my gaze scanning for Jackson's messy blond surfer head of hair.

I made it to the centre of the foyer with no luck. Cat hand landed on my arm, squeezing and pulling my attention to her.

"It's not good, right?"

I tugged her into my chest and wrapped my arms around her, ducking my head to make sure no one else heard us, but also painting a picture of the loved up couple we were.

"Any other day, I'd say it'll pass." I pressed my forehead to hers, staring into her concerned gaze. "But today's the worst day for a scandal."

"We won't let it detract from the launch." She kissed me, quick and fast, meaning to reassure. I wish it had worked. "You've got a team of people trained for this at your beck and call. It'll be okay."

I hummed noncommittally. Making plans without all the facts would be pointless. I needed to get the bad news from the horse's mouth.

Thankfully, we found him in a corner, frantically whispering into his phone, his eyes wide with panic. Jackson's tie hung loose around his neck and he dragged a hand through his hair, sending it further into disarray.

"Of all the times not to screen me, Ros, now's it. Pick up." When he hung up, he turned, catching sight of us nearby. He winced. "How much did… you know what, I don't care."

"What's going on, man?"

"Nate, I love you, but not right now." He spun in a slow circle, his head swivelling left to right as he scanned in the foyer. His frown deepened the longer he looked. "Have you seen Abi? I really need to talk to her."

"I haven't, but you can talk to me." I stepped in front of him, blocking his path. "Maybe I can help."

He clapped me on the shoulder, a smile flashing across his face for a flicker of a second. Then the frown returned and he brushed past me.

"I wish you could."

Then he was gone, leaving us staring after him with questions swirling.

Cat's hand tightened in mine. "C'mon, let's go find our seats."

"But—"

"You know where he lives." She tugged on my hand. "You can question him later."

Only I didn't get the chance. The asshole snuck out halfway through the film.

#

CATRINA

I practically had to hold Nathan in his seat through the film. It would not have looked good for all four of them to sneak out. A quick glance down the row confirmed that both Abi and Mona were dealing with the same problem.

Shaun and Finn couldn't keep their eyes on the film either.

It made me furious at the press.

Like why today? Couldn't they have held off for just one day and let the film launch?

Of course, I knew better. Over the last few months, I'd learnt how screwed up and instant gratification-focused the industry was. Didn't mean my hope for common decency would ever fade.

One day, they'd stop hiding in the bushes outside restaurants to catch us off guard. Or tailing us through traffic like we were going to do anything more exciting than go grocery shopping.

Accepting Nathan into my life had been eye-opening —

and sometimes terrifying — but I wouldn't change it for anything.

Even if he kept staring out the window instead of making good on his heated promises on the carpet.

"So I was thinking…" I let the words trail off, hoping that would be enough to grab his attention.

He hummed in response but didn't so much as side-eye me.

My eyes narrowed on him. "We should let the divider down while we fuck. I'm sure your driver would enjoy the show."

"Whatever you want," he said, tone flat and unengaged.

"You're going to regret saying that later." I shook my head.

There was nothing else for it. I'd have to take matters into my own hands.

Hiking my dress up and over my knees — I slid on to the limo floor and crawled forward, ignoring the burn of carpet against my knees. It took my hands landing on Nathan's thighs for him to finally look at me. His eyes widened, seeing me kneeling between his open legs.

"Cat, what are—"

"Nope. You had your chance to talk."

I had no intention of letting him off the hook that easily, not after spending the last few hours watching his eyes glaze over. I didn't really care what he had to say at this point; I just wanted my boyfriend to pay attention to me for more than two seconds.

"You promised me mind-blowing sex on the way home, Nathan." My brows quirked. "Are you seriously going to let tonight be the first time you renege on a promise?"

"You're right." He groaned. "I'm sorry. It's just everything with—"

Tired of waiting, I unzipped his pants and freed his cock. For a second, Nathan's mouth hung open as I gripped him. He instantly hardened and I dragged my hand down, pumping him until that surprised look faded, replaced with a familiar fire.

"Now are you paying attention?" I asked.

He swallowed. "I'm all yours."

Satisfied, I wet my lips before leaning forward and licking the tip of his cock, swirling my tongue around until Nathan's lips twisted with pleasure. He shifted in his seat, trying to control himself as I sucked him deeper into my mouth.

My lips and tongue worked in tandem against him while my hands massaged his length, relishing in the small tremors that ran through him.

For the last twenty minutes, I'd sat in silent anticipation, waiting for him to reach for me. My panties were soaked before I got on my knees but now my pussy ached with the need to be filled.

Nathan's eyes fluttered close as I increased my pace, focusing on pleasuring him rather than the burning need to sink down on his cock. His soft moan encouraged me to keep going, exploring every inch of him with my mouth. I took my time, licking and sucking until he bucked against me.

His hands found my hair and he grabbed handfuls, guiding me over his length, fucking me as much as I did him. I moaned around his dick, making sure he felt every vibration.

His breathing became laboured and he tensed beneath me. I pulled away before he could come and met his gaze.

"Fuck," he breathed. "That was …"

A smug smile spread across my face. I crawled into his lap, pushing my panties to the side. Forget stripping, there was no time.

I sank down on his cock, both of us sighing in pleasure as he filled me one delicious inch at a time.

"Less talking. More fucking."

Nathan gasped, grasping my waist as I started riding him, finding a slow and steady rhythm that left us both trembling with pleasure.

"I can get on board with that," he muttered, his voice hoarse. His gaze tracked down my front, his brow furrowing at my dress blocking his view. "This has to go."

I chuckled as he scrambled for the tiny hidden clasps. A couple of rolls of my hips and he gave up unbuttoning my dress with a disgruntled grunt. He resorted to pulling the fabric tight behind me instead, using his grip on my waist to keep the dress back.

The way his blue eyes darkened as I sank onto him only heightened the pleasure spiralling inside of me.

The limo filled with our pants and gasps.

It would be a miracle if the driver couldn't hear my strangled moans through the partition. A couple of months ago, I would have cared. The embarrassment would have burned through me, but the deeper I sank into Nathan's world, the more I came to savour these moments of quiet between us.

It was rare that we were truly alone. We needed to grasp them whenever we could — even if it meant a limo driver overhearing me scream Nathan's name.

We moved together, our hips meeting in a perfect rhythm that hit me right in the core. His grip tightened as I rode him harder and faster until we were both lost in the pleasure of it all.

I closed my eyes, giving in to the sensations coursing through me as Nathan's fingers dug into my flesh. One last thrust and I came apart around him. Burying my face in his shoulder, I screamed his name. Nathan followed me over the edge, panting against my neck.

We stayed like that for a few minutes, connected as we rode out our orgasm together.

"I'm sorry I zoned out on you," Nathan whispered a little while later, his lips grazing my ear. "No excuse. I promised you I wouldn't exclude you ever again."

I straightened up and took in his grim expression. "You're worried about your friend. I get it." I brushed his hair back with a smile, caressing his face. "If Jackson needs us, we'll help him together, but until he asks, there's nothing you can do."

"But I—"

I pressed my fingers to his lips, silencing him. "If you were in his shoes, would you want your friends clamouring around you, or would you want them to focus on the business while you got your head screwed on?"

"I'd want them to help, obviously."

My brows climbed. "Oh? So if you'd slipped up and lied to the press about me, you'd want your friends to explain the situation? Not you?" I kept my voice quiet, but Nathan would have to be obtuse to miss the deadly undercurrent in my tone.

"Fuck."

My meaning finally sunk in and he slouched deeper on the seat, taking me with him. He dragged a hand across his face and sighed.

"I wish I could hate how often you're right."

I laughed. "Liar. You love it."

I do." He smirked, but his amusement was short-lived. "But I'm worried about him."

"Me too." I thread our fingers together and lift our hands up to eye level. "But until he asks for help, it's just us so please don't shut me out."

Nathan smiled, his eyes shining with a love that never ceased to steal my breath. He cupped my cheek and leaned forward, capturing my lips in a soft kiss.

"I promise," he whispered, his forehead pressed to mine as he stared into my eyes. "If you promise to keep reminding me when I fall short?"

I grinned. "You couldn't keep me quiet if you tried."

Nathan chuckled. "I love you, Icy."

"Love you too, Playboy."

I'd never cease to marvel at the mysterious turn my life had taken. From a one night fling in a bar to the hardest game of resistance I'd ever played, all to find this: the love of my life. If I could do it all over again, I wouldn't change a thing.

If you enjoyed *Acting Counsel*, please consider leaving a review on your preferred platform.

Next and last in the Kings of Screen series is Fashionably Fake following the fallout from Jackson's lie. Will Ros bail him out or will he be forced to face the music?

ROS

Jackson Levi was dead.

Not literally, but if he knew what was good for him, he'd delete my number and retract his stupid statement.

Us, in a relationship? No one would believe it.

I'd woken up to forty missed calls, a hundred or more texts, and countless voicemails. Most of them from Jackson fucking Levi.

A month ago, the Scottish actor had been fun. For a time, a very very short time, he was my friend. I could always count on him for a good laugh. Shit at work blew up? One text to Jackson and I'd laugh. Bad date? I'd open my phone to find a stupid meme waiting for me. I could enjoy myself, never feeling like he'd want something in return and be my normal dorky self.

I knew there would be no way he would ever be interested in me. Men only ever wanted to use me and, let's face the facts head on: I had no money, no fame.

Yes, I had connections, but they were all in the fashion realm and none of them would have the first clue how to help an Academy Award-winning actor.

Over the summer, he'd become the perfect distraction from my shitty, unpredictable life.

And then he'd ruined it all.

I lay in bed for over an hour, scrolling blurry-eyed through the messages and headlines. The more I read, the more my blood pressure spiralled.

> JACKSON
>
> We need to talk. ASAP.
>
> ABI
>
> Don't go to work today. The vultures are descending.
>
> JACKSON
>
> I panicked. I'm sorry, but we need to talk.
> Stop screening me.

I snorted.

Yes, Jackson, every time I miss a call, I'm screening you.

Couldn't possibly be that he was three hours behind, and I'd gone to sleep at a normal hour for the first time in weeks. My world totally revolved around the entitled asshole.

Okay, I didn't mean that.

Things were great until he'd asked me out and that wasn't a crime. Unfortunately.

I didn't like it, but I could forgive it. The awkwardness would fade out, maybe by the next time I saw him, and we'd go back to being friends. But telling the press I'd been his girlfriend for six months? That I couldn't forgive.

I dialled Abi, laying there with my eyes covered like some stupid childish game where it would all go away if I couldn't see it.

"What the fuck happened last night?" I asked the second she answered.

"I'm still getting all the facts but we can't find Jackson and he's not answering his phone," she said, her words almost drowned out by a sea of voices and low music in the background. "I'm still at the production company afterparty. Can you hear me?"

I grimaced, my ears straining. "Just about."

"Hold on."

I shifted onto my back and waited, staring at the ceiling like it might magic up a time turner. Shit, I'd give my favourite Gucci jacket for a way to go back in time and stop the idiot from opening his mouth.

A couple of seconds later, the party sounds cut off. "Better?"

"Much."

"Good. I've probably got five minutes before someone starts hammering on the bathroom door, so let's talk quick." She blew out a breath. "Are you okay?"

I pursed my lips and considered her question. "I don't know yet. I'm still in bed so I have no idea what's waiting for me outside the apartment."

I rubbed at my eyes, tiredness hitting hard. It was unusual for me to see this side of 7 AM after a gruelling month at Paris Fashion Week. The least I deserved was a week of long lie-ins and late starts. Instead, the universe threw a scandal at me the first chance it got.

"Why did he say it?"

"One of the magazines is claiming he had an affair with a married woman." Silence fell for a second and I could imagine my red-haired best friend chewing her lip, destroying whatever was left of her lipstick. "I think he panicked. Shaun and Nathan are pissed at him for not walking away."

My brow furrowed. "I might join them."

He had other options, but he'd chosen to drag me into it.

Why? I'd have to return one of his many calls to find out. Or at least listen to his voicemails. Neither of which appealed.

I might do something stupid. *Like agree to play along.*

I shivered at the thought. Even pretend monogamy would be a step too far for me.

"The guys don't think it's true," Abi said. "The married woman, I mean. Not him saying you… you know."

I hummed in response.

What the hell was I meant to say to all this? Thanks for turning my life upside down for your own gain? Fat chance of that.

"But it's sweet though, right?" she continued, rambling through my silence. "You were the first person he thought of when he needed help."

"You're a terrible matchmaker. Don't even try it." I threw the covers back and climbed out of bed, scowling at the dark sky outside my window.

I had another two weeks before preparation chaos started for New York Fashion Week in December. As much as I'd love to throw the covers over my head and hide from the world, I couldn't and, honestly, I didn't want to be that person.

My mother had tried it for years – burying her head in the sand and ignoring my father's cheating, as if that would make it go away.

Abi went suspiciously silent.

"I might have pushed you at Finn, but that doesn't mean you need to return the favour, Abs. Jackson is my friend." I winced. "Was my friend. Remember when you tried to set me up with the guy from your agency?"

She groaned. "Don't remind me."

"Oh no, I think you need reminding."

I stepped into the silent kitchen and flipped the coffee machine on. It had been five months since Eva moved to LA in June to be closer to Abi and I still hadn't gotten used to it. Probably never would.

"The date went horribly. He threw every red flag in the book at me."

"I remember. You don't have to remi—"

"And then!" I said louder than necessary. "He turned into a stalker." I leaned against the counter, staring at the peeling off-white paint on the cabinet in the tiny kitchen. "So tell me again how great your matchmaking skills are?"

She sighed. "Fine. I'll keep it to myself."

I nodded. "Good choice."

"But that doesn't mean Jackson will."

"Abi!" I pinched the bridge of my nose, desperation leaking from me. "Can we not? He fucked up, and he needs to fix it before he turns my life upside down, but this changes nothing. I wasn't interested in ruining our friendship a month ago and I'm not interested now."

"I know. I know. I just think…"

"Stop." The coffee machine started spitting out my energy nectar, so I found the will to dig up some patience. "We're not doing this. He has a **PR** team or whatever, he can handle it."

"What if he can't?" she asked, her voice quiet.

Then he's royally fucked… but on his own. A pang of guilt sliced through me at the thought.

"Then it's not my problem."

If it's not your problem, why are you still talking about it?

"Even if you could help the guys salvage their launch?"

My eyes narrowed. "Wow! Abs, tell me you are not pulling the emergency card?"

"What if I am?"

"Then I haven't had enough coffee, alcohol, or sleep, and I need to hang up before you do it."

"No, don't hang up."

My head tilted at the panic in her voice. "You're avoiding something."

"Am not." Her voice hitched, giving her away.

"Hmm."

She sighed. "I'm avoiding Finn."

"Explain. Now."

Abi had been head over heels in love with the Irishman since before filming wrapped on Married Blind. The only time she'd avoided him was when they'd broken up before the show ended. She couldn't say no to the man, and they were nauseously cute together.

"I've been nursing the same drink for the last few hours, and he's getting suspicious."

"Why would he get suspicious over a drink and why aren't you downing all the free booze like you're twenty-one again?" Then a lightbulb went off. "Oh my god! Abigail McCarthy, are you motherfucking pregnant?"

"Yes," she mumbled, her voice ridiculously low.

As if Finn would be eavesdropping on her in the bathroom. I almost laughed. Almost.

"That's amazing! Congrats!"

"Thank you," she whispered, her tone sheepish.

"Does Eva know?"

"No."

I grinned. "Oh, she won't let you live that down."

"Which is exactly why you're going to pretend I said nothing."

"Sure I am." I chuckled, but quickly sobered.

"But that settles it. I am not getting involved with Jackson Levi." Abi and Finn had only moved in together in August last year. Mona had a baby two months ago. Cat and Nathan just got engaged. I would not be rounding out the final piece in the Kings of Screen puzzle. No way.

"Ros!"

"No! Absolutely not. There's clearly something in the bloody water down there."

"Not every man is your dad."

"That would be impossible." I rolled my eyes, trying to shrug off the emotions thoughts of my father always elicited before they could fully settle again. "Doesn't mean I need to tempt fate though, does it?"

"I don't know, it might be nice."

I snorted. "Nice is not the word I would use."

Ulcer-inducing, definitely.

"I like my life. I don't need the man or the ring. I'll be the fun aunt who swoops in, spoils your kids, and then leaves you with a sugar-fuelled child with a slight addiction to Christian Louboutins."

"And I get that, but —"

The doorbell sung out, cutting her off.

"Hold that thought. Someone's asking to be murdered."

Before I could take two steps, the pounding started.

"I'm coming!" I scowled in the general direction of the front door.

Knocking on my door before 7 AM. Definite death wish.

The pounding continued, grating on my last nerve. *To Hell with stranger danger warnings.* I'd seen enough slasher films to know better, but I was ready to go full psycho on the idiot trying to bust down my door at the ass crack of dawn. Consequences be damned.

I swung open the door.

Just Jackson on my welcome mat, arm still raised to pound again.

For a split second, the last month ceased to exist, and a smile tried to claim my lips. Staring into his wide hazel eyes, I almost, *almost,* invited him in.

Then reality caught up.

I froze up while this war waged inside of me. Just stood there, mouth agape, emotions swirling from happy to annoyance to anger and back.

This is why I don't get up before the sun.

And that, ladies and gentleman, is why you check the peephole. You never know who is going to darken your door

— axe murderers, religious zealots, the mob, or idiot actors who can't keep fiction separate from reality.

I needed a vat of coffee to deal with him. And maybe a getaway car on standby. Fuck.

Abi squawked in my ear through the phone I had mercifully not dropped, demanding to know who it was.

"I have to go."

"What? Why?"

"I'll talk to you later. Congrats again."

I hung up, never taking my eyes off the asshole smiling at me like he wasn't here to sweet-talk me into doing his bidding. Hell the fuck no.

"Why are you here?

AUTHOR'S NOTE

When I started writing romance, I never thought I would write a book like Acting Counsel: a romance between an attorney and the celebrity client she couldn't have.

But then the Johnny Depp and Amber Heard trial happened. My muse fixated on Camille Vasquez and the rest was pretty much history.

Something about the way she handled herself in court caught my attention and started the wheels turning. She seemed to represent the badass, strong-willed, smart women I love to feature in my books.

As a result, Catrina Sinclair was born. The perfect counterpart to laid-back Nathan Logan, a self-assured A-list British actor.

Acting Counsel went through various iterations to get the balance right for their "forbidden" relationship and there were times in the months leading up to release where I questioned absolutely everything. Lovelies, I knew it would be a hard book to write, but I was NOT prepared.

I'm so proud of how far Cat and Nathan's story has come and of myself for the things I pulled off while writing this books. I decided to quit my TV job to travel full time, I put my house on the market and started the process of moving out and selling everything I own. It was a rollercoaster couple of months and, in future months and years, I'll look back on this book and remember my resilience.

Dear reader, I hope you enjoyed Nathan and Cat's story as much as I loved writing it.

Happy Reading!

Morgana x

ALSO BY MORGANA BEVAN

True Platinum Series (Rock Star Romance)
(Rhiannon)
Chasing Alys–Ryan (Resistant to Love)
Charming Daphne–Matt (Force Proximity)
Winning Nia–James (Second Chance)
Enticing Mel–Dan (Secret Baby)
Needing Emily–Emily (Accidental Marriage/Runaway Bride)
Defying Ella - Jared (Close Proximity / Snowed-in)

(The Brightside)
Braving Lily - Lily (Opposites Attract)
Daring Ceri - Alex (Second Chance)
Marrying Olivia - Lewis (Accidental Marriage)

Lovers Knot
Rockstar Regret - Nick (Forced Proximity)

Kings of Screen Series (Hollywood Romance)
Between Takes (Enemies to Lovers)
Married Blind (Marriage of Convenience)
Acting Counsel (Close Proximity, Forbidden)
Fashionably Fake (Fake Dating)
Lights, Camera, Baby! (Accidental Pregnancy)

ABOUT MORGANA

Morgana Bevan is a sucker for a rock star romance, particularly if it involves a soul-destroying breakup or strangers waking up in Vegas. She's a contemporary romance author based in Wales. When Morgana's not writing steamy celebrity romances with gorgeous British rock stars and movie stars, she's travelling the world, searching for inspiration.

She enjoys travelling, attending gigs, and trying out the extreme activities she forces on her characters.

Find Morgana online at morganabevan.com.

Morgana's Facebook Reader Group: facebook.com/groups/498919364708263